Boru launched himself, hurling a blood-curdling shriek that exploded on them, startling the hreenu while momentarily freezing the maneaters. Time slowed; Boru watched the man's sword arm swing gradually back as his saddle hreen half turned to strike with its shoulder. Casually Boru's blade clove the beast's face, then took the man in the neck, sweeping him from the saddle.

The next man had nocked an arrow, loosed it, and Boru struck it aside with his sword as his mount recovered. As he charged he saw the man's wide staring eyes, sagging mouth, saw his hand go to his sword hilt. His hreen reared, but before its front hooves could strike, its throat opened, gushing blood. Boru thrust the rider through.

The leader sat frowning, sword in hand, ten meters away.

"Who," he said hoarsely, "or what, are you?"

THE WALKAWAY CLAUSE

THE WALKAWAY CLAUSE

JOHN DALMAS

A TOM DOHERTY ASSOCIATES BOOK

THE WALKAWAY CLAUSE

Copyright © 1986 by John Dalmas

First printing: October 1986

A TOR Book

Published by Tom Doherty Associates, Inc.
49 West 24 Street
New York, N.Y. 10010

Cover art by Tom Kidd

ISBN: 0-812-53475-1
CAN. ED.: 0-812-53476-X

Printed in the United States of America

0 9 8 7 6 5 4 3 2 1

This story is dedicated to friends who early encouraged me to write, and particularly to:

> Elizabeth Netzloff Witherspoon, teacher at Linden High School
> Richard Dean, 341st Infantry Regiment
> Marilyn Washburn Jones, Michigan State University
> Ken Duncan, Michigan State University

Those friendships were in other times, when I wore other names. It took me a while to make the commitment.

Reasoning psychotics are people with insane intentions, who apply rational intelligence to carry them out. You uncover them by the trouble they cause, if you can find out who caused it. And because reasoning psychotics like power and secrecy, they'd taken over Department Eleven, the Foreign Ministry's covert action arm.

When Bhiksu Tanaka, "Mr. Ethics," sent Barney Boru to Siegel's World to kill a king, Barney didn't question it. The contract had an approved Bill of Particulars, and if, when he got there, the job smelled bad, he could invoke the walkaway clause.

It smelled worse than bad. Barney landed unknowingly in the middle of a blood match between Department Eleven and Kyril Golovin, the Russian Stork. They were using various pieces to play, including free-moving pieces like Barney.

But if a piece learns what the game is, it can become a player. And if the player is like Barney, he'll try to take over the game.

PROLOGUE

Planets with intelligent life are classed from F to A according to the technical level of the leading culture, F referring to a level equivalent to the Old Stone Age on Earth. E refers to cultures, sometimes metal-using, that have significant agriculture, herding of domestic animals, or the like, without cities and without large-scale commerce. At the top of the scale, A indicates large-scale commercial and industrial space activity.

So far only five worlds have been classifiable as A when first contacted. (Only Earth had originated a faster-than-light drive.) A planet must be at least a well-developed and reasonably stable B world to become a full member of the Confederacy. Then of course it rather quickly becomes an A world, complete with warships. A number of B and some C worlds, or nations on those worlds, have been made associate members pending attainment of sufficient political unity and sanity for full membership.

Numberous B and many C worlds have not been offered associate membership because of their political conditions, and a very few have declined membership. Most of these non-members are open to commerce in certain categories of commodities and services, the categories varying with the planet and nation.

Since 2386, the Cultural Protection Law has prohibited contact with planets classed D or lower. The sole exceptions are small authorized study projects and undercover police monitors.

Some unauthorized "leakage" occurs of course, through smuggling and other criminal activities. But as these are subject to severe penalties, they are small, very covert, tend to occur at only one or a few locations on the restricted planet, and in general are of a nature that does not draw attention. Therefore their effects are almost always minor, and assimilable by the culture.

There have been exceptions. . . .

ONE

"Mr. Boru!"

Bjorn "Barney" Boru woke up like turning on a light, and rolled to his feet on the polished wood floor.

"Vacation over?" he asked.

"I have an assignment for you."

"Twenty minutes," Barney said.

"Excellent." The terminal went gray.

With quick movements he hung the single sheet on two wall clamps, put the sleeping pad atop the long storage chest, making a couch of it, and padded to the bathroom. Its south wall was a sliding glass door standing open to his balcony, twenty feet above the plunging hillside, giving a tree-framed view across the wooded, park-like Los Angeles Basin.

The whole cottage was virtually a balcony, cantilevered from the ridge. A bird chirped cheerily, then sang; another answered. Early morning sun glinted on scattered ponds and the windows of medium-rise clusters below, showing here and there among woods, lawns, and meadows. Although it was the summer monsoon, clouds and the almost daily thundershower were a few hours away yet.

Boru wiped the day's growth of stubble from his throat, scalp, and strong face, leaving only eyebrows. After that he let the shower beat on him, first hot, then cold, and dried with a rough towel—an old-fashioned indulgence more pleasant to him than blowing dry. Finally he donned shorts and body shirt, pressed on his shoes, and left, jogging down a moist, humus-dark footpath that descended steeply across the face of the hill among trees and bamboo clumps.

It was an exclusive neighborhood, owned by the higher guilds and restricted to their members. He shared his cottage with another Equity agent. They both were away—off planet—most of the time, and seldom overlapped.

At the foot of the hill, the trail joined a broad paved walk, softer and more resilient than the foot-packed path. There were a few other early risers—occasional joggers and runners but mostly people walking to work or to shuttle stops in the fresh morning air, umbrellas furled but ready. A few minutes later he arrived at Hollywood 3791/0086, its fountain splashing and sparkling, and trotted through the entrance.

No one was in the entry except the security guard, who glanced up at Boru, then back to his newsfac. The elevator was all Barney's too, all the way to the twelfth-floor penthouse. The receptionist, no longer young, smiled at him.

"Good morning, Mr. Boru. Did you enjoy your vacation?"

She really wanted to know, so he really told her. "Hi, Maria. Yeah, it was nice to relax with almost zero chance of getting hit. Hike, swim, sit and talk with strangers on the beach. But work is more interesting." He glanced at the wall clock.

"You can go in," she said.

Bhiksu Tanaka stood small and trim, a security phone in one hand, looking westward out the window. The view was bounded on the north by the long wall of the Santa Monica Mountains and in the distance by the Pacific. He nodded his almost bald head to Barney, and the agent sat down carelessly in one of the chairs.

"Ms. Fong," the old man said quietly into the phone, "please tell Mr. Chatterjee that he must decide things like that for himself, guided by written policy." His words were gentle and precise, the intention behind them total. "It is not your job to intervene from the ignorance of distance, as you both know. I realize that you are new on your post, but you have been most thoroughly trained and so has Mr. Chatterjee. You are a communicator; he is an agent. You are not to make decisions for him or give him advice, he is not to ask you to, and I will not again point this out to either of you.

"This is true in all cases, and it is most *vitally* true of walkaway decisions.

"Now, do you have anything further to say about Mr. Chatterjee's mission that I should know? . . . Good! I really believe you will do just fine. Pass my words on to Mr. Chatterjee. Good day."

He tucked the phone in the side pocket of his loose white jacket and turned to Barney. ''Mr. Boru,'' he said, smiling, ''have you ever killed a king?''

The cab slid to a position above the rooftop, then lowered itself gently onto the landing pad. The man who got out was of ordinary height, and his bishop's crown of wispy hair graying. Despite his expensive mode of travel (the cab's registry was Geneva, Switzerland, the dropoff Melbourne, Australia), his clothing was that of a modestly successful professional or businessman. His thick waist suggested a lack of athletic competence, but it would have been dangerous to act on the assumption. He was still quite strong, albeit his stamina was now only ordinary. And if his quickness and flexibility were not what they had been, they were nonetheless exceptional. His coordination was superb, precise, and his trained skills remarkable and deadly.

Yet he could stand unnoticed in a group of six or eight, and might have been the last man taken in choosing sides for a softball game at a bank picnic.

The senior of the three men who met him bobbed his head in respect and followed rather than conducted him into the elevator. The other two trailed with the luggage.

Their destination was familiar to Albert Haas. He'd been there before, but as a consultant. He hadn't been active as an agent for sixteen years—not since he'd been off-loaded by Department Eleven. The usual procedure would have been to mindwipe him, for he had a great deal of sensitive information. But he had arranged a safeguard that they had decided not to risk, resulting in a standoff. He had agreed to be inactive as an agent, doing consulting only, and they had provided a very comfortable pension without tampering with his mind.

Within the commercial justice field, Nemesis Ltd. had distinctly the inferior reputation among the Big Four, from the standpoints both of ethics and the quality of staff agents. But financially it had been very successful: it was open to more marginal jobs than more ethical firms would consider. And when it needed an agent of exceptional skill, Nemesis offered top dollar to the handful of illicit freelancers good enough to survive.

Also it had certain special connections, which was why Hass was there.

The suite in which Eldred Pelham received Mr. Haas was very expensively furnished and appointed; it would have been appropriate to an upper-level executive of System Mining and Manufacturing. And in a way, that's what Pelham was. Nemesis Ltd. was a fully-owned subsidiary of SM&M, a fact virtually unknown even within Nemesis and carefully unmentioned by the few who knew. In fact, the existence of Nemesis was scarcely known outside the profession except to the upper executive strata of outsystem mercantile corporations. And to these only if their operations extended outside the Confederacy.

There were, of course, many such corporations. Intersystem commerce, high technology, and government were the principal economic activities of Earth.

It was not that the basic activities of Nemesis were illegal. But the commercial justice field disliked publicity, and the way that Nemesis operated was not creditable.

"Well, Albert," said Pelham briskly, "it is a pleasure to retain your services."

Haas looked at Pelham with something like distaste. They'd known one another from before Nemesis. Pelham in turn felt slightly repelled by Haas. Unlike his staff agents, Haas felt personally dangerous to him. He'd agreed to use him only under external pressure.

"You have not retained my services until we agree on the assignment and the terms," Haas replied. "In writing."

Pelham smiled smoothly. "I'm sure you'll find the payment attractive. And as for the assignment—there is always something attractive in evening old scores, *nicht wahr*?"

TWO

(Excerpts from the *Staff Manual of Equity Ltd.*, by Bhiksu Tanaka)

1. Basics of the Business

Equity Ltd. is a justice firm.

There are those who consider ''justice firm'' a satirical euphemism, for our basic function is execution—assassination if you will. Yet the term justice is appropriate.

There were, when I last counted, eighty-four member and associate worlds in the Confederacy, all of them with more or less technologically advanced cultures. These, in turn, do business with several times that many worlds outside the Confederacy, most of them relatively primitive.

The primary activity between worlds is commerce—trade and the communication of ideas. Thus the purposes of the Confederacy are the regulation of trade and provision for the common defense. Within the Confederacy there is a code of rational law to protect the individual person or firm from criminal commercial practices. There is also a system to enforce that code. And there is a navy to protect the Confederacy from outside forces, should any appear.

In commerce with *unaffiliated* worlds, however, such protection does not obtain. And the adage, ''Let the buyer beware,'' although excellent advice, is hardly an adequate substitute. Many business transactions with ''bush worlds'' are carried out to mutual benefit and satisfaction on no other basis than the honor of the transactants. But a party of good will and reasonable caution can be grievously and wrongly injured, even to bankruptcy, by the carefully plotted criminality of someone with whom he does business.

In the absence of appropriate law, then, execution has been turned to as a crude means of justice. Execution removes the criminal from the commercial environment. And knowledge that execution is a possible response to seriously criminal trade practices undoubtedly discourages and reduces such practices.

The existence of justice firms is, of course, an invitation to unscrupulous wealthy persons and firms to seek our services for unjust assassinations. To some extent this is discouraged by the very high costs of justice services. It is further limited in that, of course, we never never accept any proposal for execution of a target within the Confederacy.

Unjust executions are further limited by requiring any applicant to document that the proposed target is, in fact, culpable—has committed a serious crime against the applicant. This documentation, termed ''the bill of particulars,'' is not of course subject to contest by the accused or his representatives, who do not even know of the proposal. And in fact, because the accused are on non-Confederacy worlds, we have inadequate or no objective case data against which to compare the particulars listed.

But our evaluators—those who appraise the bills of particulars—are highly trained, apprenticed, and alert. They have encyclopedic summaries, thoroughly accessed, of most unaffiliated trade worlds. And not infrequently they detect and challenge inconsistencies in bills of particulars. An untruthful bill of particulars is subject to rejection with no reconsideration, and the large application fee is not refundable.

Nonetheless, a skillful construction of lies, or a fabric of dishonestly selected truths and omissions, sometimes results in acceptance of an unjust proposal of execution. Thus the walkaway clause is included in every contract. If a justice agent, in ''casing the target,'' finds the situation substantially different from that represented in the bill of particulars, or if he simply develops substantial doubt as to the justice of the intended execution, he is authorized *and required* to ''walk away'' from the assignment. On his return, he is required to present a bill of justification with which the client is confronted. The client may then forfeit his entire deposit. He is allowed to contest the agent's action, but in the case of Equity Ltd., at the time of this edition we have never overruled an agent's exercise of the walkaway clause.

When a proposal of execution is rejected, whether during evaluation of the bill of particulars or by an agent exercising the walkaway clause, the rejecting firm notifies all other justice firms. The likelihood of the proposal then being accepted by another justice company is poor. In fact, any further proposals by that client will be looked at quite minutely.

What, you might ask, prevents an unscrupulous mercantile corporation from employing a freelance assassin and bypassing justice safeguards? The key is the Justice Agents' Guild. The Guild, in the tradition of guilds, has a limited, highly skilled membership. Its members enjoy very lucrative contracts with justice firms, and active membership is limited to persons with justice firm employment.

The Guild strictly forbids executions by members and others not acting on justice contracts—that is, on approved proposals. It actively and severely disciplines the few, in or out of the Guild, who violate this regulation, and itself proposes justice contracts against out-Confederacy offices of offending companies. This has

markedly restricted unjust executions
as well as protecting justice firms
and Guild members from unfair trade
practices. . . .

5A. Communications: Security

Despite the essential and highly sophisticated security systems available for computers and communication
equipment (and we at Equity Ltd. enjoy
the best), there often are advantages
to writing something on paper and handing it to someone who peruses and then
burns it.

Beyond that, as a means of transporting confidential information, there
remains the human mind. The mind, of
course, is more or less accessible to
various combinations of cleverness,
ruthlessness, and technology. It can,
in turn, be protected from forcible
entry by conditioning of various kinds,
generally injurious. The most reliable protection is death.

Equity Ltd. does not, however, em-
ploy agent death as a security procedure. At the very least it is expensive
in terms of recruitment, training, and
group morale, not to mention personal
and familial loss.

Most basically, however, it is unethical to disenfranchise the agent from
his body, or impair his mind in any
irreversible way. And it has become
increasingly obvious, since the pi-
oneering work of Dr. N.A. Kubiak some
decades ago, that ethics is not a cultural arbitrary which can be ignored
at convenience, but a natural power

operating in the physical universe with a force comparable to that of gravity, if often less immediate.

Mindwiping, broad or selective, was long popular with intelligence agencies. It is quite harmful to the recipient, and Equity Ltd. abjures the practice. It is not analogous to erasing the memory of a computer, and the memory is not actually removed. It is simply the application of extreme pain, usually by electric shock, accompanied by hypnotic command, sufficient that the treated person does not remember and cannot be gotten to remember, even under extreme coercion. Unless, of course, he is implanted with a key phrase or other ''trigger to tell,'' in which case, when it is activated, he will tell compulsively.

Fortunately the long-time rule of small-cell project organization, and the ''need to know'' rule, are almost always sufficient for the security of information and are easily applied. In a majority of cases, Equity Ltd. sends out one-person missions, so that the agent has no confederate to protect from discovery. . . .

6C. The Nature of Ethics

. . . The importance of ethics was so long overlooked for three primary reasons.

1. There was no valid ethical theory to provide reference data against which empirical observations could be evaluated.

2. Until relatively recently, theories regarding ethics had confused ethics with *morals*: Morals are cultural rules, often arbitrary, which coincide with ethics only to limited degrees. Thus studies of morals do not disclose useful universal laws. Within a limited time scope, morals provide more or less workable local guides which, in the absence of a science of ethics, are essential but never really adequate to the life and function of a society. Especially in areas of rapid cultural change, moral codes tend toward obsolescence, maladjustment, and consequent disregard.

3. The relative nature of morals, and the confusion between morals and ethics, have since classical antiquity increasingly discouraged the study of ethics as futile.

Thus the *practice of ethics*, even in the age of the faster-than-light drive and of computers based on complex organic molecules, has been comparable in sophistication to the agriculture of the Ukrainian waldsteppe during the Late Stone Age. Now several decades of effective research into ethics are substantially impacting the academic fields of psychology, sociology, anthropology and xenology, and have begun to filter into politics and personal life.

But by and large, ethics as a modern technology has had relatively small effect on the world of corporate business. The fear persists that to dis-

continue unethical practices in the
sometimes ruthless contest will risk
one's standing in the management hi-
erarchy and possibly founder the corporate ship in the heavy weather of
competition. . . .

THREE

Barney Boru put the rented flier down in the landing space
outside the garden-like grounds. Sprays rose from sprinklers
located among the trees and shrubs; the Monterey country
was north of the true monsoon region, and summer rains were
irregular. Behind him to the east, the early sun peered over a
higher ridge; below, to the west, fog covered the coast and
lower hills, and filled the canyons with soft whiteness.

He passed through the sprays at a jog and found Artemus
Kabashima on a small mat, his old legs folded comfortably
beneath him in a lotus. Kabashima turned his parchment face
to his foster son.

"Would you care to be seated?"

"Thank you, father." Boru lowered himself to the floor.

"You have come to say goodbye?"

"That's right. I'm going on a long assignment."

The gray head nodded.

"I didn't want to leave Earth on last week's goodbyes. I
wanted to see you again before I take off."

The dark eyes regarded him calmly. "I am glad. There is
something specific you wished to say to me?"

Boru nodded. "I feel that I may not return. Although I
have had no premonition of death."

"Ah." When Boru said nothing more, the old man asked,
"Would you like tea?"

"Tea would be nice."

Kabashima reached and struck a small gong, the note sounding mellow but clear. A moment later a girl appeared.

"Yes sir?"

"Maralies, we would like tea, please."

She bowed and backed into the house. The old man chuckled. "There is an amusing symmetry in customs scorned being re-embraced by a later generation." The dark eyes fixed the blue. "Is there something further you have to say?"

Boru nodded. "Yes. To thank you for your training. I never sought satori or experienced it; I practiced neozen only to become a master warrior, though it has helped me in everything I do." The look between the two men was mutually comfortable, without defensiveness, condescension, or resentment. "And while I have not become a master of neozen, I've certainly become a master of the deadly hand."

Again Kabashima chuckled. "Tanaka thought you might."

"Uncle Bhiksu?"

"Bhiksu Tanaka sometimes sees the future. Not pictures, to my knowledge, but sometimes he knows." Something passed over the old face—decision. "You do not know all you might of your background. I have never considered it important before, but now I feel you should know.

"When you were not yet two years old, Bhiksu Tanaka brought you to me. He said, 'Your children are grown. Would you take another? He is of the best stock, though who his father is, I am not at liberty to say.' " Kabashima grinned. "I looked at you and said, 'leave him with me.' He thanked me. 'I believe he will be a master karateka,' Tanaka said, 'indeed a master samurai.'

" 'By his lineage?' I asked, for I knew that Tanaka lends importance to that.

" 'His lineage and more,' he answered. 'I sense that purpose in him. He will be an honor to you.' "

Kabashima crowed with laughter. "What is honor? And who bestows it? I asked him that, and it irritated him. Tanaka is an eclectic, and very able. But he does not know neozen, although he has informed himself in it."

Smiling, the old man sat quietly then, encouraging the younger to speak.

"So Uncle Bhiksu brought me to you," Boru said thoughtfully. "I'd always assumed I'd come from a foundling home, or from some serving girl. I assumed that if I was the child of some friend, you'd have told me."

Quietly Maralies brought two cups, small and delicate, and filled them from an exquisite pot. Her technique was very good—exact and unobtrusive. When she had left, the two men sat silently for a while, one age thirty-four, the other of indeterminate years—perhaps ninety, possibly a hundred. The only sounds were the chirping of a bird, the occasional plink of a bamboo wind chime, and the slight inhaled hiss of sipping hot tea.

"And there is something else?" Kabashima nudged.

Again the blue eyes met the black. "Yes. I've seen a lot in my short life, on various worlds. I've seen a number of men of force and exceptional ability, and a lot more with ordinary— endowments. I've been exposed to quite a few lifestyles and philosophies. My understanding has grown and my priorities have shifted.

"After accepting my new assignment, I made a decision."

The old eyes, the thin lips, smiled at him. *What does he know?* Boru wondered. *Does he know my thoughts? What I'm going to say next? Can he do that?* He'd wondered before. It sometimes seemed that way.

Boru went on. "For most of my life I've known that neozen is very—powerful. I had few of the problems of other children. Excelling was easy for me, and still is. Yet observing you, I knew that I was sampling only the fringe. But I had what I wanted.

"Now, as I said, my priorities, my values, have changed. When I've finished this new contract, I'm quitting as a justice agent. I'm going to join an order and see where neozen can take me."

Kabashima nodded acknowledgment, his eyes still smiling. They finished their tea more in silence than in talk, then Boru left. Each had said what he'd needed to say. And if it had always been easy to be around his foster father, it was also easy to say goodbye when it was time.

FOUR

Barney Boru carried his mission orders only in his mind. He also knew the summary on Siegel's World thoroughly. And he'd had a four-week crash course in the language of Lokar, one of its many kingdoms, the one in which he'd operate. Language training was a considerably developed technology, and Boru a quick study.

Currently he was recording an off-the-cuff, spur-of-the-moment monologue in that language which could be critiqued by a program in his travel computer.

"Som goss ne' tuulikran, ya' tokk kalissen . . ."

Someone knocked.

". . . tu vriinje gaart," he added, got up and opened the door.

"Yes?"

The man who'd knocked was middle-aged and overweight. "You're Mr. O'Bannion?" he asked Boru.

"Richard O'Bannion," Boru said. "Who gave you my name and stateroom number?"

"One of the crew."

"What's his name? It's against policy for crew to give that information unless authorized."

The intruder grunted. "It's easy to get around little things like that."

"It's going to be easy for me to complain to the master-at-arms about the improper and unwelcome interruption. Now what is it you want, Mr.—?"

"Jeong. Tomaso E. Jeong. I saw you work out in the gymnasium this morning. You're quite a gymnast."

"What's that got to do with you?"

"Gymnastics are popular with professional martial artists.

Excellent for flexibility, and they can do gymnastics when they don't want to be recognized through the practice of their katas."

Boru looked the heavyset, reddish-haired man up and down, slowly and deliberately. Jeong was probably a gofer for someone. "Interesting. So you concluded that I'm a martial artist."

"That's right."

"Okay. If that's all you've got to tell me . . ." Barney started to close the door, not to get rid of the man but to get his reaction. Jeong shifted his body in the way.

"It's not," Jeong said. "I'm with the government—Criminal Investigation Division." His right hand moved into his loose jacket, and at that moment Boru hit him in the throat with stiffly extended fingers. The heavy body dropped to the carpeted corridor deck. Barney grabbed his feet, pulled him into the stateroom, and closed the door.

The man was heavier than he looked, more muscle than fat. His mouth was open, little gasping sounds coming from it. Briskly Boru frisked him. In an inside jacket pocket was a small cylinder; he removed it with his handkerchief. It might have passed for a pocket communicator, but it was not for communicating. At close quarters it could provide a spectrum of physiological effects, from slowing reactions somewhat, to temporary paralysis at medium settings, to death. In another pocket was a flat case with an identification document. Criminal Investigation Division. The picture matched the man's face, of course, and the name *was* Tomaso E. Jeong—a perfect document, even to the minute notch in the small letter *e*'s.

Boru tossed the ID case on his bunk, then checked the setting on the stunner, thrust it at Jeong's face while depressing the stud, and put it in his own pocket, still wrapped in the handkerchief. Without grunting, he hoisted Jeong into a chair.

"All right," Boru said casually, "what's this all about?"

"You're in trouble now, bastard," Jeong croacked sluggishly. "You attacked a government official, and worst of all, a C-man. If you know what's . . ."

Boru overrode him sharply. "Jeong, if you were a C-man, none of this would have happened. We'd still be talking at the door or you'd have gotten your information and left. Now let me rephrase my question: Why did you come to see me?"

"I'm supposed to investigate anyone I suspect of belonging to the Frihetskara."

"Um. And you think I'm Frihetskara?"

"You fit. Skinhead, doing gymnastics—and what you did to me there in the door. You're a trained martial artist." He paused, moving a slow hand to his throat. "You hurt me," he husked. "Do you know that? You're a trained martial artist."

Boru grunted. "You should take a course in logic sometime, Jeong. Find out about differences, similarities, and identities. Martial artist does not equate to Frihetskara or any other terrorist group. Why were you reaching for your stunner?"

"You were a presumed martial artist who was being hostile and uncooperative."

"Uncooperative? You hadn't ordered me to do anything, nor established your authority if any. Who do you really work for?"

"I already told you—the CID."

"Come off it, Jeong. A C-man would have had his ID in his hand when he knocked. Then he'd have come right to the point instead of playing a little game. And he wouldn't have stopped me from closing the door unless he was prepared to arrest me on the spot and press charges." He eyed the man wryly. "There *are* field personnel I've never met, a lot of them, but I know the procedures and the style. You're an imposter, and that's a criminal offence, you know.

"Now who do you really work for?" He paused, peering closely at the round face. "A justice firm? Not Equity or Catharsis or Faraday. They may be a bunch of glorified assassins, but they don't use turkeys." He'd been watching the man's eyes. "Nemesis? You're a gofer for Nemesis!"

"Kiss my ass," Jeong growled.

"Who do you work *with*, Mr. Jeong of Nemesis?"

"No one. I work alone."

"Even Nemesis wouldn't send you out by yourself."

"Shows how much you know."

"Do you realize you've practically admitted working for Nemesis? While carrying CID identification?"

"So where's your witnesses? You're not CID either. It's your word against mine."

"Um." Boru went to the room communicator and punched in a number.

"Master-at-arms," said the speaker.

"Officer, I've got a criminal in Room B-16, disarmed and out of operation. Would you come and get him, please?" He disconnected.

Jeong glared at him. "You're a fool, O'Bannion. You've assaulted a C-man using karate and then a stunner, a proscribed weapon, and *you* call the MAA!"

"A proscribed weapon with your identification on it."

"Identification? You're crazy!"

"Fingerprints, Mr. Jeong. Yours. You must have noticed I've only handled it with my handkerchief."

The small mind looked at that for a moment, along with the rest of the situation, and submerged into silent resentment. A minute later there was a firm knock on the door. "Master-at-arms answering your call!" said a voice.

"See?" murmured Boru. "That's how a pro does it." He raised his voice. "Just a moment, officer." He stepped to the door and opened it.

Jeong spoke at once, still hoarse. "Officer, arrest this man for assault on a federal officer!"

Boru smiled slightly. "Officer, would you like to hear a recording of everything that was said?"

Jeong's face froze. The MAA looked from one to the other. "Let's hear it."

Boru ran the recording accessor back, then forward, checking at a couple of points until he heard his own voice say, ". . . kalissen tu vriinje gaart," noted the setting and played it from there.

"Mr. Jeong," said the MAA when it was done, "you are under arrest." He handcuffed him, then helped him to his feet. "You'll find our facilities reasonably comfortable. Mr. O'Bannion, I want you to come along too, and bring the recording."

"Of course," said Boru, "just a minute." He punched in the setting he'd noted, then touched *Preceding* and *Erase*. The record of his language exercise was gone when he removed the matrix cube from the machine.

After supper the MAA, still in duty uniform, was waiting for Boru outside the business-class dining room.

"Good evening, Mr. O'Bannion." He advanced a strong

hand, which Boru met and shook. "Could we go somewhere and talk?"

"I thought we had everything handled. Am I charged with anything?"

"Not at all. But there are some things I'm very interested in."

"Um. All right, I guess I can do that for you. How about your office? It's private, and you'll be able to record there if you want."

"Just what I had in mind." The MAA gestured and Boru walked beside him. Courteously the officer carried on a friendly, casual conversation as they went, so no one would think Boru was in custody. His office was small and orderly; he closed the door behind them and they sat.

"First, Mr. O'Bannion, I must tell you that this conversation is being recorded on trideo. My name is Peter, incidentally. Lt. Peter Hrudny. I checked the computer on Mr. Jeong. We tank it up from the public data bank each time we dock on Earth, including priority three government data okayed to approved space-commercial terminals. The Justice Ministry has a Tomaso E. Jeong, but this man isn't him. I also learned that you are not a Ministry man." Hrudny's watchful eyes found no trace of reaction in Barney Boru's. "At least," he went on, "your name was not included in the data we were allowed."

"Of course. I never claimed to be CID, or any other department in the Ministry."

"True. You seemed to imply it but you didn't say you were."

Boru allowed himself a slight smile.

"So then, who are you?" Hrudny waved his hand to forestall Boru's reply. "I know, you're Richard O'Bannion. But who is Richard O'Bannion? Surely not the business consultant you claimed to be on the ship's register. You're too knowledgeable about the intelligence field."

"First," said Boru, "I'd like to know why you're asking. Am I required to answer? If so, on what basis?"

The young officer shook his head. "You don't have to say a thing. But you are a somewhat—irregular person. First, Jeong sought you out; that's interesting all by itself. Then there's the effective way you handled him—not just physically, but also the way you got him to say so much and got it all on the cube.''

Hrudny took in Boru's casual, matter-of-fact expression, his aplomb. *I wonder what language he was recording in, just before his confrontation with Jeong,* Hrudny said to himself. *Interesting that he wiped it before giving me the cube. Obviously confidential.*

He offered Barney a cigarette, and when it was declined, lit one for himself. ''You see, one of my duties is to inform the port captain, at each stop, of any passenger going ashore there whom I suspect of possible criminal activities.''

Boru smiled. ''And you're wondering whether I'm someone you should warn them about.''

''Exactly.''

''Fine. Just for the record, let me assure you that I'm not. Now ask me your questions.''

''Again, let me remind you that we are being recorded. Your name please?''

''Richard O'Bannion.''

''Your employer?''

''That is classified information.''

''Classified? Are you saying that you work for the Defense or Foreign or some other government ministry?''

''I'm saying that the identity of my employer is classified information.''

Hrudny frowned. This wasn't beginning very productively. He did not want to finger this man needlessly to the port authorities. If he *was* government, it might critically disrupt his mission.

Boru took the initiative. ''Suppose I just talk,'' he said— ''tell you what I properly can. First''—he held up a finger—''I *am* a consultant, a security consultant.'' He paused, examining the MAA as if evaluating how far to go. ''Cornfields,'' he went on, ''is not my ultimate destination; I think I can safely add that. Cornfields is my jumping-off point within the Confederacy; I'm headed outside.

''Just because a planet is outside the Confederacy doesn't mean we have no interest in its government, its commercial activities, or its people. There are individuals and groups on some of them who are important to us, in one way or another.

''And I'd better add here that by 'us,' or 'our interest,' I do not necessarily refer to the Foreign Ministry or any other government agency.

"My employer and I are quite interested in a planet which I will not specify, in a system I'll leave unnamed. Like lots of them, it is not a peaceful world, nor technologically sophisticated. Skullduggery is a way of life there—Niccolo Machiavelli and Lucrezia Borgia would find kindred souls there in its palaces and bourses—but their security and intelligence technologies are relatively primitive. They can be substantially improved without introducing advanced, culturally incompatible equipment.

"So there is use there for a security and intelligence consultant, both from the point of view of the local welfare and our own long-range benefits."

Boru folded his hands on his lap in quiet signal that he was done. Peter Hrudny's gaze found no barrier—neither curtain nor hostility—in the eyes. And although he knew that proved nothing, he was influenced by it. Boru saw that and stood up.

"I hope that's enough for a decision, Lieutenant—Peter. I've already stretched security policy about as far as I can, and I have work to do."

"Of course." Hrudny opened the door, ushered his guest into the corridor, and watched him walk away. O'Bannion certainly managed to sound government, but it was very possible that all he'd said was misdirection. Interesting though. If he had to bet, he'd bet that Cornfields was as far as O'Bannion was going, but he wouldn't give any odds on it.

At any rate, he wouldn't mention him to the port captain there.

FIVE

From *Technical Report 2359:05:31 of the Kubiak Laboratory for Human Studies:* An exercise in the Planning of Sane Cultural Development

The kingdom of Lokar, on Siegel's World, seems on the face of it to be a very unremarkable country on an unremarkable DH planet. Yet ''psychosocial'' tests made by the third expedition gave Lokar the highest social evolution latency score ever reported. Thus, small and primitive though Lokar is, it has the *potential* to become unaided a planetary and extra-planetary leader, according to the tests. A rare quality.

It is not, however, in a class of its own in this regard. An occasional historical or current culture has scored in the same high band, if less far up in that band. Almost all cultures that have so scored, however, subsequently made certain decisions—took certain routes deliberately or by accident or default—which more or less locked them into a consequent social decline. This is true even though, technologically and economically, they may have flour-

ished for a century or two afterward—
in some cases for several centuries.

Such decisions or non-decisions, of
course, were a response to some immediate opportunity or difficulty, in
ignorance or carelessness of the prob-
able long-term results. And the most
important reason for research into the
dynamics of societies is to enable the
recognition of optimum decisions or
reasonable approximations thereof.

A major step in that direction is the
ability to recognize destructive decisions, many of which can appear necessary, unavoidable, and even con-
structive, at the time they are made.
Part of that ability is the ability to
recognize the decision maker who is
likely to make destructive decisions.
And as you should be well aware by now,
we have the know-how to do that.

With regard to a state like Lokar, we
know how to strengthen it—how to sta-
bilize and reinforce the attributes
that make it special—and how to reduce markedly the danger of destructive decisions. Theoretically we even
know how to reverse the effects of destructive decisions if they are not
too immediately extreme and if their
results have not progressed (or rather,
regressed) too far. It is our progress
in this general area that we will look
at in this planning exercise.

Applying our own improved understanding of mental and social dynamics, we
have reanalyzed the raw test data on a
large number of cultures. For the most

part, the rankings of those cultures
did not change appreciably. What *did*
change was the predictive value of certain elements in historical cultures
with regard to subsequent cultural
changes. And these results are in remarkable agreement with theoretical
results. For example, interdependent
covariance analysis . . .

Cornfields had no native intelligent life form; it was a colony
world. Politically it was autonomous within the framework of
the Confederacy. Economically, Boru was sure, it was or
could be controlled by one of the major banking combines. It
took a lot of money to establish a viable colony, and the outfits
that provide that kind of investment insist that things be set
up to ensure long-term profits. Which to them meant the ability
to control what goes on there if necessary.

Cornfields had docking facilities for ships as large as the
great bulk carriers used in the grain and ore trades, but a liner
like the *Admiral Horta* would seldom actually land there.
She had too little to load or unload; it was cheaper to send
down a shuttle. So Boru entered the shuttle's passenger cabin
with thirteen others and sat down.

A signal beeped and flashed, and after a moment the seat
restrainer activated—perhaps an insurance requirement left
over from the days before mass proximity phase, when reaction engines were still used close to planets.

Casually he looked over the thirteen other passengers. Twelve
of them he dismissed as irrelevent to him—new immigrants,
or colonists returning from trips. The thirteenth, he felt confident, was not. To look as inconspicuous as number thirteen,
you had to try and you had to know how. Boru doubted that
anyone else on the shuttle had noticed the man at all. If they
had, they probably wouldn't be able to describe him afterward.

From the man's rumpled clothing and the bag he'd secured
in the overhead rack, he'd arrived immigrant class. To anyone who might actually look, he could easily seem a new
office employee for one of the agro-brokerage firms. Boru
decided he was a C-man assigned to an investigation on
Cornfields.

It didn't occur to him to wonder how he'd come up with that idea. But clearly, it was unlikely that someone would create so exactly the appearance of an immigrant unless they were going to stay there; there'd be little point to it.

Albert Haas's senses and intellect functioned invisibly behind his dull face. Now he half-turned in his seat, as if seeking something in a pocket, his eyes again passing over Barney Boru. *He's noticed me*, thought Haas. *He is definitely the one*. Haas did not deceive himself that he would necessarily spot an agent, especially on brief, casual contact. There might still be another on board, but that one fitted the description Jeong had given him and was very probably the O'Bannion he'd been told to expect. Surely Department Eleven knew who O'Bannion really was—what he looked like—yet they hadn't told him. Department Eleven played strange games sometimes, even with itself, with its own people.

But Jeong! Jeong must have been Nemesis' own peculiar aberration; Department Eleven wouldn't have had someone like that on staff, even as a gofer. He'd assumed that Jeong's apparent stupidity was a front—a facade. Imagine gratuitously exposing one's self to a suspected justice agent, apparently for no better reason than to show how clever one had been to have spotted him. It was fortunate the *dummer* had reported before confronting O'Bannion.

O'Bannion might well take a disguise after landing. But on Siegel's World, O'Bannion would be a large man among the locals, and there'd be the violet-blue eyes, the snub nose and wide strong mouth. He was unlikely to hide them successfully.

Boru consolidated key items of his luggage into a large musette bag and slung its strap over one shoulder. The rest he checked in terminal storage. It was likely he'd have to take a hotel room by the time the evening was done, but before he did that, he would look for Wan Larmet, the smuggler who would be his transportation to Siegel's World.

It was the growing season on Cornfields. The evening air was warm and humid, the sky grading from rose-streaked violet in the west to near night in the east. The ground, heated by day-long sunshine, would keep off any evening chill for several hours. And from the stockyard a few kilometers out of town came the strong odor of steer manure, like hot rubber.

He walked past the bored gate guards onto the paved street

bordering the space port. On one side was only the tall mesh fence that circled the field. On the other were restaurants, bars, small hotels, trucking firms. Farther on were warehouses. There was little traffic.

He'd been told that the place to find Larmet, or get a line on him, was a bar and steakhouse called the Kansas Feedlot, near the port. A strange name. Boru wasn't sure what a feedlot was, but Kansas had been a political subdivision in the old North American federation before the reorganization. After walking a ways, he could see it a short distance ahead, its quaint sign sporting the fluorescent outline of a bovine head with tireless jaws that chewed robotically in flashing red.

Inside the Kansas was semi-dark, a sizeable barroom in front, the larger dining area behind it partially screened by a wall. The barroom was well occupied but not crowded. Somewhere in back he could hear an argument, noticeable by tone rather than loudness; the bartender and bouncer were giving it half an ear. The clientele seemed a mixture of spacers and laborers, with a few young farmers of the kind that come to town half-hoping for a fight.

Boru stepped to the bar, and the barkeep came over to him. "A draft," said Boru. "House brand." The man drew it. "I'm looking for someone," Barney continued, "a pilot named Larmet. Wan Larmet."

"You picked the right time. He's back there now, feeding his face."

"How'll I know him?"

"Short and stocky, bobbed red hair: a heavy-world hominid. Dressed like a bum but he never asks for credit."

Boru nodded and carried his beer into the dining area, where he stood by the entrance looking around. He found Larmet and the argument at the same time, the smuggler exchanging hostile words with two other spacers seated at the same table. Standing behind the two were two more. The language was not Terran, the trade language of the Confederacy. Other diners glanced their way now and then, curious or annoyed; probably none were able to follow the dispute.

Boru stood back to watch, putting his musette bag on the floor just inside the door. One of the seated spacers laid a large heavy-bladed knife on the table, his hand resting beside it. Abruptly Larmet lunged to his feet, simultaneously throwing the solid table to one side, the knife sliding off and across the floor in a crash and scatter of dishes and glass. One seated spacer went down beneath the table, the man who'd shown the knife went over backward in his chair, but the two on their feet reacted quickly. One lunged for Larmet, who met him with a heavy hooking punch that knocked him onto the overthrown table. The other went at him with another knife, which slashed Larmet's arm as he grabbed the man's sleeve. He clubbed the man with his right fist, once, twice, then twisting, threw him over one hip.

The other three were regaining their feet, two flashing steel in their fists. Boru intervened without warning, feet and hands swift and brutal. One man had time to fumble out a gun, swinging it toward Boru, but Larmet's heavy fist took the gunman in front of the ear and he went down like a hammered steer.

For an instant their eyes met, Boru's and Larmet's, and as one they hurried into the barroom, Boru snatching up his musette bag enroute. The bouncer, club in hand, let them pass: they were aimed at the exit, and that was exactly where he wanted them to go.

Outside, Larmet turned left, jogging.

"Where are we going?" Boru asked.

"Which one are you?" Larmet countered.

Which one of who? Boru wondered. "The one that saved your ass in there," he said. "Name's O'Bannion. I hope you're Larmet."

"Wan Larmet. I'm headed for my ship and then for Thegwar—Siegel's World." He looked over his shoulder at Boru. "O'Bannion, it's now or not till next week for you. I'm raising ship tonight. Those guys back there have friends—a whole ship clan—and they'll all be around till sixday. I don't intend to be back till they're gone."

"You've got yourself a passenger."

They slowed to a brisk walk as they approached the gate. Larmet had lost considerable blood and was clutching his left arm, pressing the cut closed. "Okay," he said, "I'll show you where I'm parked. After that you'll have just fifteen minutes to get your gear and get aboard. Then I'm pulling the picket pin and getting out of here; those Balthions are mean bastards."

Boru grinned. "I've got all I need to take with me right here." He clapped the musette bag with one hand.

The gate guards looked a bit more interested when Larmet walked through with blood brightening his disreputable jumpsuit, but they didn't say or do anything. Now that the action was over, Boru thought Larmet might get shaky or weak, and watched for it as they crossed grass and concrete toward a small pot-shaped ship waiting on its pad in the thickening night. But when they boarded the *Slengeth Buëd,* Larmet was still as tightly wired as when they'd left the Kansas.

"That's your bunk," he said, pointing at a door. Then he opened a small locker and took out a white metal case. "I need you to tie up this damn arm." While Boru opened the aid kit, Larmet peeled the jumpsuit down to his waist. Blood was flowing again until he repinched the cut closed. Boru scissored off a six-inch length of surgical sponge, bound it snugly on the thick bicep with absorptive bandage, then taped it.

Larmet tied his jumpsuit sleeves around his waist like a sash and began the pre-takeoff procedure with his hairless torso bare to the waist. "Where'd you learn to fight?" he asked Boru.

"Here and there over the years."

"Right. Forget I asked; I'm not myself." He said nothing more as he worked. About five minutes later he had Boru take the auxiliary pilot's chair, sat down himself and tapped the power switch on his radio.

"Traffic control, this is *Slengeth Buëd.* I want an okay to lift out. Over."

A bored voice answered. "Hold it a minute, *Slengeth Buëd.* . . . All right, *Slengeth Buëd,* you've got an okay to lift."

Larmet's experienced fingers jabbed keys. They rose slowly in mass proximity phase, accelerated smoothly upward above the broad and fertile plain, the lights of the town shrinking, drawing together, losing identity, disappearing. The terminator came into view westward. Seconds later the horizon was a sunlit arc.

"So we're on our way to Siegel's World," said Barney.

"You got it, O'Bannion." A few minutes later Larmet eased in the tensor control and they flashed away.

SIX

Dear Editor:

In your evaluation of Assembly Bill 2389:147 to relegalize human cloning, you cited the classic instance of the Robert Lemoyne clone. To be sure, only seven of the 50 scions showed sufficient interest and ability to obtain doctorates in mathematics, despite all being educated together in the Marcellus Academy.

However, the commonly held idea that all were pushed toward a mathematical career is untrue. They did a standard Marcellus curriculum, with free choice of scholastic emphasis. In fact, for almost 17 years *they did not even know from whom they had been cloned.*

Thus a record of 14 pct becoming Ph.D. mathematicians is really highly remarkable, even though only two of the seven have had outstanding careers and none have shown the brilliant originality of their progenitor.

I knew and personally worked with members of the Lemoyne clone, and in fact all of the test clones, as chief counselor in the Marcellus Academy. I had access to all of the clonal performance data, which were highly diverse within clones, and I massaged those data in every way I could think of.

And I must perforce agree, without reservation, that new procedures of cloning will not produce the kinds of results we had hoped for and became disabused of. Neither personality, proclivity, nor intelligence are duplicated in cloning, *so neither, then, are they strongly influenced genetically*. The considerable circumstantial but never truly compelling (merely attractive) data that had led us to hope otherwise are no better now than they were then. Which is to say, no good at all.

Yet somehow there *is* an unquestionable connection between cloning and success in the activity for which the clone was selected. Although the study persons were sequestered to age seventeen on the extensive Marcellus estate and not told the talent for which they had been cloned, invariably performance in the progenitor's specialty area was significantly greater than that of randomly selected (within intelligence classes) non-clonal control groups raised and educated with them, and of groups cloned for other attributes. For example, of the 20 scions of the David Markel clone, eight grew up to play World League basketball, three becoming major stars. Even among males in the 2.1 m height class, that was statistically far above the

means, significant at approximately
the 10^{-4} probability level.

That the cause is not genetic, nor some
strange side effect of the cloning process itself, does not make it less
real. Yet while it is undeniable that
the scions of Ching Mee Chao have a
hugely disproportionate ability to
play the piano or otherwise perform or
compose music, some of the 40 displayed
little interest or talent. What *is* the
factor at work?

I feel that, despite the failure of
cloning to produce duplicates of progenitor intelligence and talent, it
is desirable to relegalize human cloning for *licensed research*. And the
research I would like to see done would
be directed at identifying the unknown factor or factors in clonal performance.

The problems of legal identification
of clonal individuals have been exag-
gerated and can be solved without invasion of dignity. And certainly they
are more severe with the bootleg cloning that occurs on a small scale outside the law. They should not be a
factor in the question of legalizing
cloning.

However, I reluctantly consider our
discourse an exercise in futility.
Your presentation was needless and my
response useless. The irrational emotions which were able to prevent or
inhibit human cloning for centuries
were overcome, those decades past,
only by enthusiasm rooted in hopes and

expectations. The irrationalities persist. The enthusiasm, on the other hand, was lost when the hopes and expectations failed to materialize. Thus I do not expect to see cloning relegalized in my lifetime.

Bernadette Silverman
Terra 91285—A—3716
Emeritus Professor
Marcellus Academy

SEVEN

Larmet put the *Slengeth Buëd* in landing mode at one hundred fifty meters, then hovered to give Boru a close-up look at the scene. They were landing on the night side of Thegwar—Siegel's World. According to Boru's briefing, this was a remote fringe of Lokar, a back-country outpost. The sky was moonless at that hour, but snowcover made the most of the starlight, and visibility was decent. In the distance was a broad ice-bound river. A small moatless castle stood some one hundred meters east of the spot where they would land. Near it to the north, a hamlet—a loose assemblage of log huts, sheds, and barns—crouched beneath the cold dark; it might have housed a hundred people. Rail fences and stone piles marked fields which in summer grew crops. About two kilometers away in three directions, dark forest stood.

In the fourth direction loomed a high plateau, its base no more than a kilometer behind the castle. Its precipitous and broken slopes in part were forested, in part too steep for stands of trees. Here and there, sheer cliffs stood black and forbidding in the midst of snow.

"Damn!" said Boru. "My information was that it's autumn here. Looks like winter to me."

"It is autumn," Larmet replied. "When winter gets here, you'll see the difference. Of course, it's a lot worse up here at Jussvek than you'll find down south at Tonlik."

He turned on a powerful search beam and played it over walls and windows of the castle, finding cracks in window shutters, the embrasures of the gate tower. "This is how I let them know I'm here," he said. After a minute a door opened; someone waved a torch overhead in the courtyard and disappeared back inside. Larmet switched off the beam.

Still he did not land; he was thinking about something else. There were limits to what it was all right to tell O'Bannion, and till then he'd discouraged questions, using generalities and refusals. But he liked the man, and he owed him: O'Bannion had saved his ass in the Kansas Feedlot at risk of his own. Larmet felt he should at least put the man on his guard, tell him something.

"You know that question you asked me?" Larmet said. "About what I meant when I asked you which one you were? Well, I was told to expect two guys. One would be a Richard O'Bannion, the other a Herman Heidemann. Both of you were coming here to Siegel's World. One would contact me and a week later the other one would. But I couldn't remember which was which; I hate to write stuff down.

"So I asked you, which was a stupid thing to do.

"Anyway, the first one—that's you—wasn't supposed to know about the second guy. Why, I don't know. But the second guy, Heidemann, would know about you. If this sounds sinister, maybe it is."

Larmet brooded for a moment. He had one more thing to say and wondered if he'd said too much already. If he'd read things wrong, misjudged his man, O'Bannion might turn his ass in, and Wan Kubia-Dek Larmet would become carrion.

"And there's something else you ought to know," he went on. "I am a freerunner, like I said, but I'm on a retainer, too, which is why I base on a hick planet like Cornfields. I may be putting my balls in a vise, telling you this, but while I do this run for Exotic Products Ltd.—they operate this connection as a front for Department Eleven, the undercover branch of the Foreign Ministry."

He lapsed into glum silence. After a minute or so they

lowered toward the stone-hard frozen field, landed, and sat waiting, brooding over coffee. Boru was suddenly very uncomfortable about this job. First of all, jobs on Class D worlds were almost unheard of—illegal as hell. A job on a Class D world could get the company busted overnight. And while Bhiksu Tanaka undoubtedly rated ethics and justice above legality, you don't waste the company.

Still he hadn't questioned the assignment: Bhiksu knew what he was doing. But did he this time? Bhiksu would never put a second agent on this job without telling him. And Department Eleven? Department Eleven had more nuts than a squirrel hoard. Bhiksu would *never* have anything to do with them.

Never say never, he reminded himself. *You accept never, you stop looking.* Looking—*look* and *act* were the things to do. You could grind yourself in with a lot of figure-figure. Look: see how it is. And act: act according to how it is. Ideas don't come out of figure-figure, they come in spite of it.

That much of neozen was real to him, even though he still got stuck in a wallow of figure-figure now and then. Meanwhile he didn't like the looks of this assignment, or the smell.

Well, he told himself, *you like a game; you've got an interesting one here.* He turned to Larmet.

"Wan," said Boru, "the information you gave me just now—I didn't have any of it, and I'm damn glad you told me. It could save me from getting hung out to dry."

Larmet was still caught in the mental backlash of having disclosed. He'd survived so far on the policy of "keep your mouth shut"; now he'd violated that policy drastically. "It's okay," Larmet said. "I owed you."

They gave their attention to the window then, to the scene outside. After a bit, a group of four Lokaru and two animals started across the field toward them. Larmet and Boru put on thermal jackets, and when the group was almost there, they went out, the door sliding shut behind them with a soft but solid thump. The temperature was well below freezing, an icy breeze blowing. The Lokaru wore fur parkas, open and with the hoods back. They wore swords on their belts, although it was little more than a hundred meters from the castle, and Boru wondered if it was that dangerous around there or simply custom.

Like Larmet, the Lokaru looked as human as Boru. But the

pack animals, *peernu*, were clearly not horses, merely somewhat horse-like. They could best be described as resembling large, powerful, brown llamas with soft dense fur. On their heads, Boru could see where horns had been cut off.

Earthmen were long since used to finding their own kind on Earth-type planets. There were variations of course, according to the conditions and history of planet and locale, but all were *Homo sapiens,* or genus *Homo* at least.

The intelligent felids found dominating some worlds had also been of a single genus. And on a few high-gravity methane planets, intelligent oviparous reptiles had been found, again of a single type.

More than three and a half centuries earlier, when science had recovered from the shock of finding humanity on another planet than Earth, there'd been a few years of contention among theorists. Then a third and a fourth world with man had turned up. Parallel evolution didn't remotely account for the observations; the genera *Rattus, Canis, Populus* etc. were not native on any of them, although things ecologically and structurally equivalent usually were, and in the parlance of spacers and colonists got labeled "rats," "dogs," and "cottonwoods."

When most of the populations of *Homo* native to various planets proved interfertile, almost the last resistance expired to acceptance that they were from a single source. Three hundred years later, Boru and Larmet could take these things for granted, even though there remained nonconformities in the data that gave the theorists migraines.

"Khua chot, Larmet!" the leader greeted.

"Khua chot! Ya' bis foira, Vinta," Larmet answered. The Lokaru chuckled or smiled, and Boru helped Larmet put chests of trade goods onto the pack saddles, where the Lokaru quickly lashed them. Then they walked together to the castle, the two house servants leading the thick-pelted peernu. The two warrior types talked with Larmet, and for the first few exchanges Boru had difficulty understanding the locals. They spoke more rapidly than Larmet, with whom Boru had practiced aboard the *Slengeth Buëd,* and less distinctly than the training tapes. Pronunciations were different too, and the tonality—a distinctive dialect. But even so, by the time they reached the gate, Boru was following the basic flow of the conversation.

Among other things, they said it was a warm autumn. But when winter arrived, which would be soon, it would be severe, because the winter pelts of the something or other were especially thick and rich. The something else were so fat they could hardly run, and took quickly to the trees where they were easy to shoot.

Two casual guards stood at the gate. When they'd all passed through, one of the guards tripped a heavy ratchet, and an iron portcullis fell with a thud, its sharp bars striking hard into frozen, broken ground. Glancing back, Boru saw them swing shut the heavy, metal-faced timber gates, then slide beam-like bars into place to secure them.

Inside, the rampart was lined with stone huts and sheds built against it. The central house, two stories high, was of large stone blocks. Bright sparks rose from one of its several chimneys, to dwindle, darken, and float down to the snow that covered roof and ground twenty centimeters thick. A small mountain of firewood was heaped outside. Their two escorts paused on the low stoop until the two house servants had unloaded the trade chests, then opened the doors and they all entered.

A sense of unruly energy and boredom met Boru inside. Four more men sat around a table with a game board in the center and a jug at each of two corners. Light was from a large fireplace and half a dozen pitchy torches in wall brackets. Whatever other odors there might have been were drowned by acrid woodsmoke. A stout woman in a coarse ankle-length dress turned to stare as they entered, then bustled out. One of the men got up from the table.

"Larmet!" he roared, "Welcome! Welcome! Good to see your ugly face!" He met them halfway, pumping the smuggler's big paw with his callused sword hand. He was almost as burly as the spacer, and taller. When he clapped Larmet on the shoulder with his other hand, the smuggler winced.

"What's the matter?" the man said laughing. "Getting tender with years?"

"A little disagreement in a beer hall. I overreached myself; there were four of them, and I got stabbed. Luckily my friend here had just come in the door, looking for me. Ask him for a demonstration sometime; he's a master of weaponless fighting."

The man grunted, his eyes narrowing as they moved to Boru. "Fighting with bare hands is pleasant enough, but in

Lokar it's the sword that counts." He examined the agent, then grinned, showing yellow teeth with a gap on top, and stuck out the sword hand again, this time to Boru. "I'm Karn Kinjok, master of Jussvek."

Karn, thought Boru, *one who holds title to more than four hundred sixty hectares.* A *juss* was an estate outside any administrative district. *Vek* meant mountain and probably referred to the plateau behind them. So, very roughly, the man was Lord Kinjok of the Mountain Freehold. Boru let the powerful Lokarn know that his own hand, if less massive, was equally powerful. At least.

"I'm Richard O'Bannion, of Earth."

"O'Bannion. Plainly you're no woodcutter, yet your hand is like iron. You must be a swordsman." He turned to Larmet. "It's been awhile, trader. I've got some prime furs for you." His eyes creased. "Including two gontru, both adults. It's going to be a fierce winter for them to have come down off Vekyorn."

He looked at one of his men. "Orlin! Bring the furs here!" Then handing a jug to Boru, he asked, "And what brings you to Jussvek?"

"Business."

The bright brown eyes fixed on him. "And what is your business?"

Apparently Lokar didn't have a strong tradition of respecting the privacy of strangers, Boru decided, even here on the frontier. "I train fighting men," he improvised. "And especially I train the trainers—the men who train others."

"Oh ho! You must be good then!" Kinjok boomed.

Boru shrugged. "Not bad."

A grin flashed again on the homely face, and Kinjok looked to the youngest of the fighting men in the room. "Frelek! Would you like to fight?" He turned back to Boru. "That's like asking a wolf if he likes to eat."

Frelek had risen at once to his feet, tall among these Lokaru, with wide shoulders, an obvious natural athlete whose thickly callused swordhand was visibly larger than the other: his training had started very young indeed. His face was scarred, not by blade but apparently by fists in brawls. "My pleasure, lord." Then he bowed slightly toward Boru with just a touch of mockery. *The bastard's sure of himself,* Boru thought.

"Hah!" Kinjok's grin was ferocious, and he fetched Frelek a clap on the shoulder that would have staggered many men. "Your pleasure? Maybe so! But what if it's his pleasure instead of yours?"

The young man's mouth drew down, and there was no humor in his eyes. "I'm a Lokarn. And better than that, I'm from Jussvek. And beyond that, I was trained by Galther—his best student by his own report. It will be *my* pleasure."

Kinjok's eyes gleamed as he looked again to Boru. "What would you say to a friendly fight, O'Bannion? With Frelek here? It's a rare opportunity for us to see an off-world fighting man display his wares, or to see young Frelek really tested."

"Maybe." This time Boru grinned. "It's good for youth to be proud, but they have to be ready for occasional surprises."

Frelek scowled; Kinjok laughed. "And you, Frelek—have you anything to say about the pride of older men?"

"I have something to say about off-worlders," he began.

Kinjok dropped his grin. "No insults to race!" he said sharply. "You know better, by Voroth! Would you have these men think we do not teach our young men at Jussvek?"

The fire left the young man's eyes, leaving them hard and sullen, and Kinjok's tone eased. "O'Bannion," said Kinjok, "the sword is the weapon for a Lokarn. And since you say you train fighting men, I am curious to see you fight. But you are my guest, and did not come to my house to brawl. Are you willing to fight this young bull? I must tell you he is very good, and while I prefer that neither of you be badly hurt, there is always that danger."

"I'll tell you what I'll do," Boru answered, "to avoid bloodletting. Give me an iron rod from your smithy, about sword length, with a handguard welded on. Frelek may use his sword if you wish. We will imagine the rod is a sword, and if I give him a stroke that would kill with a sword, the fight is over."

Kinjok almost laughed with delight at the combination of brashness and psychology. The man had to be good to dare it, but even so . . . "And if he gives *you* a mortal stroke with his sword? Suppose he runs you through?"

O'Bannion shrugged. "Then the fight is also over."

Frelek's intensity was gone; the body was ready but the spirit had lost its certainty. Kinjok looked back and forth between the two men, suddenly thoughtful. "Vinta," he said to one of the men, "give . . ." He groped for the name.

"O'Bannion," Boru said helpfully.

"Lend O'Bannion your sword. If it gets damaged, I'll give you your choice from the armory, and the colt Neetha."

"Neetha? Wait a minute," Vinta said with a grin. "Let me go out and weaken the blade first." He drew his weapon and laid it on the table for Boru, who took it, hefting it, feeling the balance, examining its double edges. It was a bit shorter than his samurai sword back home, but heavier—thicker, to provide the necessary strength against breakage while still providing two cutting edges. With his own sword, a skilled and flexible wrist made two edges out of one, cutting on both strokes.

But the difference was unimportant to him, more a matter of martial aesthetics than of combat effectiveness. He nodded to Kinjok and took a casual stance. Frelek drew his sword and faced the off-worlder, his tongue unknowingly licking dry lips.

"All right," said Kinjok, "this is to be no death fight, but an exhibition. I prefer neither of you dead or hurt. When I shout 'Stay!' both stop at once. And do not fail to stay when I call it."

Boru nodded, eyes on Frelek. There was no sign that the younger man had heard his master. His face seemed darkened, sculpture instead of flesh, except for a muscle in his jaw that flicked arrhythmically.

"Get set!" ordered Kinjok. "Start!"

Frelek, instead of feeling out his adversary, learning his moves and responses, attacked with abrupt fury, his blade striking and thrusting high and low. Boru parried easily, let a long thrust slip past his ribs only centimeters from them, and sweep-kicked Frelek's feet from under him. Eleven seconds after the command to start, Frelek lay panting on his back with Boru's sword tip at his belly. That was about eight seconds longer than it would have taken if Boru had been willing to kill him.

And Kinjok knew it. "Stay!" he shouted, although Boru had stayed already.

Boru stepped back and bowed to his prostrate opponent, then turned to Kinjok. "I'm sorry to give you no more display than that. But Frelek is very good, too good to extend the contest needlessly. It is dangerous to play with someone like him.''

Frelek regained his feet and stood with sword in hand. "Put it away!" Kinjok snapped. "Now!" The man sheathed it. The host looked back at Boru.

"You didn't try once to cut him. You only parried."

"Anyone who needs stone walls has enemies and needs good men around him. Why waste one? I have no bloodthirst, and no grudge with Frelek. And besides, I demonstrated a principle that's too little appreciated anywhere I've ever been. Two principles.''

"What are they?"

"First, the body is the true weapon of the will and mind, and the sword is only an extension of it. And second, control is more powerful than anger.''

Kinjok looked thoughtfully at Boru, then turned to Frelek. "Sit!" he snapped. The young man sat. The Lord of Jussvek examined him. "Drink!" The young man reached to a jug and raised it to his lips. "And don't brood!" Kinjok finished.

The man was troubled, and Barney knew why: his champion had been totally outclassed. His cultural image had been severely damaged. "Are there many like you where you come from?" he asked Boru.

"To tell the truth, very few. My people are traders, not warriors. On Earth, I'm a master warrior, one of a handful. Although anyone that Larmet brings to Thegwar is likely to be a fighter.''

Kinjok examined Boru, then nodded to himself. "Mordon!" he bellowed toward the kitchen. "Durnis! Prepare food for my guests! Two of them!''

Meanwhile Orlin had come back accompanied by a house servant. He had arrived while Frelek was still on his back, and had put down the litter-like pallet with its three large bales of furs. Now they picked it up again, and made as if to set it on the table.

"Not there!" roared Kinjok. "For the sake of Voroth! Our guests will eat there! Put it on the floor," he added, pointing to a place better lit than most. When they had complied, he untied the bales, and Larmet sorted through the furs, piling them by species and apparently by size and quality, speaking an offered price for each into his pocket calculator. Occasionally Kinjok took brief exception, as a matter of principle, but his heart wasn't in it. Boru decided that Larmet was quoting prices higher than could be had from anyone else, and had left the man without a game. Larmet might well be buying at a loss—on a reduced margin at least—to retain this contact on a planet where off-world contacts were illegal.

With no real dickering, or even any close appraisal of the furs, the entire procedure took less than half an hour. It was over and the bales retied by the time two women came in with large platters and food enough for a squad of marines. The others sat and helped them drink, while Larmet and Boru ate supper. The roast reminded Boru of venison, and there was a hard-crusted loaf of coarse dark bread, a sort of butter or soft cheese, and potatoes with thick gravy.

"Potatoes!" said Boru. "I'll be damned!"

"Yeah," Larmet replied, "you find them in the damnedest places. They originally came from Deiwaanis, you know. My home world."

"Sorry, shipmate," Boru replied, "but potatoes are from Earth. That I'm sure of." He cast back into his memory. "They were first grown by aborigines in America, on Earth, who called them 'batata.' When a more advanced culture found out about them, it spread them all over the planet. About four centuries before space flight."

Larmet eyed him. O'Bannion sounded like someone who knew what he was talking about. Of course, good liars sounded that way too, but he didn't think O'Bannion would lie needlessly, even if he did work in a covert field. "Next thing you'll be telling me you guys invented gravy," the spacer said.

Boru grinned at him. "Everyone invented gravy. Everyone who didn't want to waste good grease." He turned to look at his host. "Lord Kinjok, is it all right in Lokar to talk business while eating?"

Kinjok looked surprised. "Of course! Talk away!"

"I need to go to Tonlik. That's why I came across the stars to Thegwar. And I'll need to buy clothing, weapons, equipment"—he groped for the word—"and a peeran from you."

"And an escort," Kinjok added.

"Escort? What for?"

"To help keep you alive. These stone walls, as you said,

weren't built for pleasure. In winter we're still sometimes visited by barbarians from the north.''

"How many men will I need?"

Kinjok looked thoughtful. "I can only let you have three, but we seldom see large parties anymore."

"How many days to Tonlik?"

"If you don't need to hole up through bad weather, about seven days to the settled districts and maybe four or five more to the city."

He looked at Boru as if wondering whether he should say more. "It's none of my business," he went on, "but you're an off-worlder, and that could get you in trouble. You speak well, damned well for a foreigner, but. . . . Once you get to Tonlik, there are people there from all over Lokar, and from foreign kingdoms too. You can blend right in. Say you're from some other part of the country—from here at Jussvek if you want. People in Tonlik won't pay any attention.

"But along the way, people will say, 'I wonder where he's from?' If you stop at the next holding, Jusstoniss, a day's ride south, they'll say, 'He's not from the Vek; we know their speech and most of their folk.' And they might guess too well, which could be bad for all of us. You'd better camp, and not stay at holdings for at least the first few days—best not till you get to the settled districts."

Boru nodded, chewing.

"My people won't talk," Kinjok continued. "We don't like attention." He took another swig of the raw liquor in the jug between them. "We're a long way from the king, up here, a long way from anywhere. Do things our own way, like trading with Larmet here. They'd have me in their prison for that if they knew."

He paused, then continued reminiscently. "It used to be almost like an independent country up here. When I was a young man, we didn't even see a tax party more than every three or four years, and they never dared to come with fewer than thirty soldiers. We wouldn't let them in. Cleaned us out when they did come though. Now they come every spring without fail, with their string of sleighs, before the ice goes out on the river."

"What kind of man is Trogeir?" Boru asked. "What kind of king?"

"What is there to say? He's a king. Kings act like kings."

"I was told he's a dangerous man to deal with—treacherous and ruthless."

Kinjok shrugged. "Anyone's dangerous with that much power. He's businesslike, that much I can tell you from experience, businesslike and thorough. His tax parties come every year now, as reliable as winter. But they don't land on us like a pack of trolls like they used to. They come in, count the furs that we haven't already sold to Larmet here, count the calves and kids and foals, measure the grain, figure the tax, take their tithe in furs, give us a receipt, and leave. It's 'Lord Kinjok' this and 'Lord Kinjok' that, and 'King Trogeir sends his greetings,' and 'thank you, Lord Kinjok, may Voroth favor you.' It's not like getting conquered and looted anymore.

"We even get something in return now. Seven or eight years ago Trogeir led an army up into the barrenlands and demonstrated it around for the barbarians to see—mass battle drills and things like that. He came away with a treaty. We never see any big barbarian forces anymore—just a few renegades now and then. Haven't stood a siege for eight or ten years."

He stared glumly, then hit the jug again. "Things are changing. When you have king's men coming around every spring, you get the feeling you're not free anymore. Sometimes I wonder if I wouldn't rather have the barbarians; you can fight them and win, and not worry about dying of old age."

He shook off the mood. "Larmet! Let's see what you've got in those chests. It's a nuisance, you know; anything that looks off-world we have to take out and hide in a cave in the mountain before the tax party comes, but there may be something."

He decided on some jewelry, which Boru was sure Larmet took a loss on, and some superb steel knives and axes that could be rehelved to look local. The smuggler then paid for the rest of the furs with gold and silver. When the dealing was over Larmet went back to his ship instead of staying overnight: Even in this remote backcountry it was best to lift ship before daylight. Also, Boru suspected, there'd be the local equivalent of lice in the bedding, which the smuggler would rather do without.

Kinjok and Boru walked with Larmet through the now still air to the *Slengeth Buëd*, where the spacer made his farewells to the Lord of Jussvek beneath the flickering cold luminescence of the aurora. Then Larmet turned to Boru.

"O'Bannion," he said, "you're a good man in everything I've seen, starting with the Kansas. I haul people here and there, now and then, and generally I'm glad to see the last of them. I don't much like agent types, as a rule.

"But you I wish well. Take care of yourself and remember what I told you about the second man and Department Eleven." They shook hands firmly. Then Larmet boarded, and when they'd backed off a few steps, he lifted. They watched him out of sight.

Boru shivered. The temperature, he decided, must be fifteen Celsius degrees below freezing and headed downward. Autumn in Lokar—this part of Lokar anyway.

"Larmet's all right," Kinjok said quietly, staring upward. "The only off-worlder I ever saw that I actually liked until you, and I knew a few in the old days, off south when I was young. If he was any of the rest of them, I'd tell him to stay away. Dangerous to have him come here these days."

They turned and trudged toward the castle, last week's snow crunching under their feet.

"Maybe I'm getting soft in my middle age," he added to himself.

EIGHT

Except for one afternoon on his vacation, Boru hadn't ridden horseback or equivalent for three years. Fortunately for his thighs, peernu were relatively slab-sided.

The trail roughly paralleled the Great River, often shortcutting its looping meanders, sometimes following the high bank above the timbered floodplain or above the river itself. It saved many kilometers, compared to riding on the river ice.

At first, when they'd left the Jussvek clearing, they'd ridden through forest that could almost have been on Earth, in Finland or Manitoba. There were straight needle-leaved trees like northern pines, interspersed with patches of slender, naked, green-barked trees that in summer would be aflutter with leaves. Beneath were scattered dark saplings that on casual observation might pass for Earthly spruce or fir.

But after a time the trail had entered an extensive burn, too large to see across, where the milliard spikes of fire-killed trees stabbed from a thick low growth of shrubs and knee-high seedlings toward a pure blue bowl of sky.

It was cold, in a way that Boru had never experienced before. Vinta, the senior of his three escorts, had commented, when they'd mounted in the first gray of dawn, that it was starting to feel like winter. They wore their traveling clothes fur-side in. So far it didn't seem to have warmed, although it was now full daylight. The sun was still hidden behind the brutal bulk of Vekyorn, the high plateau. A moment's mental arithmetic told Boru that at this season and latitude, with only thirty days till the solstice, the sun wouldn't climb higher than about twenty degrees above the horizon at noon.

Meanwhile the peernu plodded through the clouds of their own breath, the dark hair of their necks and shoulders white with rime frost, the frozen moisture of their own exhalations. The mustaches of the three Lokaru were chunks of ice. This trip would be a time of adjustment for Boru—adjustment to the 30.6-hour days as well as the climate.

Here and there, animal tracks crossed the trail, while others followed it. Vinta pointed out old prints of several large animals, the name of which translated most nearly to "wolf." A pack of six, Vinta said. Another animal, a *hreen*, left very large cloven tracks. Kin to the peernu, he added, but much taller. Sometimes they'd attack a man in spring, when there were calves, and in early autumn during the rut.

As the party finally approached the edge of unburned forest again, they saw a hreen, nearly black, standing perhaps two meters at the shoulder, with long legs and a longish neck. Short horns jutted forward. It watched their approach, giving no ground; when his escort drew the short bows from their saddle boots and strung them, Boru followed suit. But as they came almost even with it, some fifty meters off, it turned away, and jogged easily, loosely, not looking back. It angled toward the forest's edge and disappeared among the trees.

By Terran standards, the region was subarctic in climate but not in latitude. Even this late in autumn, daylight lasted for some ten Earth hours, and they would use all of it and more. Three times before midday they dismounted and led their mounts to rest them, each time walking a kilometer through the hard shallow snow. Boru's sore thighs and buttocks were ready for the change; he was sure the peernu were no more grateful than he for the break.

Gradually the day warmed until, in early afternoon, they threw their parkas across the peernu's backs in front of the saddles as they walked the animals a fourth time. Boru estimated the temperature then at no colder than perhaps minus ten or twelve Celsius.

"How deep does the snow get in winter?" he asked.

"Oh, about to here," Vinta answered, holding a hand out at face level. "In great winters—about one in ten or twelve—it gets maybe twice that deep, and about as often no deeper than this." He held out his hand waist high.

"How do you get around when the snow is too deep for a peernu to carry you?"

The man laughed. "As little as necessary. On skis. We keep on trapping and hunting for furs, but we do no needless traveling."

"What do we do if we get a big snow now?" Boru held out his hand waist high.

"We won't." Vinta eyed Boru quizzically. "Don't you have snow on your world?"

"Sure, although not where I come from. In some places—in the high Sierras for example—a meter or more will sometimes fall in one storm."

"Huh! Here it doesn't fall like that. We have lots of snowfalls, but mostly like this." He spread the thumb and fingers of his mitten to indicate six or eight centimeters. "But by winter's end . . ." He shrugged.

It made sense to Boru. He'd studied a map, and it was several hundred kilometers east to the ocean, with mountains in between. The year on Thegwar was 1.71 times as long as a Terran year, and the seasons were long in proportion, with a thirty-two degree axial tilt. Spring was a long way off. He'd make his hit or walk away, as the case might be, and be back on Earth long before the snow melted here.

Late in the day the trail became a rough and narrow road wide enough for sleighs or wagons. Vinta explained that it was a portage by which river cargoes bypassed the falls and rapids of Toniss ye' Kivvors. Just now it was marked only by the tracks of hunters and trappers from the holding called Jusstoniss, near which they would pass in the morning.

Some kilometers farther they dismounted for one last hike. The long winter dusk was settling, and a steep ridge rose perhaps two hundred meters above them. On foot they climbed the diagonally slanting road, the distant boom of a mighty waterfall in their ears, the light fading, the temperature sinking toward arctic again. At the top, Boru would gladly have made camp, or even continued walking. But Vinta gave the order to mount, and they rode another hour, down into a draw and up the opposite ridge, and then once more.

There they camped at a small crude corral where the frame of a large lean-to stood partly roofed with bark. They finished the job with saplings, then two went out to cut young firs on whose tops their mounts could browse, while Vinta and Boru gathered firewood. Finally they prepared supper.

"What about wolves?" Boru asked. "Any danger?"

Vinta shrugged. "When the snow is a meter deep and food hard to find or catch, they might threaten a man out alone. But a bow would hold them back, and they'd still their gnawing bellies with their own dead. Of course you'd want a fire by your side while you slept. For us, so early in the season, you can rest in peace. At worst they may trouble the peernu. If they do, we'll hear about it and I'll set a watch to throw firebrands at any that come near."

They talked until supper was cooked, then filled their bellies. Finally each man rolled up in a heavy fur robe, feet toward the fire. For a few minutes Boru lay awake, replaying his day before he went to sleep.

"Who are you?" the king demanded.

I am Richard O'Bannion, thought Boru.

The king shook his head. "No, *I* am Richard O'Bannion, king of Lokar. *You* are Brian Boru, King of Ireland, defeater of the northmen." He opened the cupboard, took down a large photo album, and beckoned to Boru.

I wonder if I should correct him, Boru thought. *My first name is really Bjorn, which is Norwegian, and I'm not the king of anywhere.* He followed the king out onto the loading dock where they sat down on the edge, dangling their legs.

When the king looked at him, it was like looking in a mirror. "They call *you* Richard O'Bannion because you look like me," the king explained. He spread the album on the table and Boru leaned forward to see. There were his mother and father, and they both looked like Boru and the king. The only way he could tell them apart was that his father had a beard and wore a kilt, while his mother was smooth-faced and wore a leotard. There were other pictures, but Boru didn't know who they were of. They could have been his parents at different ages, or the king or himself. It seemed to him that they were of other people—aunts and uncles, brothers and sisters.

He turned the page and there was just one picture—another look-alike except for the oriental eyes. It was Kabashima, dressed not in pants and shirt, or kimono or gi, but in a dhoti wrapped around his loins.

"Good evening, father," said Boru.

The old man smiled, touched finger to lips, then motioned him to follow. Boru trotted along behind him up the long tunnel that curved steadily clockwise so that he could see only twenty meters ahead. Water and steam pipes lined the overhead and the outside wall. The tunnel ascended slightly as if to take one spiraling up to the surface. Once and again the tunnel was partly blocked with old junk, mostly plumbing, made of iron, of all things, rusty and scaling. Kabashima was no longer with him, and Boru knew that it was now up to him alone.

With some distaste he picked his way through the junk and into the park. There, declining an invitation by a group of youths playing basketball, he approached the pool. It was circular and perhaps ten meters across, with knee-high curbing, and the men in it wore rubber waders to their armpits. A—something—swam in powerful circles below the surface, its scarcely submerged back forming a wave to mark its passage. Boru watched for a bit as the men tried to trap it in the net they dragged, but the something avoided it, surging past them.

They're afraid of it, Boru thought. *They'll never catch it while they're afraid*. He jumped in, the water above his waist, breasting purposefully toward the surging wake. At his close approach, the something burst out of the water, not at all sharklike, instead like a great tangled snarl of wire, a spinning, snapping tangled mass of barbed wire from some agro colony. And ugly! But he felt no fear or even distaste, and as it spun, it shrank.

He stood feeling more sure and powerful than any king, than any Brian Boru, watching it spin and shrink until, with a small inaudible pop, it disappeared like a soap bubble.

Boru half woke, then slipped back into sleep, not to dream again, until a high keening wakened him. The others had wakened too, and Vinta saw him raise his head.

"Wolf," said Vinta.

Another wail answered the first, nearly as high-pitched, and another higher yet, almost ultrasound to Boru. One dropped out and a fourth entered in, in a sort of round, one voice rising, another in mid-cry, another falling, each voice distinctive, making the night electric. They might have been a kilometer away. Boru crawled out of his sleeping robe, out of the lean-to. Overhead, between the treetops, he could glimpse the aurora shimmering and pulsing in the sky. He didn't even feel cold for several minutes, until the chorus ended.

After relieving himself, he returned to his robe and remembered his dream. Not all of it, but the fountain, the wading men, the powerful surging wake. And the decision, plunging in, and the ugly tangled snarl emerging to spin and shrink and disappear.

Dreams, he'd always felt, meant nothing more than one's subconscious rolling around in sleep; Kabashima said the man who sought wisdom in dreams was looking in the wrong direction. But Boru was glad he'd dreamt this one, and glad he remembered it.

NINE

Because the nights were so long, they began their subsequent travel days long before dawn. On the third day, the pain of riding was notably less, and on the fourth, Boru rode comfortably.

On the fourth night came the snow. Vinta had sensed its coming in advance, though Boru could see no sign of it in the sky. Even when they made camp, the stars showed sharp and clear between the treetops. Fourteen hours later, when they broke camp in the darkness, fifteen centimeters of new snow covered the old—a heavy fall by local standards and still coming down. They loaded their pack animals and rode off into a veil of falling white.

By midmorning the snowfall had thinned; by midafternoon the sun was shining. But the peernu were wading now in snow well up toward Boru's knees.

In late afternoon they came upon fresh tracks of hreenu leading up from the river, turning then to follow the trail ahead of Boru and his escort. Vinta grunted a stop and examined the tracks, while the other two Lokaru looked around worriedly, hands on sword hilts.

"Looks like half a dozen or more," Boru suggested.

Vinta nodded.

"Are they more dangerous in herds?"

Vinta's sober eyes met Boru's. "They don't form herds. These are maneaters." He saw the confusion in Boru's face. "Not the hreenu; they eat plants. But there's a—brotherhood of crazymen that live wild in little bands, hunted by the kingsmen. I've never heard of them so far north before, nowhere near this far north. They live down near the edge of the settled districts, and raid farms there. Sometimes several

60

bands get together and make a big raid.'' He paused. "They eat man-flesh."

He peered around, narrow-eyed. "It's their pride that they tame hreenu and break them to the saddle. Maneaters are the only way you'd have half a dozen hreenu walking together in a line like this."

Without speaking further, he turned his peeran and back-tracked the hreenu trail toward the river, putting distance between the maneaters and themselves. After a little the trail led down onto the ice, but instead of turning downstream, Vinta led them across the river into timber on the other side.

"Too visible, traveling on the ice?" asked Boru.

Vinta stopped, nodded, and turned in the saddle. "Narl!" he ordered, "I want you to stay behind us a hundred meters and keep your eyes and ears sharp. If you see or hear anything more than a jay, anything that might mean someone else riding around out here, ride hard and catch us. If you're attacked, holler, as loud as you can."

The youth's face paled beneath its outdoor color. "Let Britto," he said. "He's the lightest. He has the fastest peeran."

Vinta's face hardened. "*You'll* do it."

The kid's scared spitless, thought Boru.

"Wait a minute," said Narl, and there was desperation in his voice. "Let's think this through. The smart thing to do is turn back north and head for home. The country south may be full of maneaters!"

"Bullshit!" Vinta retorted. "All the maneaters there are probably don't come to more than thirty or forty, maybe fifty. You want to go back to Jussvek and tell Kinjok we gave up because we saw some tracks? You'd be better off fighting the maneaters!"

Britto had been scowling at Narl; now he looked at Vinta. "Hell, I'll be rear guard if he doesn't want to."

Vinta shook the offer aside. "I told him to." His eyes hardened on Narl. "You got any more to say?"

The youth flushed and shook his head, turned his mount and started backtrail, reaching for the bridle of his pack animal as he came even with it.

"Leave Ginniti with us," Vinta ordered. "You don't need him with you, and if you need to run, he'll either slow you or you'll have to leave him behind."

The youth withdrew his hand, his flush darkening, rode a

few paces back, then stopped to let the others continue ahead of him out of sight.

"The son of a sow was going to run away," said Britto to Vinta.

Vinta grunted. "Don't say it unless you know it's true," he answered, but no one, including Vinta, thought otherwise.

"Are these maneaters good fighters?" Boru asked, "or do they just have people scared?"

"I've never seen one," Vinta replied, "but I doubt they're any better, man for man, than we are. If as good. They're crazy, that's the difference. Don't give a damn what happens to them. A couple of guys in a tax party, three or four years ago, had been in a patrol that ran into a band of them. They said the maneaters were wildmen in a fight. The kingsmen beat them, but they outnumbered the maneaters two to one.

"They captured two of them, and after a day or so the maneaters got so they'd talk to them. Both had been stolen by maneaters in a raid, along with three other boys twelve or fifteen years old. Those that stood up to the torture pretty well were invited to join. The initiation was to eat manflesh; actually that was only part of it. One of them wouldn't, and they didn't ask him twice, just poked his eyes out and left him afoot in the forest without even a knife.

"The two of them ate and did whatever else they were told, so of course they could never go back among decent folk again. That stuck them with the maneaters from then on—the only people that'd have them.

"Then, in the fort where they were holding them, they got hold of a dull old table knife. One of them managed to shove it up under his buddy's ribs into his heart. Then he tried to do it to himself but passed out before he reached the heart. He died the next day."

Vinta stopped talking and rode grimly. Boru wondered how he himself would act if he ever got into a situation like that. Taboos could be compelling, and the taboo against cannibalism was one of the strongest.

That night they made no fire, even to cook, and Vinta assigned sentry duty, each man to stand his watch along the backtrail as long as he could stay awake. He stood first watch himself, then wakened Boru. In a fireless camp they slept crowded together under their combined sleeping robes, sharing heat. When Boru got up, the others stirred, half waking.

He buckled on his sword and rode his still-saddled peeran down the track that Vinta pointed out to him, parallel to the trail they'd come in on. There, some hundred meters from camp and fifteen from the trail, he sat to watch from the concealment of a sapling thicket.

Cold as he soon became, it was hard not to doze. He kept his mittened hands inside his parka pockets, then worked his toes in his fur boots, for the activity as well as warmth. Finally he undertook to enter the neozen aware state, in which subjective time is controlled by the person and drowsing does not occur. But he failed to attain it, drifting instead into upright sleep, waking with a start. He couldn't have slept more than half a minute, he decided, a minute at most, or he'd have started to fall.

He wondered how long Vinta had sat on watch. One hour? Three? The man was good—smart, level-headed, responsible; he'd not have given up as long as he could hold off sleep.

The longer Boru sat there, the easier it was to stay awake, and he tried again for the aware state until he was there, outside of time. Eventually a snowflake drifted down, and then a few more, little more than flecks. At length they stopped. He was aware of cold feet, a chilled body, as if he were outside them. His peeran's head hung down in sleep, but occasionally its body shifted beneath his own.

Suddenly there was movement down the trail, but it did not startle him. Men came riding in the night on tall ungainly hreenu reminiscent of camels and even more of moose. In eerie utter silence they rode by—five mounted men followed by two pack beasts, swords in mittened hands, the leader's eyes ahead on the trail, the others following dully, unalert.

And these are the men we feared, thought Boru.

As the last man passed, only fifteen meters distant, Boru launched himself, hurling a blood-curdling shriek that exploded on them, startling the hreenu while momentarily freezing the maneaters. Simultaneously his sword slicked from its scabbard. The last man let go his hold on the pack string line and was going for his sword as Boru cut him down. The next man, wheeling, closed with him. Time slowed; Boru watched the man's sword arm swing gradually back as his saddle hreen half turned to strike with its shoulder. Casually Boru's blade clove the beast's face, then took the man in the neck,

sweeping him from the saddle. The large animal crashed
down as Boru's peeran recoiled.

The next man had nocked an arrow, loosed it, and Boru
struck it aside with his sword as his mount recovered. As he
charged, he saw the man's wide staring eyes, sagging mouth,
saw his slow hand go to his hilt. This hreen reared, but before
its front hooves could strike, its throat opened, gushing blood.
Boru thrust the rider through, and man and beast fell heavily
together against a tree, then to the snow.

Already the fourth man was fleeing. The fifth, the leader,
sat frowning, sword in hand, ten meters away.

"Who," he said hoarsely, "or what, are you?"

Boru matched gazes with him. The man spoke like the
voice on the language tape; with an upper-class accent, maybe
an aristocrat gone bizarrely and criminally depraved. Boru
dug the nervous peeran with his heels, closing the distance
between them.

"To these I was death," he said. "To you—we'll see. Get
down!"

The man nodded carefully and tossed his sword into the
snow, then started to get down on the off side of his hreen,
where Boru would lose sight of him for a moment. Instantly
Boru rose in his stirrups and lunged, slashing downward,
backhanded, across the tall beast's back. The man fell sound-
lessly as his mount backed, wheeled, and galloped off.

Boru calmed his own animal, patting its shoulder with a
thickly mittened hand, then dropped to the snow. He searched
the final dead man, not sure what he was looking for, perhaps
an energy weapon concealed. The only weapon he found was
a sheath knife, razor sharp and balanced for throwing.

It was the first time Boru had fought in the neozen aware
state. Now it had slipped from him, leaving him alert only in
the more usual sense. He remounted and trotted toward camp.
Vinta met him on foot, bow in hand, Narl and Britto close
behind.

"They're all dead but one," Boru called. "One rode away."

Vinta surprised him with a grin. "They're *all* dead," he
said, displaying his bow. With his other hand, bare, he
jabbed a finger against his thick neck below the ear. "When
you yelled, I piled out of the lean-to with my bow and a
fistful of arrows. Then this fool came riding like a blind
man—I don't think he saw me or the camp—and passed

about ten meters off." He chuckled and shook his head. "At that it was a lucky shot, him riding full tilt in the dark through the trees."

Vinta told the other two to follow, and they jogged through the snow to see the carnage. It would give them something to talk about at Jussvek, assuming they ever got back there.

On the second day after the encounter they met scouts from a large force of kingsmen, who insisted they bare their chests to be checked for a telltale tattoo.

Yes, Vinta said, they'd seen tracks of maneaters, but he told nothing more. And the kingsmen, their attention on wiping out maneaters, didn't question them about their business. Six days earlier they'd engaged a combined force of some thirty maneaters raiding deep into a border district, killed many of them and scattered the rest. They intended to track the survivors and end the problem.

Boru was impressed with the discipline, bearing, and toughness of the troops as well as their basic good manners.

Two days later, the four entered farmlands. Before nightfall they came to a town with an inn, and in the morning parted company. Vinta and his men turned back north at once. Kinjok had warned them not to get drunk; it might loosen their tongues. Boru continued south toward the capital.

TEN

Tonlik, with a population of forty-five thousand, was the major seaport, the metropolis, the center of commerce, and the capital of Lokar. It was also, Boru noted, treeless and generally unaesthetic.

The avenue he rode on wasn't bad—wide enough that on special days an army could parade down it with room at the sides for crowds to stand and watch. But on this winter evening it bore only occasional wagons, a few "equestrians," and scattered citizens hurrying on foot in the cutting wind.

By contrast, most of the streets that entered it were little or no more than alleys close-pressed by buildings. He wondered how safe they were for ordinary pedestrians at night.

It could be worse, he told himself. He'd been in Klumon on Taji's World and visited towns on Pandit's and Johanson's, in cities that could be described as medieval, even if they were technically C class. At least here the street didn't have slops and garbage dumped from windows and balconies. There was dung of peernu, to be sure, but not of humans. The pungency of wood smoke from the city's chimneys was the predominant odor.

Before long the avenue brought him to what was obviously Krogaskott, the great citadel which was the seat of royal government in Lokar. Its massive wall surrounded and largely hid its buildings. The square before its broad open gate was some ninety meters wide, and as long as the wall looming over it—roughly a hundred and fifty meters between ponderous defensive corner towers. Evident but unobtrusive, erect and impassive, serveral guards watched, swords at their sides and bows in hand, near the gate where tall pikemen stood. Like the troopers in the field, these men were clean-shaven and professional looking.

Killing a king, Boru reflected, might take some doing. There'd be a problem of access and a problem of escape. But it didn't occur to him to doubt success. He had certain advantages: physical skills beyond any expectation here and therefore beyond likely limits of protection; sophistication— knowledge of the techniques of cultures where assassination was a refined technology; and then there were patience and surprise. Surprise was a key factor. In pretechnological societies, many might wish to kill the king but few could make the opportunity to do it. Almost any serious assassination threat would grow out of certain known factions, and depend on the connivance of identifiable persons or connections that could be watched.

Boru, on the other hand, enjoyed the status of an unsuspected agent with an unsuspected motivation. They would not be watching for such as he.

At least that was the assumption.

Just now he was a stiff and hungry agent, having been on the road for fifteen of the last eighteen hours, and his peeran was weary. Despite a raw wind in his face, the nearness of journey's end and a threat of storm had kept him moving. Tonlik was some twelve hundred kilometers south of Kinjok's wild subarctic holding, but wintry nonetheless. A bitter gust of wind swept the square, generating a whirlwind of gritty snow, and Boru reined his peeran toward two buildings, a stable and an inn, side by side across the square.

Several stolid peernu stood riderless and waiting before the inn, chewing their cuds. His own mount had long since brought his up and had no more to chew. Boru swung stiffly out of the saddle and tied the reins to the hitching rail, then crossed the low stone porch and went in. Two men were talking just inside, and stepped aside to let him through.

The innkeeper, Nars Lorf, was not thrilled with the new customer—a pinewoods savage wearing furs, and bloodstained furs at that. Nor was Boru's speech reassuring, for he'd practiced diligently the backcountry dialect of Jussvek, to make himself believable as a native. But when Boru laid an undeniable gold korbin on the counter, apprehension was suspended. Even when he stabbed his heavy-bladed skinning knife into the wood between the innkeeper's fat hand and the coin, Lorf's sudden interest was not dampened.

When they'd finished dickering, Lorf had a serving boy lead the man to his room. It didn't surprise the innkeeper that he'd gotten away with overcharging for the tiny sleeping cell, but he *was* a bit startled that the man, who called himself "Barni," did mental arithmetic quickly and accurately without so much as glancing at his fingers, and even understood the king's recent decimal currency. When the frontiersman came back down a minute later, he'd shed his saddlebags and other gear, but his sword still rode at his thigh and his eyes were still hard. Lorf was glad to see the street door close behind the man, who might have been truculent at finding so little room for his money.

Lorf shouted to the potboy to mix him a mug of hot punch, then went to speak to other customers and forgot about the man from the north.

Outside, Boru allowed himself a grin. He enjoyed a game with someone like the innkeeper. Unhitching his peeran, he led it to the stable next door and ordered a stall, feed, and rubdown for the animal. He assumed the stablekeeper was overcharging, and beat the price down a bit as a matter of form. But the man was no weasel like the potbellied innkeeper. Boru then asked after an eating place—''the best around''—and the lantern-jawed face studied for a moment.

''Next door is pretty good,'' he answered. ''I eat there. But the best around is the Larilia Tavern, eight or nine doors on by. Costs though. They've got fancy cooks, foreign foods, musicians, a pretty woman dancer from the southern lands, a couple of women that cleans it every night—and you pay for all of it twice when you buy a meal.''

Boru grunted his thanks and left.

The Larilia Tavern could almost have passed for some supper clubs on Earth—one of those that attempt a medieval atmosphere. It was actually fairly clean, there were forks and spoons as well as knives, and the drinks were served in glasses instead of metal or ceramic mugs. Even the music was not too unlike some that could be heard in certain exotic clubs in Los Angeles, Brussels, or Djakarta. It reminded Boru of a record he'd heard once, of Renaissance music from Provence.

The lights, though, were bowls of oil with burning wicks that a fire marshal would never approve; the solid, rough-hewn ceiling beams were sooty from their smoke.

Without staring around, Boru studied the clientele. A few glanced at him, curiously or idly. They were clearly upper crust—merchants, professionals, and court officials he supposed. It was the kind of place to know about.

The waiter collected the tab when he took the order—a practice that hadn't been mentioned in his briefing—and the meat arrived a bit overdone on the outside though properly juicy red within. He hadn't realized till then how ravenous he was.

Selena stepped in from the back room and looked the small crowd over before telling the musicians what she wanted. Most of the faces were familiar, men who ate there occasionally or often. There were no women among them; in Lokar, women rarely ate in public houses.

One man, though, she was sure she'd never seen in the Larilia before. It was his garb that caught her eye and stopped it, but what held it was something else. Cautiously she probed, then thoughtfully walked to the musicians and spoke quietly.

Miku, the leader, was surprised at her instructions: usually her dancing was not flamboyant, for the style of the house was conservative. It was a place for conversation more than entertainment; people met there, things were discussed, deals were made, all over the finest food and drink of any public house in Tonlik, which meant in all of Lokar. But Miku nodded. He admired Selena, thought himself in love with her, and felt fortunate indeed to have her infrequent favors.

Two of the instruments were essentially the same as the Terran flute and lap harp. There was also a simple drum and something resembling a lute. The flute began, and Selena glided onto the slightly raised dance platform. Her basic style was that of Gzarim, a country five thousand kilometers southwest. And given the level of transportation on Thegwar, Gzarim was known more by fable than fact to even the more sophisticated Lokaru. So if she called herself Selena of Gzarim, no one disputed her. And if some of her techniques resembled Terran ballet more than those of the sultan's seraglio, there was no one to point it out.

She began to dance, and a few sets of eyes turned to her, but conversation mostly did not pause; they'd seen her dance before, most of them, and there were things to talk about. As she continued, though, more eyes were drawn, and the murmur of voices thinned. Normally her dances were modestly sensuous; this one was increasingly sensual. At every opportunity her glance crossed Boru's, and if the encounters were fleeting, he knew they were not accidental.

The musicians caught the unaccustomed energy and emotion, and their playing became increasingly electric. No one in the room was talking now; all eyes were on the woman. When after a prolonged climax she finished, she did not simply curtsy deeply, but folded into a low and graceful ballet position that epitomized submission. The customers stood as one, applauding, Boru included. Gracefully she rose, bowed, momentarily caught Boru's gaze, then disappeared into the back room.

He finished his meal absently. Who the hell was she? he asked himself. From Earth probably, yet supposedly Lokar had deported all off-worlders. And she definitely seemed to recognize him. It was vital that he question her; his security was endangered if not already blown. He waited until the musicians broke for a beer, then walked over to them. "What's the dancer's name?" he asked.

The flutist, Miku, didn't answer at once, staring at the roughly dressed, somewhat alarming-looking stranger. But he could think of no good reason to refuse an answer. "Selena," he said reluctantly.

"Where is she from?"

"Gzarim." Miku doubted this backwoodsman had ever heard of it.

"When does she dance again?"

"When she has rested. It'll be awhile; probably a quarter hour yet."

Hours on Thegwar were half again as long as Terran hours, Boru knew. He nodded curtly, and this time sat at a small vacant table close to the dance platform. Miku felt alarm at this and thought of going for the bouncer. But what could he complain of? To wear a sword, if unusual, was not unlawful so long as it remained in its scabbard. Would the man be angry when Selena came out in moments instead of after a quarter hour? But he hadn't lied, only misled, hoping the man would leave. For when she came out next, it would be to play, not dance.

The flutist had just finished his beer when she appeared again, her own flute in hand. His eyes moved to the stranger, but the man sat quietly. The musicians went to their stools, and after a few quiet words began to play unobtrusively. She was easily the best musician in the group, with solo passages to demonstrate her virtuosity. But after one piece, and before they could begin another, Selena excused herself. To Miku's chagrin, she went to the backwoodsman's table and sat down; worrisome behavior. She didn't even look back.

Boru watched her approach; she even sat down gracefully.

"You dance very well, Selena," he said in Lokarit.

"I wasn't sure a man dressed the way you are would appreciate it."

He grinned. "Any man would. Where did you learn to dance?"

"In Gzarim. My home place. It's a long way from here— five thousand kilometers."

"Hm. I thought you might be from someplace a lot farther than that," he said. She examined her nails. "I think," he went on, "we may have things to talk about, of mutual importance." He switched to Standard Terran for his next two words: "Don't you?"

She looked at him. "I'm sure we do," she replied in Lokarit.

"My name is Barni," he said. "When are you off tonight?"

"Not for an hour. I have three more dances."

"You dance beautifully. I recognized some techniques. I hadn't expected to see anyone from, uh"—he grinned again—"from Gzarim here in Tonlik."

She smiled slightly in return. Something was bothering her, something he'd just said. "Where can we talk freely?" he asked.

"I don't know. This is not like—Gzarim. There aren't any—any cocktail lounges." She used Terran for the concept.

"Right. I've got a room in the Three Bulls Inn, but you'd be conspicious going in, and it doesn't even have a chair. It hardly has a bed to sit on. Where do you live?"

"I have a room near here, in a private home. But I don't know how I'd get you in. They'd never allow me to bring in a man."

"Do you have a window?"

"Of course. But it's an upstairs room—second floor."

"Tell you what. I'll go to my place and get rid of this sword. Then I'll meet you here and walk you to your place so I know where it is. You can show me the window. If I can't see a way to get in, we'll figure out something else."

She gazed absently at nothing, thinking.

"Is there anything wrong with that?" he asked.

"Not really. I was just wondering what to say to Miku, the band leader; he usually walks me home. This is a pretty law-abiding town, but women don't walk out alone at night. He's really nice." She looked at Boru. "And interested in me."

"Shows good taste. Tell him I'm walking you home. He's already overawed by the rough-looking frontiersman. Tell him—hell, you'll think of something."

She nodded, moved as if to stand, then paused. "Did you like my dance?"

His grin was boyish in his two-week-old beard. "You've got it, trouper," he murmured in Terran. Then in Lokarit: "It was lovely. Exciting."

"I danced it especially for you."

"I wondered. I hoped so. There was a message in it, you know," he said more seriously. "It said, 'I recognize you.' "

"It said more than that," she answered. "It said, 'God but I'm glad to see you. I was afraid you'd never get here.' " She broke their gaze then, got up and went back to the other musicians.

Boru watched her go. *But that doesn't tell me how you knew me,* he told himself, *or what you're doing here.* When he'd finished his beer, he got up and left.

He timed it so closely, they wouldn't let him back into the Larilia when he returned; they were getting ready to close. She looked worried when she came out, then relieved to see him there. He took her gloved hand in his mitten.

"What did you tell Miku?" he asked as they began to walk.

"That you'd been a sailor on the ship I came to Tonlik on; that we'd become friends on the voyage. He's jealous of course. But in Miku, jealousy takes the form of sadness instead of anger, and he knows he has no claim on me."

They strode along on the packed and lumpy snow and turned down the first side street that entered the square. It was wider than some, but still narrow and unlit, with densely shadowed walkways between buildings—truly dark on this cloudy winter night.

"I can see why Miku walks you home. How far is it?"

"Less than a block now. A long block though." A dozen buildings farther on she stopped. "This is it."

He looked it over. It was brick, narrow, and two stories high, with a loft beneath the steeply sloping roof.

"They don't need another boarder, do they?" he asked thoughtfully.

She smiled. "Good try," she whispered back, "but no balloon."

"Um. Where's your window?"

She led him down an alleyway between buildings, only wide enough for a large wheelbarrow full of firewood. "There," she whispered, pointing, "the small window by the corner. There's another window around the corner in back." She paused and looked at him. "Doesn't look very promising, does it?"

Boru reached out and touched the walls on both sides of the

alleyway. Something more than a meter apart, he decided; maybe a hundred twenty or a hundred thirty centimeters. He placed a foot on one wall and the other against the opposite, to hang there spread-eagled between them just above the ground. "I think I've got it solved," he said, and jerkily worked up a little higher before dropping to the ground again. "Assuming your window isn't frozen shut."

Her dim face was thoughtful in the darkness. "Can you make it up that high? It must be seven or eight meters."

"About six," he said. "And these rough brick walls make it a cinch. Run upstairs now and open the shutters. Then be ready to open the window again when I get there."

She stared at him for a moment, then nodded and hurried out of the alleyway. He waited for several minutes, eventually wondering if she'd been drawn into an unavoidable conversation inside. *Maybe she's starting a fire in her stove*, he speculated. *They're not likely to have central heating here for a long time to come*. He'd removed his hood to look around, and a claw of cutting wind whipped down the alleyway, chilling his scalp through its short stubble. It occurred to him that the whole situation was ridiculous. It was a wide stretch between walls, six meters up to the window, and they could just as well talk while walking around in the streets. The weather wasn't *that* bad, certainly not compared to what he'd traveled through.

He heard the window then, looked up to see the shutter swing out. She looked down and waved. He reached to the sides and began inching upward. Hell! He could drop that far without feeling it or losing his feet.

It was more strenuous than he'd expected—he hadn't been working out—but two minutes later his fingers hooked over the windowsill and he clutched it, letting himself swing into the wall as his left hand reached to join his right.

The hard part was getting in. The bulky parka dragged against the rough bricks and the window was almost too narrow for the gymnastics involved. When he'd gotten his shoulders in, she grabbed his waistband in back and pulled until his hands reached the floor and he somersaulted the rest of the way. As he got up, she closed window and shutter, and they stood an arm's length apart, looking at each other in the light of a single oil lamp. Her lips moved, formed a soundless word, and suddenly they were in each other's arms, their lips meeting.

"God but I'm glad you're here," she murmured against him. "I knew you'd come some day, but I didn't know if I'd last that long." She stepped back, holding his shoulders, his eyes, then stepped into his arms again. Soon their hands wandered, until after a while they lay naked together, touching, kissing. There were tears on her cheeks.

"You're crying," he said. "Is anything the matter?"

"No," she said, half laughing. "I'm happy. Don't you know women? I'm so relieved and so terribly happy. I was beginning to think I'd been abandoned." She pulled at his body. "I don't want to wait," she whispered as he moved to position himself. "I've waited too long already." She reached down between them. "I want you now."

They lay side by side in the flickering light, holding hands in silence. There were not even snapping sounds from the stove, for the wood was not resinous, and the pieces only slender faggots from the city's coppice forest. Their urgency gone, each lay in private thought until, after a bit, Boru spoke.

"How long have you been waiting here?"

"Nearly four and a half years—Thegwar years. More than seven Earth years." She squeezed his hand softly. "It was a long long time. Until tonight. Tonight changed my perspective on it; it's over."

"Who told you to expect me?"

"Hagop. Hagop Valenzuela." She sensed his lack of comprehension. "I guess you don't know him; Foreign is a big ministry. Hagop was deputy ambassador for information to the royal court of Lokar." She paused. "How much did they tell you about my situation here?"

"Practically nothing. How about filling me in?"

"Well, I was—am—basically a dancer. I loved dancing and music, and majored in them in the secondary grades. But maybe I didn't love them enough, because at seventeen, when I'd gone as far as I could at Marcellus, they decided I didn't have enough talent, or enough drive, to send me to one of the major dance or music schools. Instead I got office training and ended up in the secretarial pool at FM.

"Then one thing sort of led to another and they smuggled

me to Siegel's World. Smuggled because they didn't want to account for me to the authorities—Trogeir had been getting more and more difficult for years—and the idea was for me to pass as a Gzarim dancing girl. After that I was to become Hagop's mistress, which would make communication easy and get me into some pretty high circles.

"I never really knew what the ultimate purpose was of all this: the good old 'need to know' principle. Or maybe there wasn't much to explain; FM is great for just accumulating data on the premise that some of it will turn out useful." She turned on her side and put a hand on Boru's arm. "Maybe I'm boring you," she suggested.

"Keep talking. This is interesting."

She removed the hand and lay back. "Well, it was clear to me from things I'd seen and heard as a secretary and over- heard on the way here that FM was really unhappy about the Cultural Ministry: about the way CM interpreted and enforced the cultural protection clauses in the Vienna Accord. FM had decided years before that Lokar was the most promising country and culture to work with on Thegwar. But Lokar was just another kingdom here. One of the larger and stronger, but there were—are—no major powers on Thegwar: a couple of empires that can hardly rule themselves plus a lot of small kingdoms and a few big ones like Lokar with a lot of wilder- ness. Transportation, communication, military technology— everything was too primitive.

"So what they wanted to do was introduce gunpowder and cannon making in Lokar, and steam engines for pumping, which would allow the Lokaru to get into serious coal mining and large-scale iron mining. Things like that. Then Lokar could build military-industrial dominance on Thegwar in just a few decades as a class C culture. But all Culture would allow was introduction of the horse collar, the windmill, improved rigging for ships—things like that. Things that would have big long-term effects but start slow."

She raised on one elbow, looking at him. "But just days after I arrived, before they even had me move in with Hagop, Trogeir chopped the embassy here—gave them twelve days to pack up and move out. I hadn't been identified as FM person- nel, so Hagop asked me to stay, keep a log of anything I could learn, and they'd send someone to pick me up later. I wasn't very eager to stay by myself, but he promised me that if I did, when I got home they'd set me up with a pension and an education of my choice. I couldn't turn that down, but I never imagined it would be so long."

She stopped talking and lay back down. He let the silence be for a moment before he asked: "How were you supposd to get information? D'you have a contact in the palace?"

Selena frowned. "They *didn't* tell you much, did they? It turned out that I'm part of the Marta Aspgaard clone. She's a psychic, a telepath quite famous in the psychological literature becaue she's so precise and reliable. I was the only scion out of thirty that showed the talent, and I wasn't really interested. To me it was a nuisance, not a gift—handy at times, but it set me apart. A lot of people resent you if they know about it—I found that out early. Most people have secrets, or thoughts they think of as discreditable. And I found the flows of angry or frightened or sad people—lots of people—very unpleasant.

"Fortunately I could turn it on or off, like closing your eyes. And because 'pathing people so often upset them if they knew, it seemed to me unethical to 'path unless there was some good reason."

"How do you use it for intelligence gathering?" Boru asked. "Do you listen in on cabinet meetings? The king's private conversations?"

"Nothing like that. There are too many minds around, too much psychic noise and no fine tuner. It helps a lot if you can see the person. Hagop had already arranged for me to dance at the Larilia—it was a watering place for embassy and government officials. It would give him an opportunity to 'meet me'; then we'd 'get interested in each other' and he'd move me in with him. So when the embassy got chopped, it was decided that I'd simply stay on at the Larilia. I'm probably the only person in Lokar who makes a living dancing. When a customer comes in, one I know might have something or one I don't know, I scan them and listen in on their conversation. Conversations are the easiest to 'path because they're vocalized."

"Is that how you noticed me?" Boru asked. "Telepathy? I don't recall thinking anything that would be all that—diagnostic."

She chuckled. "You didn't. It wasn't telepathy." She put

her hand on his thigh, and he raised himself on an elbow. But instead of kissing her, he asked, "So how then?"

"I almost didn't. It's been—sixteen years, and your clothes didn't help any. And you don't expect to run into a Terran in Lokar. But the face was familiar, even with the red stubble." She stroked his cheek. "And then I remembered."

She paused, and when he didn't respond, nudged him verbally. "You still don't recognize me, do you? From the academy."

"The academy?"

She frowned, wondering if she could have been mistaken. "The Marcellus Academy. I was there when you were. In different buildings and classes maybe, but I couldn't help but notice. There must have been twenty or more that looked just like you. And twenty-nine others that looked like me."

He fell back on the bed. "Holy Jesus!"

Her hand withdrew. "What's the matter?"

"You just explained half the things I ever wondered about myself." After a few seconds he got up on his elbow again and looked down at her face. "I never lived at the Marcellus Academy," he said, "at least not that I can remember. Maybe as an infant, but I doubt that too. And I never knew I was part of a clone. I grew up thinking I was an orphan or a foundling—something like that."

"Oh!" she said, her voice small. "Look, I didn't mean to say anything that might hurt you."

"You didn't! God no! You don't happen to know what clone I belong to, do you?"

"Um. I'm sure I heard. After they let us know. Hm-m. Who were those good-looking athletic blond boys?" Her hand drifted again, fingertips dragging. "Cloned from some martial arts master. Not an oriental name—Irish I think. . . . Started with a K, but it wasn't Kelly. Keenan! That's it, Keenan! Does that sound right? Like anyone you ever heard of?"

"There was a James Keenan in England," Boru said, "years before I got into martial arts. James Keenan. I've seen him mentioned in the literature but never saw a picture of him. An eclectic with special interest in the kung fu praying mantis style." Boru laughed quietly. "My god! It's a wonder my foster father didn't spot the resemblance. I guess Keenan didn't perform all that widely for a man of his professional stature. Mainly in Britain, I suppose.''

"I'm glad I didn't upset you," Selena said.

He grinned, his teeth showing in the lamplight. "You didn't." He rolled onto his side and reached for her. "Now let's see—where were we?"

Before he left that night, Boru told her that his mission was not to pick her up—that he was corporate, not FM. But he promised that when he left Thegwar, he'd take her with him if she wanted.

He was not entirely frank about his mission, saying only that he was to insinuate himself into the palace. The best way he could think of to do that was to get hired as part of the royal guard or other household staff. He also told her that he expected another agent to show up with unknown motives who might be hostile to him, and that the person might be middle-aged, of medium height, and bald.

After he dropped from her window to the frozen alleyway, it occurred to Boru how embarrassing it would have been to sprain a knee or ankle. But he had a definite ally now. He had no doubt she'd be helpful, if with nothing else than what she knew about the royal government. Getting her to Jussvek afterward might be a lot harder than promising it; even getting himself there could turn out to be quite a game. But she was physically strong, and he knew damn well she had to be tough.

That deputy ambassador, Valenzuela, was a camel's rectum, leaving her here like that. Seven years! Knowing how FM operated, or more exactly how its Department Eleven worked, the odds were five to one they'd never send a pickup for her.

Boru came out of the shadowed side street into the broad open square. The walls of the royal fortress loomed dark and somehow mysterious, its great gate closed now, the guards gone. But eyes no doubt watched from the towers, and certainly from the gate towers. Inside was a king, a living man, whom Uncle Bhiksu had sent him to kill. Undoubtedly a man well guarded.

I wonder how Bhiksu got hold of me in the first place, Boru asked himself. *And why? Why and how did he manage to get a little baby, presumably a highly valuable experimental sub-*

ject, out of a high-security government-controlled research project? If he'd wanted a child, there must have been infants of almost every kind easily and legally available to him. It had taken connections, that's for sure.

There still were several peernu hitched to the rail in front of the Three Bulls, stoic in the biting wind, and it occurred to him to hope that none were the same animals he'd seen there three hours earlier. Opening the door, he went into the warmth and sound. The innkeeper was gone, and a hulking strong-arm type stood in his place. Customers were fewer, and most were drinking instead of eating. Boru decided to have one with them, then go to bed.

Selena followed Boru's thoughts until she lost them in the confusion of the Three Bulls taproom. *To kill the king or try to?* It seemed suicidal, and suddenly her chances for returning to Earth with Boru seemed terribly shrunken. But maybe he'd back off on the assassination; maybe she could influence him. She could try

Maybe they wouldn't take him off unless he completed the mission. It wouldn't be so terrible staying here with him. She'd only known him for about two hours, but she was sure they could make it work with each other. Even a telepath could misappraise someone now and then, but she felt sure about this one.

Barni was a nice man, even honorable, a gentle man, and physically very good. And from Earth, someone she could really communicate, share, with. Regardless of what might happen later, she told herself, she had him for now. Even a few weeks would be better than nothing.

ELEVEN

She looked around with distaste, then started down the puddled street. Warm air had moved in from the ocean overnight, and thick cold drizzle fell from a leaden sky, making the snow gray.

Most of the people she passed didn't like it either; they were glum and introverted. People from other parts of the country said weather like this was rare outside the southeastern coastal district, and unheard of north of the Toolis River.

But in four and a half local years, she'd been outside Tonlik only—she counted—four times, never far and never for more than two days. There had to be a lot of beauty on the planet, she thought, and she was suddenly angry that she'd allowed herself to get stuck in an unbroken routine at the Larilia. A routine rooted in the caution that grows out of low-intensity fear; she'd been afraid her pickup would arrive and she'd miss him. On Earth she'd be thirty-four now; she'd lost seven years. The realization made a bitter taste.

A wagon loaded with firewood thumped and splashed down the narrow street, and Selena moved close to the wall as it passed. The peernu's coats were darkened by moisture. When the weather cleared up, she'd ask Barni to rent a saddle peeran for her, and they could get up early and ride out into the countryside.

The square was less dismal than the narrow street; the tall stone towers and walls loomed softly in the thick drizzle, the guards but dimly seen beside the gate. She wondered if they felt miserable standing there in the weather, and decided that they didn't, but she did not reach to their minds to find out.

At the Larilia, the day steward's eyebrows raised when she entered so early. The place was only minutes open, still almost deserted. Usually she came in when it began to be crowded, to dawdle over breakfast, sipping her nauk and thinking god knew what.

Her eyes passed over the steward without really seeing him, although she spoke, a routine greeting on a circuit. Her attention was elsewhere. Looking around, she spotted Boru at a small puncheon table cornered and shadowed by two walls. He rose as she walked toward him. Without seeming in the least naive or vulnerable, there was something youthful about him, and it occurred to her that he was the same age as she.

"I was wondering if you'd be here," she said quietly as they sat down together. "There aren't many clocks on Thegwar. Most people go by the hours rung in the palace bell tower, and all the clocks in town get set by it. I suppose if the bell ringer ever forgets . . ."

He was grinning at her, eyes alert, and somehow she blushed, just slightly. "You look like someone who's been up for hours," she said to cover.

"I rest fast," he replied, then lowered his voice confidentially. "I checked out my peeran to see he's being properly cared for, then went to the palace and applied for a job on the guard. I'm surprised what a businesslike twenty-fourth century operation they have over there. They've got a waiting list, but where you stand on it is based on the test and interview they give you, so I ought to be at the top.

"Actually I held back a bit on the swordsmanship—avoided some of the more refined techniques so they wouldn't get too curious about where I learned." He looked up, saw the still lethargic waiter gazing blankly from the kitchen door, and signaled to him. The man, instead of coming over, disappeared. "After I finished at the palace, I went out and got a job," Boru continued. "So I'm ready for an early lunch."

"A job too? On your first morning?" she said. "You move fast."

He smiled and put a hand on one of hers. "We both move pretty fast. And you are now talking with the day bouncer at the Rambling Bear Tavern. I start at eight tomorrow."

"The Rambling Bear? I don't know it."

"It's got a lot different clientele than the Larilia. It's on Cordage Road, down near the river. Sailors, dockers, guys from the shipyard, assorted working men of one kind and another—that's what the owner told me. It's probably just as well that I'm big by Thegwar standards.''

She nodded. "It's helped that I'm small by Earth standards. Is the Rambling Bear a pretty tough place then?''

"The owner doesn't seem to think so, but I suppose it gets that way now and then." He grinned again. "It'll help to keep the job interesting. The next thing I want to look for is a place large enough that you and I can move in together. If you'd like.''

The waiter was coming over, so she answered with a hand squeeze. Selena gave her order, then watched Boru as he questioned the man and gave his. She looked at the muscular hands resting on the table, the steady eyes as he talked. The strong face was bereft now of its seedling beard, no doubt to make the right first impression on the clean-faced, shaven-headed guard officers at the palace.

When the waiter left, she switched to standard Terran, in an undertone. That would hide the subject and content, and if anyone's ears were too sharp, let them think the language was Gzarmuk. "Why do you want to get into the palace?" she asked.

For a long thoughtful moment he regarded her, saying nothing. "Never mind," she said, "I understand the need-to-know principle.''

Boru examined his reaction to her question. Interesting. He *wanted* to tell her, which was not only needless but seemed unwise—dangerous. She *didn't* need to know, and actually he hardly knew her.

"I was sent here to kill the king," he said quietly. "To execute him." *And that*, he told himself, *was about as professional as Little League baseball*. But she was a telepath: she'd have learned anyway if he stayed around her. And he intended to.

She squeezed his fingers. "I learned that from you last night," she murmured, "when you were walking back to the Three Bulls. I just wondered whether you'd tell me or not." Her eyes searched his. "As long as we're coming clean with each other.''

He smiled. "I'd say we're starting out pretty damned well on that. Especially for a couple of people that're professionally into secrecy.''

"Do you know how you're going to kill him?" she asked.

"I haven't even thought about it," he said. "There's no hurry, and I need to get as familiar as possible with the layout and routines—the possibilities. I'm not interested in getting *me* killed. And there's a restriction on this job: I can only use native weapons, so finesse is important. I can't just lob a grenade and escape in the confusion. And finally I need to size up the king and the situation so I can evaluate whether execution is just or not."

She looked questioningly at him, and Boru explained the walkaway clause. "So it's not just a matter of killing someone," he continued. "In the absence of any proper legal system, we have to do the best we can to avoid unjust executions. We're a justice firm, not assassins for hire."

Selena frowned. "Justice?" she said. "What does justice have to do with killing Trogeir? Why does anyone want him killed? Besides the Foreign Ministry for kicking them out. From what I've seen, there probably aren't many places with government as good as they have here."

Her response surprised Boru; its tone was challenging. "For one thing," he answered, "he imprisoned six management personnel from Systems Mining and Manufacturing, and they've never been heard of since. He also broke several commercial contracts with them and took over their factories where farm implements were made. And he wasted, threw away, years of planning based on those agreements."

As he recited, he found himself feeling uncomfortable. For the first time he realized it was a light case to justify breaking the Cultural Protection Law for an execution. And Selena was staring at him with open disbelief.

"First of all," she countered, "I don't believe he kept any of them in prison. Or had them killed. Even if, somehow, word of it hadn't leaked, I'd have run into it from someone telepathically. And for the rest of it—how much do you suppose the takeover cost SM&M? We're not talking about some automated hundred-hectare plant. These are nothing more than big wooden sheds with work benches. Go look at them! System's total investment here didn't equal the expense account of one of their junior vice-presidents.

"Someone," she finished, "fed you a line of garbage."

Boru was stunned: that didn't sound like the Bill of Particulars he'd seen. What the hell was going on here? His attention went to what Wan Larmet had said about FM's continuing illegal interest in Lokar. FM's expulsion from Lokar had been the culmination of several embarrassments and scandals. Not long afterward the Assembly had acceded to the Cultural Rights lobby and passed legislation that removed and forbade Confederate embassies and consulates on all class D worlds and put those worlds off limits to virtually everyone. It was an enormous reduction in FM size and role.

But it didn't make sense for FM to revenge themselves on Trogeir. All he'd done was kick them out of Lokar—one country. Of course, some of the things Department Eleven did were pretty crazy, and someone that's crazy *doesn't* make sense. That's the criterion.

And it was utterly out of character for Bhiksu to send someone on an FM revenge mission. Not knowingly. Whatever was going on here, it wasn't in the Bill of Particulars.

The Bill of Particulars! He was so used to the four-square way that Bhiksu did things, everything above-board and by the letter, that he'd left his critical faculties in the closet! Uncle Bhiksu, *Mr. Ethics,* had assigned him the job; ergo, it was legitimate. At least as far as could be ascertained without field examination. Only this time it didn't look like it.

Why had Bhiksu done it? Looking at it now, the proposal had never even gone to the evaluators. He knew those guys: rational skeptics, all of them. They'd have laughed themselves into hiccups or thrown up; then they'd have trashed it. The old man had bypassed them and sent him out on a setup.

Who had that kind of leverage on Bhiksu? They wouldn't even have gone to him unless they had heavy leverage; they'd have gone to Nemesis and hoped they could get away with it there. Boru sat in a black cloud while Selena watched him concernedly.

Looking at it again, it had been out of character for Bhiksu Tanaka to say what he had: "Mr. Boru, have you ever killed a king?" And smiling, as if he thought the remark was humorous! It had surprised Boru at the moment; then he'd set it aside and forgotten it.

Boru raised his eyes to Selena's; had she been reading him? She nodded sympathetically.

And he was Bhiksu's golden-haired boy, figuratively as

well as literally. Others had commented on it: "Barney gets the tricky ones." So here he was.

The waiter brought their food and left, but Boru wasn't interested in food at the moment. "What do you know about the circumstances of FM and Systems getting booted out?" he asked her.

"Not a lot. I suppose you know that Trogeir grew up on Earth from age five?" He nodded. "Well," she continued, "maybe he came to dislike or distrust Earth and the Confederacy. Or maybe it was something that happened here later. He was king for quite a while before he threw them out. Although I guess he didn't have much to do with the embassy from the time he took the throne. He really restricted the freedom of movement of embassy personnel, their number, and the length of their assignments. Obviously he didn't trust them."

Boru pursed his lips thoughtfully.

"And when I arrived here," she continued, "the embassy staff was worried because Trogeir had discovered two Department Eleven agents on the palace staff. They were afraid then that he might do something drastic."

Boru nodded slowly as if making a decision. "Thanks, Selena. Looks like a walkaway, sure as hell. But before I leave, I want to get all the facts I can to support it. I want to be able to take it to Justice Ministry and see someone get their ass busted."

His eyes moved to the coarse bread, cheese, pickled fish, and ale on the table in front of him. "Now what do you say we eat?"

TWELVE

It was his sixth day on the job. During the first hour things normally were slow, and he was the only man out front, more tapman and waiter than bouncer. Not until noon—ten o'clock—was there business enough to justify a separate waiter, and even then it was mostly Boru who drew the beers and poured the whiskey.

Already he had his favorite customers, and got smiling to his feet when the short stocky man came in. "What'll it be, Sunto?" he asked.

The broad fierce face grinned. "Fat meat and four fried eggs. Bread and beer. You want to drink beer with me? I'll buy. I just sold whole load of wood to a square-rigged Bleesbroker. He wants to get out on next tide, so I stuck him pretty good."

"A beer sounds pretty good to me," Boru said. He gave the order to the cook, drew two mugs, then sat down with the customer. They were alone in the room.

Sunto was a barbarian from the northern barrens, interesting looking, with darkish skin, tan hair, brown eyes, and a sparse beard scarcely worth shaving or growing. His face was ornamented with raised tattoos resembling welded seams.

Boru corrected himself—*ex*-barbarian. Sunto was a businessman now, with a wagon and two peernu. He hauled and sold wood from the city's fuel forest and had a Lokarn wife.

"You and your woman marry yet?" Sunto asked.

"Not exactly. We're going to though. I got a place big enough to live together now, and moved in her things last night."

The barbarian showed big square yellow teeth—better teeth than you usually saw in Tonlik in people with more than thirty Terran years on them. Maybe, Boru thought, it was from growing up chewing lots of tough meat. Sunto probably never even heard of potatoes and grain until he'd come south and gotten civilized.

"What did you eat when you were younger, living in the north?" Boru asked.

Sunto grunted. "We herded cattle, ate lots of meat. Not cattle like here; ours were wild, dangerous. Kill a man if he lets them. Ate fish, too, and in spring, birds' eggs. In winter we killed wild peernu. Sometimes we killed *vissutonsa* too, in winter— what you call hreenu, but hreenu live mostly farther south.

"In summer we don't live in forest. In summer we live in . . . *riisu*. No trees in riisu, lots of grass, little bushes, water pools, wild flowers; lots of feed for cattle, lots of flies, too. Then we live in little tents, move herds from place to place where grazing is good.

"In fall, when it gets cold and meat won't rot, we kill lots of cattle to eat in winter. We do that in winter villages, off south where forest is, lots of trees for firewood. Keep enough calves alive to make up for cattle we kill. See how it works?"

Of course, thought Boru. The seasons are long on Thegwar. Summer that far north would be too cool for trees, but not for grass, and probably four or five Earth-months long—say six months or more of grazing. Not a real tundra then—sort of a cold prairie.

"Bear meat is pretty good too," Sunto continued, "and bear fat good to grease hides with.

"But in winter, cattle live hard, get damn thin. In bad years lots of cows lose the calves in their belly. Bad for next year calf crop."

Boru had kept one eye on the kitchen door. Now he got up and brought Sunto's lunch—what was called "second meal" of the four usual in Thegwar's long days. Sunto put butter on the heated loaf end, then stuffed a forkful of fried fatmeat into his mouth, the big square teeth and strong jaws demolishing it. "Things better here in Lokar than in my old country. Always enough to eat. More choices in life."

Boru leaned his elbows on the table with his beer mug in hand. "How'd you happen to come south, Sunto?" he asked.

"Oh, well, one winter come early, lots of early snow, it get very deep. Lost lots of calves, even cows. So we know that next winter won't be enough meat." Sunto chewed thoughtfully, looking past Boru, seeing that other, northern winter. "Wild game scarce then, too. So next fall some young men in our clan, we decide to take our skis and go far away to hunt, far off south in forest. Thirty of us.

"My clan is the Bear Clan, biggest clan in Siiksun, my tribe. Siiksun is most powerful tribe in north." He straightened slightly. "My father is medicine chief of Bear Clan—principal medicine chief of all Siiksun. Important man. He makes sick people get well. He wanted me to be a medicine chief; I got the talent. But I didn't want to do it." Sunto laughed. "I rather hunt, ride around, race peernu, run on skis, get in fights.

"So us young men leave winter village and ski a long way south. Sometimes we kill some peernu, once a hreen, and cut them up. Each time, some of us load pack frames with all meat a man can carry, and men start back for village.

"After two hands of days—ten days—we came far south to a little village and a castle with stone walls. Big mountain behind it."

"A place called Jussvek," Boru suggested. Sunto shrugged and drank deeply from his mug, then wiped foam from his lips with the back of a brown hand.

"Don't know what Lokaru name is. We call it 'Stone Walls,' first place you come to where *Kuutonsisa* live. In northern tongue, Kuutonsisa means 'bony faces'—like your people, like Lokaru. So we go to Stone Walls and ask for food. The people there were all inside castle, scared to come out, think we came there to fight.

"But the chief there wasn't scared. He comes north each spring over river ice, trades with our people for furs. So he comes out of castle, tells us to kill two cows, says come back with furs and he make good trade.

"After that, some of us want to take meat and go home. They were scared we come to king's soldiers pretty soon. Nine of us, we want to see what it's like farther south. We go along past Great Roaring Falls . . ."

"Wait a minute," said Boru, "why were some of you afraid of the king's soldiers?"

"Huh! Well, the year before in the time of first frosts, king come to our land with great army. Thousands of soldiers but no women or children! Very dangerous! They made great show, did drills, played war. Columns of fours turn into battle lines, lines charge across riisu, lances down, pivot around one end, separate, come back together—everything very quick, very—exact!

"Then they put up great tent, soldiers rode out into riisu and round up lots of wild game and kill it. The king gave huge feast, invite all our chiefs. They even invite people to come around to cook fires, feed them too.

"All were afraid that if chiefs went in tent, they get killed, but chiefs went in anyway. Nobody got killed. There was lots to eat, and the king gave a speech to chiefs."

Sunto laughed, shaking his head. "Didn't seem funny then, but funny now. King is very smart; he understands my people. I understand them too now. He told chiefs it was not all right for young men to go out and raid Kuutonsis places. He said he want to be our friend, not our enemy. He said if he comes again to our land, he wants it to be with just a few friends, and leave army at home.

"But if we want to be enemies, he would be our enemy, although he didn't want to. If we want to do killing and burning, he would kill and burn too. But he would rather be our friend.

"The chiefs came out and told this to the clans. And the clans told the chiefs to tell the king we would be his friends, and the young men would no longer raid the Kuutonsisa. They said to tell him quick and ask him to go home right away while there was still any game left in the country, some wild meat for the winter.

"So the chiefs told him, and the king hug the chief of each tribe and the chieftain of each clan. To each he gave a fine peeran for his own, bigger and stronger than ours, and a sword of finest steel. And to the chief of each tribe he also gave a silver helmet to wear.

"And to the clans, to each clan, he gave four brood mares white as snow, of strongest blood, and one white stallion. The people been seeing those big white peernu, and wished they had such animals; now they had them."

Sunto's sharp brown eyes sought Boru's blue ones, and he enveloped a forkful of eggs. "What you think of that king?" he asked after a moment's chewing.

"Well," said Boru, "I'd say he handled the situation about as well as possible. He showed his power without using force, and left without leaving hatred behind. He paid respect to the positions of the chiefs, but the gifts he gave would also remind everyone of the king and his power."

Sunto nodded. "And king has lots of soldiers. We told each other we will stay away from soldiers and won't kill anybody, won't get into trouble. No raiding.

"On the second day we pass Great Roaring Falls, snow very deep for so early, not even shortest day yet. For more than a hand of days we keep going, hardly saw any game, got very hungry. Finally came to a wide place of open land. It wasn't riisu; we knew Kuutonsisa must have made it. Here and there was little bunches of buildings. We never seen anything like that place; it made us little bit afraid.

"We decide we better go home, but need meat first. So after dark we went to nearest buildings, kill two calves, cut them up quick and put in packs, then leave. But not in secret, because they got big dogs there that come out and whoop at us until one of us shoot one with arrow."

Sunto drank deeply of the heavy spicy beer. "We worried then; we think maybe soldiers will come after us. And so far south, snow was only knee deep, easy for peernu. We were right. Two days later, soldiers catch up with us. We afraid they will kill us, so we fight. A soldier's peeran kick me. When I wake up, my bow gone, and my knife. Two soldiers and five young men were dead, three more of my people wounded, soldiers tied them over peernu. Me, I'm all right. They put rope around my neck, make me ski along behind. Then three soldiers are taking me to Tonlik through country that is farms as far as I can see. When we get here, it was almost winter but the snow had melted off ground on the south sides of buildings. I couldn't believe it! Then they put me in jail.

"A few days later I get taken to the palace; I know right away it's place where king must live. They took me to room and there he is, the king! Easy to recognize: he got big red beard and long yellow hair, while soldiers got none, maybe little on top.

"King asks me questions, I told him all that happened. There was very very tall Kuutonsis medicine chief with him, had long black hair. I never saw anyone that tall before, or hair so black. I could tell he was very strong medicine chief, because I got talent. I know. The medicine chief speaks my tongue good enough so we talk through him. King was friendly, told me we shouldn't have killed calves that belong to someone else, but I can go home to my people if I want. But there was plenty food in jail, and it's not good to travel so far in winter alone, so I tell him that, and tell him I rather stay till spring.''

Four men walked into the tavern together, looked around for a waiter, then walked to a table, talking and laughing. Boru glanced, but sat tight to hear the rest.

"So they put me back in jail. Each day before dawn we ate, and guards took us out to forest of little sprouts to cut and load firewood till dark or sometimes stay in town and shovel snow. By spring, when they let me go, I can talk pretty good Kuutonsisik. Instead of going home, I decide I want to see more, so I get job as sailor, went all over, saw different lands.''

Sunto cleaned his teeth with his tongue and finger, looking thoughtful. "But the best place I seen to live is Lokar. So now I got Lokarn wife and baby, own wagon and two peernu, house and barn, got to earn money.'' He got to his feet. "I better go back to work.'' He paid, then left as Boru went to wait on the four newcomers.

Boru would remember what the barbarian had told him.

THIRTEEN

The five sailors had hardly ordered before the trouble began. One of them recognized the two palace guards as something official by their off-duty uniforms. His well-scarred face twisted into something like a smile as he rose to look down at them.

"Hey! Whatta we got here?" he said loudly. "A coupla soldier boys?"

The older of the two guardsmen met the man's sneering gaze stonily, then turned to his beer, his eyes warning off his younger companion.

"Whataya think?" said another of the sailors. "You think maybe they're deaf? Or just scared to say anything?"

The younger guardsman pushed his chair back, but Boru in passing pushed him back down on it and confronted the standing sailor.

"If you guys came in here for some friendly drinks," Boru said pleasantly, "we're glad to have you. If you came in for trouble, weigh anchor; we don't want it here."

"Oh ho! You must be the muscle here, eh? I'll bet someone told you you're tough once and you believed him."

"My name is Barni, and my job is to see that things stay peaceful."

"Well whoop de doo!" The man looked Boru up and down, his smile gone now, mouth ugly. Boru was slightly taller, but the brawny seaman had ten kilos on him. "I don't suppose you'd care to try throwing me out, would you?"

Without answer or foresign, Boru shot a short right punch to the sailor's breastbone with the heel of his hand, slamming him across the table into one of his companions. The one nearest was on his feet instantly with a knife in his hand, but didn't attack. Things might have stopped there if the younger guardsman hadn't jumped the knifeman. Instantly a melee began that lasted six or eight seconds; when it was over, three sailors and the young guardsman were on the floor and two sailors had run out the door into the street.

The few other customers in the Rambling Bear gawped wordlessly.

Boru dropped to one knee by the downed guardsman, then looked up at the other. "Go get help! Your friend's hurt bad!"

The man nodded and loped out. Boru held a wadded handkerchief hard against the stab wound in the guardsman's neck to reduce the blood flow, scarcely glancing up as the cook's helper ran through and out the door to find a street patrol. But pressure is inadequate when a carotid is torn, especially when bleeding has gone uninhibited for several seconds. When two patrolmen arrived a few minutes later, Boru had left the corpse and was trussing two out-of-action sailors, the original troublemaker having stumbled out.

After that he cleaned up the broad pool of blood with the aid of the cook's now green-faced helper. When that was done, he sent the lad running to bring him a change of clothes; his own were badly bloodied.

*   *   *

The guard corporal they sent had trouble finding Boru, because he was looking for Barni of Jussvek, not for the bouncer at the Rambling Bear. Boru had moved from the Three Bulls the evening before, but the innkeeper volunteered that the dancer at the Larilia might know where he was. At the Larilia they told him she was off duty, but someone told him approximately where she lived. When the man found the place, no one was there, so he went back to the Larilia to wait for her, and got into a conversation with the bouncer who told him where Barni worked.

It was second meal when he found him. The message was that they'd lost a guardsman the day before, and Boru was invited to take the job.

The story of the fight had been told all through the guard, of course, and central to it was the bouncer who had demolished three sailors in less time than it took to tell. They hadn't realized that the bouncer was also the applicant chosen to fill the vacancy. The corporal looked forward to passing that around when he got back to Krogaskott.

He told Boru to be at the guardhouse the next morning at seven if he was still interested. When Boru said he was, the corporal gave him a one-time pass, good between six and seven. It would get him inside the great gate of the fortress. He must be prepared to go on duty at once.

Yes, it was required that he live in the citadel if he was single. If he was married he could live outside, as all rooms for married guardsmen were taken.

"So you're definitely going to be there then?" the man asked.

"I'll be there all right."

"Good." The guardsman's smooth, high-cheeked face was sober as he put out his hand. They gripped. "From what Sergeant Geesl said—he was the guardsman who saw the fight—you're the kind of man we like in the guards. If you have discipline."

Boru smiled. "I'm a man who likes things orderly. Predictable. Done right and on time. And if Geesl told the whole story, you know I'd rather handle trouble without a fight."

The man nodded curtly. "You should do very well. Ask for Corporal Roska when you get there; that's me. It will be my job to orient you and get you started."

He turned and walked out, cold wind swirling in around his legs before the door closed behind him: winter had returned to Tonlik, in fact if not yet by the calendar.

Boru frowned. If they required proof of marriage, he'd have no choice but to leave Selena and move into the fortress. Although as far as his mission was concerned, it was preferable to be quartered inside Krogaskott than out; it would give him more opportunity to move around the place.

He hustled food and beers around until the second-meal rush was over. At that time the proprietor came in to give him a meal break, and sat down with him for a beer.

"Villus," said Boru, "lots of things are different here from at Jussvek. What do you do to get married in Tonlik?"

The man's beefy red face curled in a grin. "The first thing you got to do is find a woman who'll marry you."

"And if I've already done that, then what?"

"Well, then you go to a priest together and he marries you. Next you take her home and . . ."

"Does the priest give us anything? Like a certificate of marriage?"

"Sure. And writes the whole thing down in the records—names and date. When did you decide to get married?"

"A few days ago. But I kept not getting around to it." He caught the tavernkeeper's eyes with his steady gaze. "Villus, I've got something to tell you."

"You want a couple days off."

"More than that."

The eyebrows raised.

"Before I started here, I applied at Krogaskott to be a guardsman. They told me it would be awhile, so I looked around and got this job with you. Now a corporal was just in here and told me I'm supposed to start tomorrow."

The tavernkeeper's smile slipped. Boru went on. "So you need to get the word out quick that you need a bouncer again."

Villus's face darkened. "Shit! It ain't hard to get a bouncer. What's hard is to get one that's friendly and gets along with people, can handle things, and be willing to wait on tables. How much they offer to pay you on the guard?"

"I didn't even ask; I didn't think about it. I just wanted to be in the guard. The pay can't be too bad though: they got a waiting list of guys that want to be on it. They jumped me up because I did real good on the tests.''

The older man's face assumed an expression of concern. ''Barni, I hate to see you make a mistake. Join the guard and you'll stand watches all through the day from before dawn till after dark. And your time off ain't even your own there; you even got to get permission to leave the fortress when you're on your own time.'' He looked earnestly across the table. ''Why don't I just, ah, raise your pay another orin?'' When Boru didn't react, he added, ''Make that two ornu. Hell, with a little more experience you'll be worth it to me. I'll tell you the truth, I been looking forward to having more time off. I figured in a few more weeks I could let you run the place until third meal, and I'd hire a day waiter to help you. I could raise you a korbin a week then.

''It's easier than being a guard,'' he added, looking hopefully at the agent. ''And you got a lot more freedom. Not so many bosses, either. I know what it's like; I was in the army once.''

''Damn, Villus, I really appreciate that, but I can't. You see, I *want* to be a guardsman. That's why I came all the way down here. And if I turn them down now, I won't get another chance.''

Abruptly Villus turned away. ''I train you and now you leave me! All right then, get your coat! You're done here!''

''You don't want me to finish my day?''

''Just get your coat. I'll pay you for the day, but I don't want you around here anymore.''

Boru nodded, went to the row of pegs on the back wall and took down his parka. When he'd slipped into it, Villus was coming from back of the bar with coins in his fist. Boru met him partway and held out a cupped hand. The tavernkeeper looked at the hand but avoided Boru's eyes as he paid him. ''And Barni,'' he said, ''I guess I ain't really mad at you. Good luck.''

Boru put the money in a pocket and took the man's hand. ''Thanks, Villus. Good luck to you too.'' The man looked at him as they shook.

''You really getting married?''

''Yep. We've even got a place to live.''

''Anybody I might know?''

''Her name is Selena. She's the dancer at the Larilia.''

"No shit?!"

"Yeah. Is that okay?"

Villus looked at him with something like awe. "I never seen her myself, but they say twenty men have asked her to marry them and she turned them all down! Some of them rich! They say she's what men dream of."

"Only fifteen," said Boru.

Villus looked confused. "What?"

"Only fifteen men asked her to marry them."

The tavernkeeper stared, turned pensive. "Well, Barni, good luck in the guard, and with your wife too. There's something about you, you probably wouldn't have stayed here long anyway, I can see that now. You're a man that big things are going to happen to.

"Come in for a drink now and then and tell me how it's going."

They shook again and Boru left. Walking down the snowy street, he began whistling.

Selena's fingers moved deftly over vivid satin, a colored thread twitching behind them. With books still relatively few and expensive in Lokar, she spent a lot of time doing needlework and practicing her flute and the approximate guitar she'd had made.

The latch squeaked, and she looked up as the door swung open from the street. Her face brightened as Boru came in, then sobered when she realized what time it was.

"What is it? I thought you'd be at work till fifteen."

Smiling, he beckoned with both hands, and she set her embroidery aside as she rose. "I start at the palace tomorrow," he answered. "In the guard. So Villus paid me off and I left to get married."

"Married?"

He nodded. "Her name's Selena—Selena something or other. She never told me her last name; last names aren't big in Lokar." He reached for her and she stepped into his arms. After a few seconds they parted.

"You're serious?" she asked guardedly. "Or was that just a figure of speech?" She opened herself to his mind. "You meant it!" she said.

"You're darned right I meant it. I want to get married! Today! Right now!"

She stepped back from him, her hands on his arms. "You don't give a girl much advance notice. What will I wear?"

"Damned if I know. Your prettiest dress."

Chagrin came over her face. "I don't have a thing to wear! I know that sounds trite, but I really don't! I have dancing costumes and I have three dresses. I never go anywhere. I've been here seven years and all I have to show for it are some bundles of notes."

"Well, okay," Boru said quietly, "wear one of the three dresses. The one you like best."

"I guess I'll have to. Unless we postpone it. I don't even know how to get married in Lokar! I don't even know that! I don't have any girl friends." She was getting more and more upset. "Seven years and I don't even know how people get married here!"

"They go to a priest. I asked."

His words, simple and direct, snapped her out of it. "And that's all there is to it?" she asked cautiously. "Don't we even have to post banns, whatever banns are? Like in olden times on Earth? There must be some requirements!"

"Not that I heard about. Let's go find a priest and find out. We'll tell him you're a foreigner and I'm from the frontier, and we don't know how things are done here."

She nodded thoughtfully, then went and examined the two dresses that hung from hangers on a rod. She took off the one she'd been wearing, poured water in the wash basin, washed her face and changed, then examined her coiled braids in a mirror.

"I guess," she said, "that's all there is to it. I'm ready." She looked earnestly at Boru. "Am I all right like this?"

He kissed her again, gently. "You're fine. Wonderful. I'm glad it's time to do it." Suddenly he looked thunderstruck. "Ye gods! *I* don't have anything to get married in! Two sets of work clothes, one of them bloodstained, and my traveling furs! Come on! We're going to Ottar the Clothiers on the way!"

Churches in Lokar are not cathedrals where hundreds gather to worship, nor is their god the creator and master of the universe. Voroth, according to tradition and scripture, had come from the sky and found the people of Thegwar living as beasts. But within them he saw a light, a soul, the potential to live higher than cattle or wolves. So he taught them speech, and gave them the Laws and Advices.

But around the world, peoples one by one went astray and forsook Voroth, deviating, some more and some less, until only the Lokaru as a people followed him honestly.

Even the Lokaru are human of course, erring and sinning. So after death, the five judges who stand behind Voroth in the Other Sphere judge each man and woman, Lokaru or foreigner, every child who dies before its time, weighing their acts, determining whether they'll spend the rest of the age in the home of light or the pit of darkness, or perhaps return to live again in their homeland and finish things unfinished. Every Lokarn from age six is taught the Laws and Advices in the home and at church.

It is a people's religion. Its scriptures and teachings are simple and relatively short. The Church of Voroth has no great holdings, no political power, no wealth. It has a Patriarch, but he has no staff except a secretary and a valet, no ecclesiastical palace, and his authority is limited to the instruction, correction, and promotion of clergy. The Church has stood for a long time without serious corruption or decadence, a major basis of morality, part of the glue and the lubricant of social interaction.

In a city built largely of stone and brick, the churches are of logs, carefully squared by adze and plane, plastered within, ornamented on the outside with intricate carvings, and painted brightly blue, white, and red. They contain an apartment for the priest and his family, a reading room for persons who wish to study the scriptures and commentaries, and a chapel for holy ceremonies and instruction.

Selena and Boru found the front stoop swept clean of snow. It too was of squared logs, well worn by feet. The carven door was heavy but unlocked; he turned the handle and pushed it open, jangling a bell. They walked into a small reception room which dimmed with the closing of the door behind them.

After a minute a middle-aged man entered from an opposite door. Bald and round-faced, he wore a robe of indigo blue that was vivid even in the half light.

"What may I do for you?" he asked.

Boru had a feeling of time suspended, a sense of having

been in this place before, of having done this before. "We want to get married," he said.

The priest turned his eyes to Selena. She nodded.

"And neither of you is married to another?"

Both shook their heads, murmuring negatives.

"Very well," he said mildly, "follow me." He led them into the chapel, a lighter room with benches in rows. Tall windows of blue glass passed azure shafts of late sunlight. With a gesture he halted the couple before the lectern.

"If you please," he said. "Sit if you'd like. I'll be back very shortly." He disappeared silently through another door.

They stood without speaking, touching only with their eyes, affected by the place. In two or three minutes the priest returned, a stout woman beside him; she smiled quietly at the waiting couple, and Boru wondered if there was a kitchen apron beneath her red robe. The priest gestured to her.

"This is my wife, Thonnara. She will witness the wedding as the maternal aspect." There was a simple dignity in the man and his words. He stepped now to the lectern, which had a narrow tray at the upper edge holding ink pot and quill. First he sharpened the nib, then uncapped the ink, the actions making tiny sounds audible in the otherwise stillness. Finally he looked at Boru.

"And you, sir, are? . . ."

"Barni of Jussvek."

The pen scratched busily, then the priest raised his calm eyes to Selena. "And you, miss, are? . . ."

"Selena of Gzarim."

Again the pen moved, at greater length, interrupted by dippings; he was entering their names in the parish records as well as on the parchment he would give them. When he was done, he looked up. "Thank you," he said. Next he blew on the parchment, paused, and blotted, first lightly, then firmly.

That done, he looked at the couple, smiled, and motioned them nearer. "I will ask certain questions," he said. "If you have any doubts, misgivings, reluctance, you must tell me, and we will stop and examine them. If your answer is 'yes,' please say 'I do.' Is this understood?"

"Yes," said Boru; Selena echoed him.

"Excellent." The priest gave his full attention to Boru now. "Do you, Barni, commit yourself to love and care for

Selena, and to provide her with the requirements of life and such enhancements as you reasonably can?''

"I do."

"To have no other woman so long as you both shall live?"

"I do."

"And do you commit yourself to honor and respect her and consider her needs and desires?"

"I do."

"To love and honor her children, provide and care for them, and teach and guide them in the ways which Voroth has gifted us?"

"I do."

"Very good." The priest turned smiling to Selena.

"And do you, Selena, commit yourself to love and care for Barni, and to make his home a place of happiness?"

"I do." Her words were almost inaudible.

"To have no other man so long as you both shall live?"

"I do." Her words were stronger now.

"And do you commit yourself to honor and respect him and consider his needs and desires?"

"I do."

"To love and honor his children, provide and care for them, and teach and guide them in the ways which Voroth has gifted us?"

"I do."

"Very good." His small smile widened. "Now turn to one another and take each other's hands."

They did, eyes large and sober.

"Insofar as you have vowed to thus be a proper wedded pair, vowed before Voroth, and before mankind as represented here by Thonnara and I, let a kiss here seal the contract."

Boru stepped to her, gently took her in his arms, felt her hands on his back. Lingeringly they kissed.

"I now pronounce you husband and wife."

They separated. The priest's wife was moist-eyed above her broad smile as her husband handed Boru the marriage certificate, rolled and ribboned. Boru dug into a trouser pocket and presented the priest a korbin. The man's composure slipped for a moment at the sight of gold, for the newlyweds by no means seemed affluent. It would have slipped even more if he'd known where this korbin had been minted—how many light years away.

He pocketed it, and hardly had his hand emerged when Selena brought a flute from under her cloak, such a non sequitur that other acts, in progress or about to be, stopped or were delayed. Raising it to her lips, she began to play. The tune began pensively, but gradually lightened, sweetened, her control, subtlety, expressiveness, all superb. *Celtic*, Boru thought, *Celtic without melancholy*, then thought no more while she played. Lightly it washed over them, gently flowed through them; it was serenity devoid of apathy, beauty without sadness.

She played for perhaps four minutes before ending, an ending which suggested there was more where that came from. The flute disappeared within her cloak again.

"And that is my thanks, Father," she said.

The priest bobbed his head without speaking and led them to the door, his wife following. At the stoop they paused. "Voroth bless you, children," he said, and then to Selena, "And thank you, my dear, for the gift of beauty. I have never heard its like."

Smiling, Selena said, "You're welcome, Father," then they turned and started down the snow-packed street, the door not closing behind them for half a minute.

Boru looked at her striding beside him, straight and sure of herself. When they'd entered the church she'd seemed subdued, and during the service she'd been timid at first. Then she'd played, and when they'd left, she'd been the biggest of them all, graceful and gracious, royalty. He felt an urge to stop, to face and tell her something, he wasn't sure what. And knowing this in her awareness, she stopped, turning to him, taking his hands. Her eyes were bright, her cheeks glowing in the cold.

"Thank you for marrying me, wife," he said simply.

She dimpled. "You're welcome, husband. Believe me. And what you were thinking a moment ago—you were the catalyst."

They kissed once, briefly. A townsman scurrying by, his eyes on the treacherous snow before his feet, never noticed, or if he did, made no sign.

Then hand in hand they went on down the street.

FOURTEEN

Villus had been right: days were long on the guard. Boru had to be at the guardhouse by 6:90 in the bitter winter dawn and wasn't off until 18:00, just two hours before midnight. Watches themselves were only a single hour long—about ninety-two Terran minutes—and there were two hours in between, but each watch section was on standby during alternate off-duty intervals.

Standby was variously occupied. One standby daily was spent in physical training and either drilling or weapons training. Another was given to education—literacy, and training in history, government, and military science. Those who had not been in the army became soldiers as well as guards, for in time of war or military maneuvers, the guard traditionally accompanied the king in the field as his personal unit.

And of course there was occasional cleaning duty in the guardhouse.

But ordinarily, if you weren't on standby or on watch, or training away from Krogaskott, you were free to come and go. Usually Boru would trot home, and spend time with Selena if she wasn't at work, or napping if she was. Sometimes he went to the Larilia to hear her play and watch her dance.

It was quickly discovered that his archery was substandard. Fortunately it did not occur to the training sergeant that a frontiersman would almost surely be an excellent marksman. He simply scheduled his recruit for lots of practice at the butts, which Boru enjoyed thoroughly. Drill was mostly military—both cavalry and foot—in the evolutions used in battle, carried out on a field reserved for it not far from

Krogaskott. They arrived there by running and returned the same way.

But his first training was in how to stand the way a guard stands—erect but not rigid, head up but free to scan around—and how to draw, present, and scabbard arms smartly, in precise unison with others. He was also familiarized with the layout of the palace and the fortress as a whole, studying a diagram and being guided around. Certain areas of the palace he was not shown, however, mainly the apartments and personal offices of executives.

Boru found himself wondering if equivalent operations in palaces and governments of medieval Earth had been so rational and efficient. It seemed doubtful to him.

On the third day, Boru was assigned a post as outside guard—one of the bowmen who stood by the great wall flanking the gate. It was generally considered an undesirable post, assigned to new men, exposed not only to the cold and wind but to any precipitation that might fall. Boru took advantage of it to work on the neozen aware state, for which he required at least a brief undisturbed period. Once in it, time was under his control, and the watch passed easily.

For him, the disadvantage of the post was that he was not in the palace. He would have to do his information gathering off duty. And even guardsmen did not have free access to the palace. They entered it only as part of an on-duty guard detail or, if on an errand, with a special pass which was signed in and out.

The other significant negative element was the officer of his watch, Lieutenant Gausa, who clearly disliked him. Gausa didn't say much to Boru, did not badger or otherwise harass him, but he commonly scowled at him when they met, and when he did say anything, he snapped or was sarcastic. Boru could tolerate this easily enough, but it inhibited data gathering: to take liberties with regulations would risk Gausa's attention, and possibly restrictions or discharge.

One day, marching back to the guardhouse in ranks, Gausa ripped Boru for too large an armswing. He would *not* have some backwoods savage making his watch look like clowns! Afterward, in the day room, Corporal Roska commented quietly to Boru: "Do you wonder why Gausa has it in for you?"

"Yeah. From things he's said, I gather it's because I'm

from the outback. But that really doesn't explain anything; it just shifts the question.''

"You've got it. The situation is that he was in the army for nine years before joining the guard. And twice, when he was in the army, he was assigned to tax collection parties up the river in the wilderness.

"You know his attitude toward duty and the king. Well, he felt the backwoodsmen were disloyal, that they withheld taxes by hiding furs and money, not keeping receipts of transactions—things like that.

"As if that wasn't bad enough, when they'd go up there, the locals were required to feed and house the tax collectors with the same kind of meals and accommodations they had themselves. So wherever they stopped, the people pleaded poverty, and all they got was thin bean soup, maybe a small boiled potato, and bark tea. And the blankets they got were always full of lice and fleas; I heard him tell about it once when he'd been drinking.''

Roska paused to look around, to see if anyone was near enough to overhear. "Let's go outside and walk around a little bit. Won't need your coat; we won't be out long." They got up and went out in the cold morning sunshine.

"But the worst was the second trip," Roska continued. "And what really bothers him is that you're from Jussvek. I've never heard *him* tell this, but they'd just left Jussvek and were traveling south on the river in sleighs. And they all had the shits bad from something they'd been fed that day before they left. Guys were needing to go so often that the captain wouldn't let the sleighs stop for them to shit. He said if they did, they wouldn't get home before the ice broke up. So they just had to pull down their pants, hang their butts over the side, and let fly.

"Well, it was getting dark and they were going along close to the riverbank when Gausa had to go. So he hung his butt over the side and some bastard in the trees let fly from close up with an arrow. Smack! Right in the ass! Joral—it was him that told me this—Joral could hear the guy's skis on the frozen crust right after. He said Gausa gave one terrible holler and that was all, and the sleigh stopped, and for a few seconds he could hear the guy's skis.

"No one chased him. They didn't have their skis on, and they were all sick and weak from shitting. And it had thawed at midday and then frozen, so the crust wouldn't have shown tracks you could follow at night."

Roska shook his head. "It was a really shitty thing to do, to shoot him like that. They had a hell of a time getting the arrow out, cutting and digging, and they didn't even have any whiskey. Just hold him down and cut and swear. Later, after they got back and he'd healed up, some bastard started to kid him about it and Gausa almost killed him.

"So that's what's behind the hard time he gives you. You're a good guy, Barni. The rest of us can see that, but he can't; when it comes to Jussvek, he's a little bit crazy.

"I don't want you to pass this story on. It's pretty much died out because those of us that know it don't tell the new guys. Because Gausa wouldn't like it, and he's a good guy too."

Boru nodded soberly, unconsciously matching the mood of the other. "I understand. And thanks. I'll keep my mouth shut; you can depend on it."

"What are you doing, dear?"

Boru answered without looking up. "I'm counterfeiting a pass to get me into the palace when I want to." The quill moved carefully on the sheet of parchment; Selena came around to watch over his shoulder. "Right now," he went on, "all I'm accomplishing over there is making a living. I'm not learning what I want to know. And Gausa isn't going to transfer me inside the palace any time soon. If ever. He's going to leave me out in the cold wind and snow."

He held the sheet up and frowned critically, then laid it back on the table and cut out a rectangle some fifteen by twenty centimeters, with the writing on it.

"Will that work?" she asked doubtfully.

Boru grinned at her. "This one's just for practice and quality control. The wording and general appearance is okay; I've got an excellent memory. And the first chance I get, I'll compare it with the real thing, to see where this one is weak. Then I can make one I dare to use."

"Can you make one that good?"

"Sure. The parchment is a good duplicate already, in weight and texture. And they're handwritten—all by the same person, I suppose, but there'd still be some variability from one to another."

She began to massage the large shoulder muscles beside his neck. "Wouldn't it be safer to steal a real pass?" she said worriedly.

"Uh uh. They're signed in and out. If one wasn't accounted for, there'd probably be a new and different set of passes made, and maybe an investigation. And if I was the investigator, about the first question I'd ask is, 'What's changed around here lately? Who's new?' "

Silently she continued kneading his shoulders. "Why do you need any more information? What more do you need to know? You've already decided to walk away and not kill him. And if class D worlds are off limits now, it was illegal to even send you."

"Honey," he said, "that's part of the reason I'm staying— that and the possible involvement of Department Eleven. I want to know what's going on. And if I don't know yet just what I'm looking for, when I find it, I'll know it. Then we'll leave."

He got up and turned to her. "Don't look so worried, sweetheart. I'm the luckiest guy I know. And part of the training I got as a justice agent was forgery. I'm pretty good at it."

The entry guard glanced at the "pass," nodded and handed it back, and Boru walked into the grand lobby of the palace. A guide, there to conduct outsiders, glanced at him, then returned to his thoughts. There was no one else in sight; it was breakfast time for most palace staff. Many areas, he hoped, would be empty of people.

Boru knew exactly where he was going. He'd prepared a mental itinerary of areas he hadn't been taken to, or wanted to see again. All he had in mind was a light reconnaissance; he needed information, ideas—something, whatever the hell it might be. If anyone questioned him, he was looking for Private Blixhofa, who in actual fact was missing that morning. He might get run out of an area, but probably no one would pursue the matter.

He trotted up the long broad staircase to the second floor, passing a couple of administrative personnel, a bad omen. At a junction of two corridors he deliberately dropped his pass. Bending to retrieve it, he glanced to see if anyone was in sight behind him. No one was, and he stepped into a short hall.

There were four doors on one side and a double door on the other. Briskly Boru went to the double door and gripped the handle. It turned stiffly; he stepped in without looking and closed it behind him.

Conference room, he decided. There was a .large round table in the center, ringed by twelve chairs, one larger and more plush than the others. *Five will get you ten it's for the king*, he told himself. The only other furnishings were two settees, one on each side of the door. They were of wood, upholstered, and with valances skirting them to the floor. Except for the valances, they reminded him of the jury benches in old holo dramas, with high seats and tall backs. For staff members, he guessed, who might be called on to give information.

On the table, each of the twelve places was provided with a stack of paper, ink pot, brace of quills, and a blotter. He examined them; it *was* paper, not parchment; someone had come up with papermaking in Lokar.

What price recorders? he thought. Having seen what there was to see, he returned to the door and was reaching for it when the handle moved. Without a moment's hesitation he dove, sliding under a settee as the door began to open.

They came in, a number of them—probably a dozen, one for each chair. There were exchanges of small talk, mixed briefly with the sound of chairs being pulled out and drawn back in as they sat down. One of the voices seemed familiar, but he couldn't place it and decided it must be a coincidence anyway. Then the settee creaked slightly as someone sat down a hand's span above his prone body. After a minute or so a gavel rapped and the small talk ceased.

"Your Majesty, gentlemen, the meeting is called to order. Will the recorder please read the minutes of the last meeting?"

Jesus, thought Boru, *I've got a front-row seat at a cabinet meeting!*

The minutes were a summary too brief to have much meaning for him. More interesting were the persons identified in them: the king; the prime minister; the senior ministers for Organization and Operations; and ministers for Executive Affairs, Organization Services, Treasury, Justice, National Services, Foreign Affairs, and Quality Control. *Quality control?*

In government? What a concept! The rest of Lokar might be medieval but government wasn't.

"Thank you, Mr. Recorder. Are there any questions? . . . Corrections?"

I suppose that's the prime minister, Boru decided. *If it was the king, they'd be saying Your Highness all over the place.*

"I move we accept the minutes as read," said a voice.

"Second," said another.

"All in favor?" There was a chorus of yesses. "The minutes of the meeting of, uh, the seventeenth of Wintercome, 682, are accepted as read. Your Majesty, is there anything you'd care to say before we begin ministerial briefings?"

"No thank you, Mr. Prime Minister."

And that, thought Boru, *is the voice that's almost familiar: the king's.*

One by one then, each minister briefed the others on activities in his ministry. There seemed to be a standard format, for the briefings were short and pithy, followed by limited questions and comments. The minister for Executive Affairs mentioned a meeting with the Patriarch and one with the harbor syndics. Organization Services ticked off a major personnel promotion, a retirement, the handling of some communication bollix, and the proceedings of a board of investigation on a malfeasance charge against some official.

"That B of I was supposed to be completed by now," the prime minister said pointedly. "Why wasn't it?"

"Initially I ordered the findings submitted by last Fiveday," the man replied, "but I extended it a week. The board ran into some contrary 'facts,' and they're still pulling the strings on that to see where they lead. It'll almost surely be finished this week, and I'll have a rundown for you next meeting."

The prime minister accepted that and went on. Treasury, Justice, and National Services followed in quick succession. The treasury was shrinking under the pressure of emergency military purchases. Charges against Lord Varthen had been proven and he'd agreed to make restitution and amends to his tenants. National Services had completed collection and snow storage of three hundred thousand khorswood cuttings for spring planting on Markil Fen, and the chief forester was confident that this would cover the shortfall in the city's anticipated fuel requirements.

When the prime minister next spoke, his voice was not as

casual as before. "All right, Palek, I guess we're ready for you. Gentlemen, the foreign minister has already reported his main item to His Majesty and I. It has major impact on your areas, so listen well. Palek, the floor is yours."

"Thank you, Larsa. Seven years ago, when His Majesty visited the barbarians, a young man among them attached himself to the army and they brought him back with them. He is the halfbreed son of a fur trader. The troopers adopted him, so to speak. He knew a little Lokarit that he'd learned on his father's yearly trading visits, and he was bright and very interested and eager.

"Although he was never formally mustered in, he became, so to speak, a kingsman, riding and drilling with the Third Cavalry Regiment. Over several years he became an 'honorary corporal.'

"Three years ago he decided he wanted to see his mother and little sister, and went north alone. Two days ago he arrived back in Tonlik with some important and serious news: the eastern tribes—all of them, from both the barrenlands and the rivers—plan to invade Lokar later this winter on skis, when the snow is too deep for the effective use of cavalry.

"I questioned him personally, and judging from the number of clans and his estimate of the number of warriors who would ride from typical clans, we can expect something like seven or eight thousand to move south against us.

"This seems to be the unknown factor we've felt must exist in the plans of the Southern Coalition. It also explains why their expected mobilization hasn't occurred yet: they're holding off their attack until *after* the barbarians are upon us in the north and a sizeable part of our army has been drawn well away from the southern border."

The foreign minister paused. "Edbar, I can see you're eager to ask a question. Maybe you'd like to know what under the sun happened to unite the tribes. Well, that is interesting. *Very* interesting. I believe it tells us something very important—adds some certainty to something we've suspected before. It seems that a great medicine man, big and fierce, came out of the barrens after the tribes had moved down to their winter villages. His magic is so much greater than the local shamans' that essentially he became the ruler of the barrenlands tribes. And—a remarkable coincidence—another similar medicine man has united the river tribes."

"Department Eleven!" someone blurted.

"I'm sure you're right—our friends in the Confederacy. This seems to confirm that they are the moving factor in the formation and planning of the Southern Coalition.

"What remains for us to do is to replan and instrument our counteractions. We're working on it now in Foreign Affairs, particularly of course in the War Office. Obviously the additional military burden will require considerable interaction with every ministry. Replanning has already begun—we learned of this only yesterday—and I'll be keeping each of you informed from day to day as needed. What I need from you today is someone from each of your staffs assigned to work with us.

"At any rate, we consider the prospects for victory to be quite good, as we know in advance of the barbarian invasion. The addition of a northern front will spread us very thin of course. We can expect severe enemy penetration, and extensive damage to the nation both north and south. But past performances of all principals points to a successful defense."

The king spoke then, quietly but with a tone of elevation. "Don't you think the off-worlders would evaluate the situation in much the same way as you have?" he asked.

There was a pause before Palek answered. "Not necessarily, Your Majesty. They do not understand or appreciate the quality of our army or the morale of our nation."

"Do you know that?"

"I cannot document it, sire, but it seems—apparent."

"Then why did they bring the barbarians into the picture? Considering the Southern Coalition's much larger population, the favorable geography for their attack, and the unfavorable geography for any preemptive or retributive invasion by our own forces, it would seem that they could defeat us handily by themselves. Yet apparently the off-worlders feel it necessary to bring in the tribes."

"Yes sire."

There were several seconds of silence.

"Go ahead, Palek," the king said. "Ask the question you have in mind."

"Knowing Your Majesty, I'm sure you had a specific reason for bringing this up. I suppose you're going to tell us."

The king's reply was delivered very matter-of-factly. "Since we learned of the plans of the Southern Coalition last summer, we've been looking for the unknown factor we were sure existed. Must exist for their invasion to succeed, or for Garvas and Prozhask even to consider it.

"Department Eleven isn't planning this war to make us exert ourselves. They want to destroy us. And Garvas and Prozhask, and particularly Bleesbrok, would never have agreed to an invasion that did not promise victory.

"We've been looking for an unknown factor, one not involving introduced weapons that would endanger the Confederate Foreign Ministry with serious scandal and its leading personnel with criminal prosecution. So whatever they have in mind, it will very probably appear to be indigenous. Now we've found such a factor, but it doesn't seem adequate to their purpose. Therefore I feel quite confident that there is a second unknown factor we haven't found yet. Perhaps even a third.

"Proceed with your planning, but keep in mind that another factor almost surely exists. Assume it. It is very desirable that we find out what it is."

The rest of the meeting didn't take long, and when it was over, the room apparently cleared of all but Boru. The man who'd sat inches above him had left without speaking.

Boru lay there for a few minutes; it wouldn't do to step out the door into a hall conversation among ministers. Then, before he crawled from beneath the settee, the latch sounded again. Two or more people entered. He heard them padding briefly around the table, perhaps picking up soiled blotters or crumpled paper. When they left, he raised the edge of the valance and peered out; he was alone.

Crawling out, he opened the door and stepped into the hall. A man with his back to Boru was entering one of the other doors and closed it behind him. Boru strode to the main hall, and two minutes later was in the courtyard, heading for the guardhouse.

He thought he knew the remaining unknown factor, or one of them: the assassination of Trogeir, king of Lokar. Trogeir was smart, and he seemed to be the pivot point of the government, perhaps a rallying point for the people.

It would be easy now to head back for Jussvek and Earth with Selena. With what he had learned, he could really blow the whistle on Department Eleven. That would not only bust them but would undoubtedly abort the war here as well.

But another thought had set its hook in his mind, a thought he couldn't ignore. Heidemann. The chances were that Heidemann was the agent he'd spotted on the shuttle to Cornfields. Whether it was him or not, Wan Larmet had said someone was supposed to follow him to Lokar a week behind. Even assuming the someone hadn't gotten away from Jussvek until Vinta had returned to escort him through the wilderness, he should be in Tonlik by now, if Tonlik was his destination. It was conceivable that Heidemann was a backup, to kill Trogeir if Boru failed or walked away. That was a long way from standard procedure, but so was everything else in this case.

After stomping the snow off his boots, Boru walked into the guardhouse and sat down on a bench by the wall, watching a group play cards around a table. Another guard came and sat down by him.

"What you thinking about, Barni?" he asked. "You look like you got troubles on your mind."

"Nope. Just wondering how things are back home." He accepted a twist of spiced tobacco-like leaves the man offered to him, biting off a chew. "Everything pointed to a heavy winter—a poverty winter. The snow up there could be ass-deep on a tall hreen by now." He spat into a convenient wide-mouthed receptacle. "I'm glad I came down here."

I'd better stay around a day or two, he thought, *and figure out a safe way to warn the king.* The obvious thing to do was write it up and have it routed to the prime minister, or maybe the king himself. But who would it go through? Would it go to some junior functionary who might diddle around with it? This place seemed to run better than that. The surest way would be to walk in on, say, the prime minister, if he could get away with it, identify himself and tell what he knew.

But they might lock him up, and it was more important that he take the story back to Earth. Writing it up seemed best. He decided that if he hadn't come up with something better, say by quitting time that night, they'd head north in the morning and mail a report to the king from somewhere along the way. That would have to do, and it would give them a few days, distance before delivery.

FIFTEEN

Though physically he did not strut, "Hosar the Weaver" managed to communicate pompous self-importance, to which his greatcoat, fur hat, and beard somehow added belligerence. And clearly he knew where he was going; it would have seemed presumptuous for palace staff to question him or proffer help.

He had passed the small, unobtrusive janitorial room two minutes earlier while going in the other direction, and hadn't even looked at it; there had been two other people in the corridor then, walking in his direction. This time the only person in sight was preceding him, unaware. Without hesitating he turned the latch and slipped inside.

There was something in the night that held away the neozen aware state. The watch dragged slowly and the cold penetrated. Boru worked his toes inside his fur boots, looked up at the waxing half moon, and realized that somehow he hadn't even noticed it there before. He wondered how much longer he had to wait.

As if in answer, he heard Corporal Jorik's nasal baritone in sharp command from the gate a dozen meters off. With crisp chop steps, Boru turned in place ninety degrees and marched briskly to a position before the gate, where he conjoined with the other three outside guards. They dovetailed to form a file of four, marched inside and through the gate a dozen steps, then spread, halted, and about faced to form a small line facing the gate, mittens on sword hilts. Other men pushed on the great gates, closing them. Still others slid the heavy beam through brackets that had each a small wheel to act as a bearing, allowing the gates to be quickly secured. Krogaskott was buttoned up for the night, although individuals could be allowed in and out the small postern gate.

Jorik's voice, still sharp but with its volume now modulated, gave the line a "right face! Mark time! March! Column right, march!" and they swung across the courtyard to the guardhouse, where they were halted and dismissed. They stomped into its warmth, mouthing their relief to be out of the cold, milling briefly before the coat wall, the weapons racks, putting away their gear.

Ordinarily Boru would have gone directly to his locker, gotten his personal jacket, cap, and mittens, and jogged home via the postern gate. But the watch had been a bad one, and he decided to stay and enjoy the warmth for a few minutes, listening to the good-natured banter of bachelor guards, some of whom would settle down to cards and conversation before going to their dormitory.

The sergeant in charge of the palace detail came in, trailed by the corporal in charge of the entry, and asked for Lieutenant Gausa. Gausa came out of the latrine, buckling his belt.

"What's going on?" he asked.

"Sir, there's a palace pass that no one picked up. Someone's inside the palace that shouldn't be."

Thick eyebrows drew down. "Or else you let someone out without logging him."

Boru had looked up from the stove, alert.

"No sir," the sergeant asserted. "It's an extended personal pass, to a 'Hosar the Weaver.' He'd have asked for it for sure if we forgot to give it to him."

Gausa pursed his wide mouth thoughtfully. "Not necessarily. What's his business here?"

"He was taking measurements for some new tapestries, sir."

"Here," Gausa put out his hand. "Let me see the pass," The sergeant gave it to him and he squinted at it, frowning. An extended visitor pass had a quick, skillfully-done sketch of the proper bearer; this sketch was of no one he'd ever seen.

A hand reached and took the parchment from him. "Excuse me sir, may I see that?" Boru had it, studying the sketch, before Gausa could react.

"What in hell do you think you're doing, Jussvek?" Gausa snapped.

The beard means nothing, Boru thought. He took in the

broad low forehead, wide-set eyes, small nose, thin lips. "Sir, my apologies, sir, but I know this man."

Kyril Golovin laid aside his pen. It was not a quill; its cartridge was the last of its box, but there was still another box to go.

Something had disturbed his concentration but he could not identify it or even locate it yet. Seeming to listen for the inaudible, or *to* it, he unfolded his long frame from the chair, then looked at the large-faced, weight-driven clock on one wall: eight minutes after eighteen. In quick decision he strode to the door, grabbing his black cloak from its peg as he passed, and donned it as he swept into the narrow, out-of-the-way hall. What was going on he had not determined, but he was on his way to the guardhouse.

Albert Haas stepped from behind the hanging mops where he had spent more than four Thegwar hours. It was almost utterly dark—a little light entered under the door. His glowing watch dial read 18:05. He stretched, bent, straightened, raised first one knee and then the other to his chest, all without showing any sign of physical or mental relief that the wait was over.

Seven Terran years ago, per his information, the king had customarily, even routinely, retired to his apartment at eighteen hours, two hours before midnight. Haas's timing was predicated on the questionable assumption that he still did.

The watch turned over 18:06. It had been designed for FM use on Thegwar. He'd kept it for more than sixteen years, looking forward to this return, to this assignment he knew Department Eleven would eventually make. He'd taken steps to see that it would eventually come to him, and then it almost hadn't.

Actually the king wasn't his primary target, but who was there to stop him, now that he was here? And after the king, *then* the Russian stork. If the rumors were right, that might be more difficult.

Eighteen-oh-six didn't allow much time for tardiness on the king's part. But by now the entry guards would have realized they had an uncollected pass, would be done questioning each other, and might already be reporting it. Allow two or three minutes for questions and answers with the officer of the watch, another few to organize a palace search. . . . There was no more time for waiting.

Haas did not approve, ordinarily, of plans with such slender time margins, or of uncertainties in such things as the target's personal routine. But he had no significant resources in Tonlik and none in the palace. It was a matter of using judgment and making do.

He left his greatcoat on the floor and put his fur hat in a mop bucket to deaden the sound, then relieved himself into it. After opening the door slightly to peer out, he quit the janitorial closet and walked swiftly down the hall. There was no uncertainty in his action. He could, without hesitating, have drawn a scale diagram of the palace. One of the more certain things in this assignment was that there'd have been only minor changes, if any, in the locations of facilities in this great heap of stone. Some uses might have been reassigned to different spaces, but the royal apartment would have remained the royal apartment because it was the only suite of rooms suitable for it in the palace.

He assumed that a guard was posted outside the king's apartment at night, so he moved to a cul-de-sac he knew of, pulled a curtain away from the wall, and with a pass key long held in Department Eleven's files, opened the door concealed behind it.

Inside he took forth a tiny lamp no bigger than a cigarette lighter, its beam guiding him swiftly through a series of passages and stairwells lit otherwise by moonlight through small, frost-coated windows. At length he came to a certain door, not the first. Pocketing his torch, he knocked loudly, waited, then knocked again urgently. High in the door a small panel opened behind a grill. Barely, Haas could discern two eyes peering out at him. He did not wait for the question.

"I have vital news about Venker Sparn, His Majesty's spy in Lorstev! I must deliver it at once and be away, or I'll be suspect!"

"Just a moment." The face withdrew. A minute later he heard the bolt being drawn; the door opened. Haas followed the man through the kitchen, past the warmly radiating cook stove and into a room where the still young Trogeir waited with an open book in his lap.

Haas did not waste time, mouthed no gloating final taunt. His only words were to cover his act. "Your Majesty! Venker says it's urgent''—Haas's hand emerged from his loose tunic with a spring-driven dart gun. There was a sharp *snap* and for a moment the king's eyes widened, his lips parting silently— ''that he be replaced''—Haas had turned with the gun at his waist; there was another snap—''as soon as possible. He's sure . . .''

He stopped talking as the valet/bodyguard jerked and began to fold. In his case the poison was superfluous; the dart had driven deep below the breastbone and through the abdominal aorta. The assassination completed, Albert Haas moved quickly back through the kitchen and into the concealed passageway.

He was not utterly without nerves, but he had abundant experience with killing. And he was a man without conscience— in that sense insane. With swift sure steps he followed another series of passages and stairwells, longer this time, leading to the food preparation area on the ground floor. The last stairwell emerged into the bakery, where a baker, long wooden shovel in his hands, was putting loaves into an oven. He glanced at Haas, then back to the oven, did a double take at a bearded stranger in a service area at night. He was shot as he turned. Straightening, he let go of the shovel, and his mouth opened. Instead of calling out, he shuddered and fell.

Haas hadn't even waited to see him go down.

A personnel door opened onto one end of a loading platform, and, unbolting it, Haas stepped out into a crystalline, iron-cold night. There was no one in sight. Jumping to the ground, he walked casually to the great fortress wall, then kept to its shadow as he walked to one of the massive corner towers. The small tower door was unlocked, as tower doors had always been, and he entered its denser darkness, climbing the stairs that spiraled upward inside.

At the first archery deck he stopped, removed his tunic and tossed it out an embrasure on the shadowed side of the tower. To get himself out the embrasure other than head-first was awkward. Turning his back to it, he dropped to hands and knees, walked his feet backward up the wall and into the narrow opening. Twisting and turning, he got first his hips in and then his chest and shoulders. But as it widened outward, soon only his grip on the inner edge kept him from chuting off the downward-slanting sill.

For the first time his nerves played him false. He went numb hanging there, numb with fear, but even that fear he remained partly outside of. After a dozen seconds he let go, deliberately, and plunged seven meters down, hitting the frozen ground off-balance sideways. There was a moment of severe pain in his ankle, then he lay stunned in the snow. It was half a minute before he got up, looked around, picked up his tunic and limped away, furtive now. He went not across the square, but across a somewhat narrower open space along the side of Krogaskott toward a mass of two-story tenements. In the cover of their shadows he began a circuitous route that would bring him around the square to his lodging at the Three Bulls.

His jaw was clenched against the pain. Before he was halfway there, he was walking with difficulty.

By the time Golovin was striding down the short, broad entry stairs, two files of guardsmen were marching across the snow toward him. He stopped as they approached, towering more than a head taller than most of them with his two-meter height.

"Sergeant!" he said, and the sergeant halted the squad.

"Yes, Lord Golovin?"

"What is going on?"

"There is a visitor unaccounted for, sir. He may be inside the palace. We're going in to look for him."

"Thank you sergeant," He stepped aside and watched the double file of men as they started again. When they had passed, he strode on toward the guardhouse. The door barely accommodated his height. The officer of the watch looked up from his desk and nodded respectfully.

"Good evening, Lord Golovin," he said. His eyes questioned.

"What has happened, Lieutenant?"

"We have a visitor unaccounted for. He may simply have forgotten to pick up his pass when he left, but he might also still be inside somewhere, perhaps a thief. I've sent a squad to search."

Golovin stood like some gaunt black bird of prey above him. "Is there anything else?"

"No sir, not really. We have a guardsman who seems to be crazy; his name is Barni of Jussvek. Lieutenant Gausa had him locked up—thought he might be dangerous."

"Where is this guard? Let me see him!"

The officer blinked worriedly, then nodded and got up. "Of course, my lord. This way."

The lockup was small, with three cells, two of them empty. The other held a glowering Boru. Golovin stared at him, thunderstruck.

"What—is he here for?"

"According to Lieutenant Gausa, the officer of the preceding watch, he began to act crazy."

"*Specifically* what did he do?"

"Well my lord, he claimed he knew the unaccounted-for visitor. Snatched the pass out of Lieutenant Gausa's hands and said he knew the man."

Suddenly Golovin flinched, paled, as if he'd had a shooting pain, and his eyes glazed. As it passed almost at once, the lieutenant continued. "He says the visitor is a dangerous off-worlder who might harm the king. Actually he seems to be a weaver named Hosar who's been measuring walls for tapestries he's to bid on."

"Thank you, Lieutenant." Golovin's voice was quiet but intense. "I appreciate your help. There may be more to this than is apparent to you. Now I want to speak with this guardsman privately. If you please."

The officer saluted, looking concerned, then turned and left, closing the door behind him. The tall, black-haired man, looking like some sane Rasputin, turned to Boru.

"Who are you?" Golovin asked in Terran.

"Barney Boru, from Earth," Boru answered. "I'm a . . ." He paused. "Look, sir, it'll take too long to explain. The guy in the palace calls himself Herman Heidemann, and he's probably from Department Eleven. He's after the king!"

"That's what you told Lieutenant Gausa?"

"Yes sir, but he wouldn't have it. We haven't gotten along from . . ."

"*Lieutenant!*"

Golovin's voice was like a projectile gun, blasting, startling Boru to silence, bringing the watch officer bolting in with sword in hand.

"Unlock it!" Golovin ordered, pointing at the cell. "Let him out!"

"Sir?"

"*Now!*"

The blast made the man jump. Fumbling the key ring from

his belt, he quickly unlocked the cell door and swung it open, nodding Boru out.

"Thank you, Lieutenant," said Golovin, suddenly mild and grave again. "The responsibility is mine."

Abruptly he wheeled, beckoning Boru to follow, and strode out. "Get your sword," he ordered, and as they passed through the watchroom, Boru grabbed his swordbelt, buckling it on as he half ran in the tall man's wake across the courtyard. Up the entry steps they went, three at a time, and passed the night guard without speaking.

It took little time, with Golovin leading, to come to the king's apartment door. The placid, burly guard there acknowledged Golovin with a salute and they strode by without pausing. At the end of the long corridor they turned into a cul-de-sac and went to the same drapery-concealed service door that Haas had used. Boru got another look at Golovin's face, grim now but alert, the eyes intense.

Golovin unlocked and opened the door, gestured Boru through brusquely, then led the way to the apartment's service door. It was closed but not locked, and they entered without knocking, as if Golovin knew that no one would answer or object.

In the living room they found the bodies. Golovin bent for a moment to examine the king. "Dead," he muttered to himself. "A dart." He gestured Boru back into the kitchen.

"Draw your sword," he ordered.

Boru did, puzzled but unquestioning.

"Now listen. What I'm going to tell you is vitally important. Do exactly as I say, *exactly*, and hold your questions till later. Lie down on the floor, right there, face down with your hand on your hilt, and pretend to be dead. You were shot and killed defending the king.

"People will come in and look at you, but you must not move. They must assume you're dead. Do you understand?"

Boru nodded. He understood *what* was wanted, though not why.

"No one will examine you or take the trouble to light a lamp in the kitchen here. Neither will happen."

Boru felt the force of the man's intention. If he said they wouldn't, they were damned unlikely to.

"So get down now and don't move. Be as dead as those two in there."

Boru got down, and before he was settled, the man was gone. *"Hold your questions till later,"* Golovin had said; Boru was asking them now, of himself, and getting no answers.

SIXTEEN

Boru lay there with nothing happening for some minutes— twelve or fifteen he thought, although it might have been fewer. What the hell kind of search were they running? The king lay murdered in the next room and seventeen searchers hadn't found the body yet. Probably with the guard outside the door it hadn't occurred to them to look there.

And what about the tall guy in black? What was he doing? Something, that was certain; he'd had something specific in mind.

Someone knocked at the hall door, a knocking that quickly escalated into pounding. He knew when it opened because suddenly he could hear voices.

"Love of Voroth!" It was the tall man. "Sergeant, have a guard put at every exit from the building! At once!"

There were other voices. One of them must have been the door guard's, because it was swearing that no one had entered after the king. Another of the voices was the sergeant's, giving orders.

"The king is still alive." It was the tall man again. "But very weak. Sergeant, send someone to bring the prime minister and Lords Mergalf and Vattenkarm. And clear your other people out into the hallway; I want nothing touched in here. Nothing."

Was that true, Boru wondered? Alive? He'd said he was dead when he'd examined him earlier. But if he was dead, then why lie?

Another voice called out from close at hand—the kitchen

door. "Lord Golovin! There's another one in the kitchen."
Footsteps approached. "It's one of us!"

The door guard, thought Boru. Other footsteps came rapidly; he sensed somone kneeling beside him, and from almost at his ear the tall man spoke. "It's Jussvek, the guard I left earlier to watch the service door." He stood, his voice less close. "Sergeant, I want *everyone* out of here, including you. They disturb the images of the past, and I must be able to recover them to see who did this."

The kitchen door closed and Boru heard nothing more. *Well*, he told himself, *we got through that step, wherever it's leading*. And the guard had called the tall man Lord Golovin. Presumably the guards, and maybe Golovin, had left or were leaving the apartment. Had they taken the king out? Probably not. That wouldn't be consistent with not disturbing "the images."

The images: Was that something Golovin made up to get the guards out? Or could he really do that? He had lots of questions to ask when the time came.

He took advantage of the wait to try for the neozen aware state. It came in no more than two or three minutes, its onset as always instantaneous—not a gradual change but a "now it's not, now it is." But this time there was an added aspect, one new to Boru. He became aware that Golovin was still there in the other room, knew it despite the intervening solid door. And the king? Nothing. Dead then. He was also aware that, outside the hall door, two guards now stood. It wasn't that Boru saw or heard any of them, he simply knew. His knowing did not include what they were doing, just that they were there. And it did not occur to him to question whether the phenomenon was real; it was too definite, too matter of fact, to question.

Time passed neither quickly nor slowly for him. At length the outer door opened, closed, and people were there, talking with Golovin. He received no words, no sounds, but they were talking. This continued for several minutes; then the kitchen door opened.

"You can get up, Jussvek. Boru."

Golovin was an off-worlder. Besides Golovin, almost no one but Gausa called him by a surname; surnames were little used for address in Lokar, and with Gausa, Jussvek was an epithet, not a name.

Boru got to his feet, looking at the four who'd come in. Regrettably the aware state had flicked off. They were all eyeing him, evaluating.

"There's a resemblance," said one of them, "but it's not *that* strong. Certainly they're not identical looking."

Boru recognized the voice: the prime minister.

Golovin smiled. "When did you begin shaving, Boru? At what age?"

Boru looked back at him, puzzled. "Fifteen. Actually I was sixteen before I started shaving every day; maybe seventeen."

"Exactly." Golovin turned to the others. "That's in Terran years. In terms of Thegwar years, he was nine. Trogeir came here, if you'll recall, when he was ten, with a rather well-established beard. You never saw him beardless or with his hair much above his shoulders. He was very much and very properly in the tradition of Lokarn royalty.

"Even though, as we know, he was not in actual fact the prince.

"Now there was something he and I never told you about his parentage, something never before relevant, but very pertinent to our present situation. We had told you that Trogeir was the grandson of Byornas Borr, Korbin's blacksheep uncle who left Thegwar with the Confederacy's first expedition here."

Byornas Borr? thought Boru. *What is this? Some kind of joke? What in hell is this all about?*

"That is true in one sense," Golovin continued, "but in another it is not. One reason Borr left was that he'd gotten involved with a language specialist on the expedition, a woman named Lisa Keenan. They had a son born on Earth, whom she named James Keenan; by that time Borr was off adventuring somewhere. His son, in turn, became a famous martial artist; on Earth, men play at the skills of war without using them seriously. The martial arts are a highly developed sport there.

"In a sense, James Keenan was our Trogeir's father, but only in a sense. You all know, I'm sure, that a gardener can take cuttings from a superior plant and cause them to root, thus making copies of the original. In Terran such a copy, or more properly all the copies collectively, is called a *clone*. On

Earth they learned to clone men, although it's now against the law.

"Trogeir, my friends, had no direct mother. He was a clone—physically a continuation—of James Keenan. There was no intervening father and mother. In a physical sense, Trogeir's father was Byornas Borr and his mother was Lisa Keenan.

"And so was this man's, for he too is a clone of James Keenan." Golovin turned to the gape-jawed Boru. "Is there anything you'd care to say about all this?"

"Holy Jesus Christ!"

"An understandable reaction." Golovin looked back to the others. "As soon as I saw this man, I recognized the face of the prepubescent Trogeir grown to full manhood. And when he told me his Terran name, 'Barney Boru,' I knew at once: he, like Trogeir, is a clone of James Keenan. Even the voice is right, if you overlook the northern accent."

His eyes shone with amusement as he looked at Barney. "Someone—I believe I know who—showed humor in naming you; someone who knew your lineage. Would you let these gentlemen hear you speak? Remembering that you need no longer affect the dialect of Jussvek."

Boru's mouth closed and he looked around at all of them. "I've got the feeling," he said, "that I've been manipulated over the past thirty-three Terran years, at least occasionally, without knowing it until just now. Maybe I ought to be mad about that, but mainly I'm curious. And while I can imagine why my face and voice interest you, I want you to tell me."

"Mr. Boru," Golovin said mildly, "have you ever been a king?"

Boru looked wryly at him, remembering another question similarly worded. "Not recently. Do you really want me to be king? Because if you put the crown on me, I'll *be* the king."

None of them spoke, and he went on. "Do you know where I was this morning during the cabinet meeting? I was in the room with you, hiding under one of the settees listening to you talk about the barbarian invasion and the Southern Coalition. Your security, gentlemen, is lousy, as also witness the body of your late king. And when I sneaked out of the meeting room afterward, I left thinking that Trogeir might easily be the best head of state in this part of the galaxy.

"Me, on the other hand—I'm pretty ignorant of government, pretty ignorant of Lokar, and even more ignorant of the rest of Thegwar.

"On top of that, I'm my own man. I do what *I* think is best, which is why I didn't carry out my assignment, which was to kill Trogeir." He looked at the ministers; they showed no sign of shock or surprise. Had Golovin told them about that? Then how had he known?

"I decided instead to get more information, enough to blow the whistle on Department Eleven when I got back to Earth. I got what I needed this morning, eavesdropping on you. I planned to write you a warning, of a possible backup assassin, and get out of here.

"But I took too long.

"So if you're thinking about putting me on the throne as a ringer for Trogeir, keep in mind first my limitations, and second, that I make up my own mind. I'd need and want your knowledge and advice, but I'll damned well follow my own principles and conclusions."

Boru looked back to Golovin. "That's my speech for now. If you're interested in me on those terms, I'm interested in the job. Otherwise there ought to be some bright, homegrown replacement who can do the job for you. You'd lose the continuity, but there'd be compensations."

He grinned suddenly, surprisingly. "How was the voice demonstration? Do I sound enough like Trogeir?"

Golovin nodded reflectively. "With a little work the voice would be excellent. As to a decision"—he gestured to the other three—"these are the men who will decide. They head the government; I am an advisor. If I seem to be in command, I am not. The semblance comes from the temporary lack of a monarch, and because it was I who saw a possible solution. Gentlemen," he said to the ministers, "what do you think of my proposal? Shall Trogeir continue on the throne?"

The senior minister for Organization, Gundith Vattenkarm, spoke, his voice quiet, his expression thoughtful. "Let's address how we could successfully convert Mr. Boru into Trogeir. Right now, beardless and with little more than stubble on his head, Mr. Boru does not look like the Trogeir people know. He looks like . . ." Vattenkarm paused. "What has your name been here, Mr. Boru?"

"Barni of Jussvek."

"Yes. To the guards, and to some of the household staff no

doubt, that face belongs to Barni of Jussvek.'' He looked at the others. ''They'd recognize him at once. Nor would the wig and beard of a wandering performer fool anyone. And we can't wait for his beard and hair to grow out; the king's presence—or *a* king's presence—is needed now, or at least very soon.''

Boru responded before anyone else could speak. ''I know someone who might be able to provide a false beard and hair that would be satisfactory. On Earth, such things have become an art. And my wife, who is less than a kilometer from here right now, was trained in the dramatic arts on Earth. I've had some training in disguise myself.

''As far as getting the actual hair for it, if you decide to make Trogeir out of Barni, you'll need to make Barni out of Trogeir. You'll need to shave him for the funeral. That'll provide all the hair we need.

''Incidentally, you need to have a state funeral for the brave guard and brave servant who died defending their king. A funeral with an honor guard of Barni's comrades. When they see his dead face in the casket, they'll look no further for him.''

The ministers' eyes all were on Boru, intent. Only Golovin smiled, his eyebrows slightly raised.

''Now the king has been struck by a dart,'' Boru went on. ''Poisoned, I suppose. Only the unusual skills of his personal advisor, and perhaps the hand of Voroth, have kept him alive. Does that fit your image, Lord Golovin? And Voroth's?''

Heads nodded.

Boru tilted his, as if examining images near the ceiling. ''So the king grows gaunt—I'll need to fast for a while—and some of his hair and beard fall out from the effects of the poison after awhile. But the king's beard and hair will recover and thicken.

''During my convalescence, I can be thoroughly briefed. For a week or two I'll be too feeble, my condition too delicate, to see anyone but Lord Golovin, the prime minister, and my nurse—the widow of Barni the guard, who has some knowledge of the healing arts, learned in Gzarim. Only an occasional servant will be allowed to enter, very quietly, to clean and of course to tell the palace staff how weak and drawn the king looks.

''Meanwhile the king's memory will be affected by the

poison, but the effects will gradually fade. Although no doubt he'll be caught for years not recognizing someone or remembering something he once knew.''

"Your Majesty," the prime minister interrupted, "I believe you've said all that I, at least, need to hear to make a decision." He looked at Vattenkarm and Mergalf. "Let's find the king's razor and get started. We can't bring servants into this: I'm afraid we'll have to do these things for ourselves. And by all means let us send for the widow of poor Barni of Jussvek. I fear we'll need her skill in rebearding the king.''

SEVENTEEN

Albert Haas was hobbling as he approached the Three Bulls. Two men reeled from the inn, and he stopped in the shadows, watching motionlessly. He preferred to be unnoticed. They fumbled the reins from the hitching rail, one swearing and one laughing, then struggled into their saddles and rode away. The assassin slipped into the narrow alleyway between the buildings.

The Three Bulls had several tiny built-on rooms across the back. Haas had rented one, not because they were cheapest but because they had private entrances into the somewhat littered and disreputable rear court. He could come and go without notice. Now he unlocked the door, went in, and closed it behind him, shooting the bolt. The lowering moon sent dim light through the one small, frost-coated window, making it glow white in the darkness. From his bag he groped a cigarette lighter and lit a fat candle, then laid and lit a fire in the small iron stove.

The things one does for one's profession, he thought wryly.

Leave a comfortable home in a lovely city to camp in squalor.
But the work is interesting.

From the same bag he brought forth a bottle and removed the cap. On the inside was an applicator, and he ran it along the edge of his beard, plucking at it, gradually peeling it loose. Once it was partly off, he recapped the bottle before the fumes became strong. The technical people on Earth had failed to visualize candles or stoves with open flames as part of the operating environment.

The wig he left on. Without the beard, no one would recognize "Hosar the Weaver." And with the wig, who would know the baldheaded ex-embassy attaché? Especially after sixteen Terran years.

His ankle was a serious encumbrance, but Albert Haas was uncharacteristically cheerful. He'd had his revenge on Trogeir. It could have been better, but under the circumstances very satisfactory: he'd cut the man down in his prime, with many years yet in which to rule. Now it was necessary to become reasonably mobile again as quickly as possible. Trogeir would undoubtedly be given a state funeral, probably with a procession, and the Russian would surely be there. The crossbow from a window would complete his assignment.

Department Eleven wouldn't be happy about the crossbow; the fools could swallow a camel and choke on a gnat. If Culture had an undercover monitor anywhere on Thegwar, it would be in Tonlik, but crossbow darts weren't flagrantly out-culture, especially if the bow was never found. They wouldn't bring on a dangerous investigation. And if they did, to hell with it: Trogeir and the Russian would both be dead, which was what they all wanted—Department Eleven and himself. And even Culture, if they'd admit it, because the two victims were a nonconformity here.

He put the beard in his bag rather than in the stove. He didn't expect to need it again, but there was always the possibility that it would still be useful. Then he took the odorous ceramic chamberpot from under the cot, and in the courtyard, filled it with snow. Back inside he sat on the single small stool and pulled off his right boot, probed the swollen foot and ankle with a finger, then dug the foot into the bucket of snow.

Tomorrow would tell him how bad it really was. He would probably need a crutch. To have any chance at all of being effective by the time of the funeral, he needed to stay off it almost entirely. It was time to make himself known to the department's only local contact, if she was still here; after seven years it was questionable. She might have been arrested, or gone native and attached herself to some local merchant.

Every minute or two he removed his foot from the snow and massaged it gently. At length he pulled one of the coarse blankets from the foot of the cot and cut a strip from the bottom. Tightly he wrapped foot and ankle, with difficulty pulled the fur boot on, added wood to his fire, and closed the draft and damper on the stove. Then, donning a short coat and his traveling cap, he limped out.

The warmth and light of the Larilia Tavern were welcome, and once he was off his feet, Haas felt almost festive. A group of five musicians were playing, but the music meant nothing to him. What mattered was that she was one of them. His optimism brightened; her picture had shown a pretty young woman, he remembered. After her seven years here, she still was. His belly tightened. It was a stressful life on assignment; he could use a pretty woman.

He ordered, and shortly began to eat. After a little, Selena got up, laid down her flute, and began to dance. Yes, she could definitely relieve his tension. He finished his meal, paying little attention to it, took his wine to a table near the musicians, and waited until she reappeared from her break. As she sat down, he approached her, hobbling, his thin lips smiling.

"You are Selena of Gzarim," he said, his voice quiet but full of hidden meaning. "I am Albert Haas. I have just arrived on a very long journey from your native land. Perhaps you'd like to hear the news from there."

My god! she thought, *my pickup! After all this time! And now I don't need him, don't want him.* Fleetingly she looked him over, avoiding his eyes. She'd forgotten how ugly some agent's minds could feel. Or how dangerous some agents were: they could kill quite brutally and casually. They enjoyed it.

His rodent eyes watched her with a hint of amusement. "Of course," she told him, and they went to his table. Maybe Barni could kill him; he was bigger and much younger. This man must be fifty or so.

"Is it all right," he said as they sat down, "to talk in your native tongue? Or might someone here take offense to hear it?"

"It's safe," she answered quietly in Terran, "but not loudly. We don't want to draw attention to it. If someone comes in who might recognize it, I'll know, almost certainly."

"Good." He appraised her insolently across the small table. Her costume covered her well, but was designed to accentuate underlying curves, and the curves were there. Even in Geneva, where he enjoyed a considerable affluence and many connections, he'd have found this one interesting. He especially liked dancers, and the small lines beginning to show on the face often meant someone who'd learned the meaning of pain, the importance of compliance.

Yes, he decided, he was going to enjoy this.

Inwardly she squirmed at his gaze. She did not read his thoughts; she did not want to and did not need to. "Why are you here?" she asked.

"My dear, surely you didn't think we'd abandoned you? I've come to take you home." He gazed expectantly. Had she been a man, he'd have been suspicious: she should have shown pleasure or relief at the end of her long isolation. But just now he was controlled by his taste for cruelty, by her apparent aversion to him, which he found exciting, and by his leverage, which it seemed to him she would hardly be able to withstand.

"Has it been so long that it's hard to believe?" He reached and took her hand in his, patting it. "Believe me, it's true. In not too many days we'll be in a ship together, bound for Earth." His eyes, his smile, were both amused and lascivious. "When are you done here tonight? No, let me rephrase that: What is the earliest you can leave? Your senior responsibility, you know, is to the Ministry. And to me, your pickup, your ticket home. This place is no longer important to you. There's no reason for you to continue here, and I have, ah, certain activities for you to perform."

If Barni doesn't kill him, she thought, *I will*. "In a little more than half an hour," she replied. "Sixty-five minutes."

He nodded. "Very well, my dear. I hurt myself tonight, sprained my ankle severely. I'll need care if we're to get away from here. I need to be able to travel as soon as possible or we'll miss our connection and both be stranded. Do you understand?

"Now I need you to take me to your home. Then you can go to the place I've been staying and bring my things. There aren't very many."

She began to see the way out of this. Barni would be at home. When they went in, she'd trip this ugly little psychopath. Barni could take it from there. "In sixty-five minutes," she repeated. "I don't live far from here. We'll make it."

"With you, my dear, I can walk as far as need be. You are a very lovely woman. Very lovely."

"All right. But I have to play now."

"Of course, my dear, by all means. Play it out. I'll leave for a short while, but I'll be back."

She got up and he watched her walk back to her place with the other musicians, pick up her flute and sit ready. The others, who'd taken a break to accommodate her absence, picked up their own instruments, and they began to play. Haas got up and hobbled out. He would put his foot in snow again. It was the only available therapy he knew of for it.

Selena was hardly aware of playing as she watched him disappear from the room. After a minute she got up again, in mid-number, nodding apologetically to the others, and slipped from the room. Haas was gone from the hall as well, so she went to the front door and looked out. He was hobbling southward; when he came to the service alley beside the Three Bulls he disappeared into it, and she went back in.

If only Barni would come in now, she thought, she could tell him about Haas. Then he could be ready for him, ambush him. The little centipede was poisonous, surely armed, perhaps with a stunner; surprise would be important. But if Barni had been coming to the Larilia tonight, he'd have arrived some time before.

As unobtrusively as possible she rejoined the other musicians and began to play. Then it occurred to her. Of course; how simple! After this number she'd go home and tell him. It would take no more than five or ten minutes.

They were not yet done when a guard came in. Selena saw him enter, but it meant nothing to her. He stood at the entrance to the room, watching them play, and when they were through, walked quickly to them. It was clear when he arrived that he had something to say to Selena, but he stood uncomfortably, not speaking. Miku watched, troubled, but did not question him.

"Yes?" Selena said at last.

"Your husband . . . Barni . . ." The words came unwillingly. She choked on her breath, and despite herself read his thoughts.

"Can we go outside?" the man asked. "I have something to tell you."

She shook her head, wide-eyed and numb.

"He was killed tonight." His voice faltered, a near whisper. "An assassin tried to kill the king. Barni tried to stop him. Someone needed to tell you."

Her face was frozen, eyes staring. The man backed away, unable to disengage from them. The other musicians were shocked. A few of the remaining customers had noticed and were looking curiously at them. The guardsman pulled his eyes away, turned, and hurried out.

"By Voroth but I'm sorry," Miku said to her. "We all are." Abruptly she stood and hurried into the back room. Miku raised his flute and began to play, rapidly, raggedly, and the others followed suit, adjusting the tempo as they got underway.

Two long numbers later she returned. Her eyes were red, her face pale and freshly washed. Without speaking she picked up her flute. Miku, avoiding her eyes, put his own to his lips and began to play a number she'd composed, a favorite of hers, sweetly sad. They all joined in, Selena too.

But her attention was not on the music. Haas had done this thing, she was sure, attacked the king, killed Barni. The man was a psychopath; he should die for this. Yet he was her ticket home, the only one now that she had. And she could not stay on Thegwar after this, without expectation or even hope of retrieval.

Oh Barni, Barni, why couldn't we go when you decided to walk away? We could have! We could! We could have been together for a long long time, and it would have been so good! She still held the flute, but unknowingly no longer played. Tears flowed down her cheeks, and the others played furiously, covering their own emotions. Then she became aware once more and tried again to play.

During the break that followed, she retreated once more to the back room and rewashed her face, then set about deliberately to recover herself. She looked around the room, noticed the wall, went to it and touched it, thumped it with her fist, feeling the impact, the solidity; looked at the floor and stamped on it. Then she looked at the door, went and touched it; the table, the shelf, the lamp flickering on the shelf.

After one or two minutes of this she went out and joined the others. Together they played, and this time the music kept her out of herself. When Haas came in, she noticed at once, but continued to play, played until the bouncer announced to those customers still left that there'd be just one more short number before they must leave. Then they played that last number, a Lokarn equivalent of "Auld Lang Syne," and the musicians went together into the back room where they kept their coats and boots.

"That man that talked to you is back again," said Miku. "Do you want us to run him off?"

"No, he's all right."

"He upset you."

"He's from Gzarim. He told me news from there. My brother . . . my brother was a prominent man. He died last year. And after that the guardsman came and told me—what he told me. It was too much. But I'll be all right now." She reached, squeezed Miku's hand. "Good friend, don't worry."

She left the Larilia with Haas, who limped excessively, in obvious pain with every step, his arm around her more for support than possession.

In her apartment she took his coat and cap, helped him to a chair, then held a splinter in the stove and lit the lamps. Haas looked around in obvious relief at being off his feet.

"Comfortable," he said. "Quite comfortable for Lokar. I'll bet you've forgotten what an upperclass home on Earth is like, yes? I'll have to show you where I live. In Switzerland, Geneva. Here, sit by me." He gestured to the chair on the side of the table next to his. "I retired early from FM, you know. I'm a consultant now. It pays far better, provides much greater freedom of action, and I'm no longer ordered by fools."

He paused to smile at her. *How incredibly false*, she thought. *If his other masks are no more convincing than that smile, he should have been dead long ago. He's a biological robot, programmed to murder, and functions only incidentally at anything else.*

"I'm sure it must be a great relief," she replied ironically, "not to be ordered by fools any longer."

He reached out and took her hand. "And how long has it been for you, my dear? Seven years?" His eyebrows arched. "After seven years on Thegwar, you deserve the company of a civilized man. And I, after a month on Thegwar, deserve the—company of a civilized woman."

"Why did you come to Lokar?" she asked. "Not to get me. They wouldn't send you here just for that."

"Yes, to get you. That was part of it. You and what you've learned." He smirked. "But there was something else—a minor little thing. I came here to assassinate Trogeir. That too. I completed that part of my mission tonight." From a pocket he brought forth the dart gun, waving it casually with its tube directed toward her. "A powerful spring drives poison darts; quite deadly. Paralysis is so quick, it might as well be instantaneous. But death," he lied, "is slow and painful. Ten or fifteen minutes of increasing agony until the organism can no longer survive it." He cocked an eyebrow theatrically. "And the victim cannot even scream or thrash around. I killed three men with it tonight, the first of them the king."

He laid the gun down and took her arm with his right hand. "But enough about death, eh? It's time to live a little." He pulled her around the corner of the table to him, his grip surprisingly, horribly strong. His mouth still smiled, but brutality and determination showed raw and naked now. She tried to get her elbows between them, to hold herself away.

"My dear, why struggle?" he hissed. "You *do* want to go home, don't you?"

For a moment she stared, then nodded, dropping her gaze. "Would you like me to undress you?" she asked.

He beamed. "What a delightful suggestion! What a thoughtful, intelligent young woman! But first, my dear, take off your own. Let me feast these tired eyes."

She sat, removed her boots, then stood, holding them out. "Part of mine," she suggested, "then part of yours."

He smiled at her, amused. "My dear, I do not wish to discourage your creativity, but understand, I am the master here. I call the dances, you do the steps. First you remove your clothes, *then* mine." He leaned back and extended his right foot. "But you may, at this point, take off my right boot. Otherwise I fear I may have to cut it off." She nodded. "But carefully if you please," he added, "very carefully."

She knelt, took his foot in her hands, then suddenly lunged, tipping him backward crashing to the floor. By the time he raised his head, the dartgun was in her hands and she had backed off two steps. He rolled carefully free from the overturned chair and sat up.

"My dear," he said thinly, "don't be a fool. I'm your ticket home, the only one you'll ever have." Clumsily he got to his knees and she jabbed toward him with the weapon.

"Don't move your hands," she said. "If you do, I'll kill you."

"No," he said, "you won't kill me. If you were going to kill me, you'd have done it already." He wagged his head. "My dear, my dear! Your chastity isn't that valuable to you, not as valuable as getting off this planet." His eyes fixed her. "No, what you are going to do is put the gun back on the table and help me to the bed. Then I'll allow you to make amends for what you just did."

She shook her head. "I was married here in Tonlik," she said. Her voice was tight, and hurt in her throat. "My husband was one of the men you killed tonight. A guard came from the palace while you were gone, and told me."

His manner changed at once, grotesquely. "Oh my poor child! My poor dear! No wonder you're upset! I didn't know . . . ." Then with lightning quickness his right hand went for the knife below the back of his collar, and the dart gun snapped. He stared, incredulous. His hand started back down toward the dart between his ribs, but had not arrived when he pitched over on his face.

The last thought of Albert Haas was sane: he wondered how he'd been such a fool.

She lay for an uncertain time across the bed, dry-eyed and dumb, to be roused by knocking. Slowly she raised her head and looked at the heavy plank door. The knocking repeated. She got up, went to it, and opened the peering slot. The man outside was the tallest she had ever seen on Thegwar. He had to bend for her to see his hawk face.

"I'm from the palace," he said. "I've come to talk to Selena, the wife of Barni."

For possibly five seconds she stared. "Someone already told me. One of the guards."

"He didn't tell you what *I've* come to say." His voice was quiet, confidential. "Your husband saved the king tonight. And while the king yet may die, it seems he will live. In any event, he wants you to come to him."

She made a decision and sought the man's thoughts. There were none! And it wasn't as if he were somehow concealing them. There simply were no thoughts to listen to, only a sense of watchfulness and power.

"Are you all right, my dear?"

My dear? My dear? She looked back at the body crumpled by the table, the expression echoing in her mind, then reached for the slide which would cover the slot. "Just a minute," she said, and closed it.

Going to the table, she picked up the dart gun, returned to the door, unbolted it and stepped back. "Come in!" she said, loudly to be heard through the thick door. The man opened it and came in, ducking his head out of habit. He saw the gun in her hand then, pointed at him, but closed the door behind him nonetheless. He could also see the body now, and paid it no heed.

"I *am* overtall," he said gently, "and I've been accused a time or two of being homely, but I really don't think you ought to shoot me on first meeting."

The wildness quieted in her eyes, but she held the gun steady.

"Who are you?" she demanded.

"I am Lord Kyril Golovin; I've come from the king."

The focus of her eyes shifted uncertainly; she had "heard" the name before, eavesdropping.

"Who is that on the floor?" Golovin asked.

"The assassin, Albert Haas. This is what he used to kill them." She found herself putting the dart gun into Golovin's outstretched hand. He examined it, found one of the propulsion springs set, and released it before putting it into a pocket.

"He knew I'm a—foreigner," she went on, "and came to me for shelter. But he didn't know I'm Barni's wife."

"Very good, very well done," he said. "You, as well as Barni, have earned the kingdom's thanks."

"Barni's dead," she countered. "What can thanks do for either of us?"

"Ah," he said, "but Barni isn't dead. You've heard a false, if well intended, report. I really think you'd better come with me."

EIGHTEEN

As one of the guards remarked, they'd never seen him at the postern gate before. He was soon back. The lad at the wicket recognized the remarkably tall, somewhat ungainly figure at a distance, although he'd never before seen the woman by his side. So he signaled his watchmates, who hurried to open the narrow, iron-faced door.

Even a lord had to identify anyone he brought in at night, and they were astonished when he named her as Selena, the wife of Barni from Jussvek. Another mystery to speculate about by the gatehouse stove. Barni's wife? Widow was the righter word. It was a heavy night, they agreed, with three men dead and the king's life uncertain.

And why was Lord Golovin bringing her here? Lord Golovin—an unobtrusive man and quiet. Although they'd heard that his voice had been like a crack of thunder in the guardhouse earlier. There was a strangeness about him, always had been, they agreed on that. It went beyond his height and jet black hair. He made people think of a wizard out of the past.

His entrance with Selena was not the last of the comings and goings: the usually quiet postern gate was relatively busy that night. Not long after Golovin's entry, four lords of the realm, members of His Majesty's government, went out grim and silent, Lord Lenkser carrying a large satchel. In about half an hour—fifty-eight minutes by the gatehouse clock—

they logged back in looking no less grim than before. A little more than an hour later, Lord Golovin left again, by himself, the bottom of his cloak cocked out behind by a sword worn beneath it.

Outside the door, before they closed it, they saw him pause, head high and swiveling back and forth, as if testing the air for smells or perhaps scanning the sky where the moon now had set. There was something about him there, his stance and movement, that caused them to watch. Then he started off, almost on a lope, paused thirty meters away to test the air again, and changed direction a bit before striding on out of sight across the square.

When they saw him next, he bore a large, blanket-wrapped bundle over one shoulder, and a dark thundercloud expression. The bundle was clearly quite heavy. This time he said nothing when they let him in, did not even nod, but strode across the courtyard toward the palace.

The guards retreated into the gatehouse, saying no more than Golovin just had, though their tongues would loosen after they'd puzzled a bit by the fire. They simply recorded his return in the log. The bundle had almost surely been a corpse, they would all agree on that, but it was written simply "large bundle."

The rising sun had lightened the battlements before the word spread through Krogaskott that the assassin had been found and had died resisting arrest. Nothing further was told officially. The body had been shown to the entry detail who, the day before, had logged Hosar the Weaver into the palace. They vouched that this was the same man—he had the same wide forehead and mouth, small nose, thick beard fuller than the norm in Tonlik.

The story went through the palace that Lord Golovin had gone out into the night and found him by Voroth only knew what thaumaturgy. Found him and struck him dead, apparently without resort to the sword, for there'd been no sign of it, no trail of dripping red, no mark of blade on head or clothing.

During ten Thegwar years at the palace, Golovin had been fairly inconspicuous for someone who was not a recluse and who stood two hundred and four centimeters tall among a people where the norm for men was one hundred sixty-seven. People *were* aware of him, and it was generally considered from his mien and demeanor that his abilities extended beyond the prosaic into the realm of the supernatural, or at least to its borders.

But in fact he had never *done* anything, or so it had seemed, and had thus occupied little of their attention. Now suddenly, by the simple expedient of sniffing the air, and seeming to find the assassin by magic, and by bringing the body in unmarked, he'd drawn attention strongly to himself, away from possibly troublesome inconsistencies in the events and explanations of the night.

And suddenly Lord Golovin was a subject in almost every conversation, along with the king and the murders. Many of the guard and the palace staff had known little about him, only that he existed and was very tall. But before the sun had swung around to the southwestern horizon and slipped from sight, it was general knowledge in Krogaskott that he'd been the king's tutor, companion, and loyal servant from childhood, an off-worlder who'd spurned his own to serve Trogeir. And from the events of the night, obviously a wizard.

Heads wagged, along with tongues. With Golovin around, woe betide anyone who attacked the king. And it was well known that only by Golovin's efforts did the king still live.

Although the magic flute of Barni's widow might well help save the king where her brave husband had failed with his sword.

Gausa, poor fellow, had stood pale and shaken by Barni's casket; then Lord Golovin had gone and stood beside him, put a hand on his wide shoulder in friendly fashion, and said something quietly. Gausa had already requested a transfer back into the army, and it had been approved.

At fourth meal, the word was passed that the king, though still unconscious and not out of danger, was holding his own. Two different servants who'd been let in with food for the king's attendants agreed that he lay as pale as a fresh corpse, but they could see his chest move. Golovin and other lords had been attending him, and once Barni's widow had been playing, her music surely as powerful a magic for healing as any Lord Golovin could bring to bear.

The king would live to rule again: that was the consensus in Krogaskott. And while the cabinet ministers looked grave as they went about the palace, the dark pall of concern lightened notably among the staff.

All in all, the production was of Academy Award caliber.

NINETEEN

Kyril Golovin accompanied the servant to the hall door, thanked him as he left, nodded good morning to the guard outside, locked the door, and returned to the royal bedroom. It smelled of medicinal smoke from herbs burned in a porcelain bowl.

"He's gone," he said.

Boru opened his eyes, swung his legs out of bed and stood up. Even with the late morning sun through the windows and a fire in the thick-walled brick stove, the tall room was chilly by Earth standards. The bed itself was warm enough with only a light quilt, for it was the stove. Or rather, the stove, broad and low and crowned with a down mattress, was the bed.

Like most Lokarn heating stoves, it was very largely an enclosed network of heating flues from a firebox at the foot. It took quite awhile to warm the mass of bricks, but once warm, it gave off hours of gentle heat, even if the fire was allowed to go out.

Nude, the "invalid" king padded barefoot to the closet and emerged in a lounging robe. Golovin was folding the blankets on the cot he'd slept on. "Well," said Boru, "we caught up on our sleep. How do we get something to eat around here? I'm famished."

"Last night," Golovin reminded him, "Your Majesty decided to fast, to simulate the effects of a coma. You wanted to justify not receiving anyone for a period of time."

Boru eyed him with pretended sourness. "Now I know why so many royal advisors ended up beheaded. They were nags!"

"Undoubtedly true, Your Majesty. But some were also

made saints by the Church—Becket for example, and Thomas More. No doubt for persisting in their duty despite despotic masters."

"Nags," Boru insisted, "all of them. Nags. We'll compromise. You can eat but I get to watch. Maybe even cadge a crust and an apple core."

He turned and padded into the short hall to the queen's bedroom, vacant for several years until now. There'd be some changes around here, he told himself. He went in and kissed Selena awake. She showed a moment's disorientation, then relaxed.

"A remarkable recovery, Your Majesty," she said, sitting up. "I'm hungry!"

Boru got off the bed and helped her to her feet. "His Royal Highness is fasting," he said, "but generously grants his subjects the right to eat. As long as they don't enjoy it too conspicuously."

"His subjects? How about his wife?"

He sobered. "The king is unmarried. But as soon as he can, he intends to marry his nurse, the widow of the noble guardsman, Barni of Jussvek."

For a moment she said nothing, then nodded. "I appreciate the situation." A quick smile broke the seriousness. "Meanwhile maybe we can sneak in a little practice now and then. It might be interesting to go to bed with a comatose king. I'll bet I could speed his recovery."

They clasped hands and leaned toward one another, kissing lightly, coolly. "You should get dressed and come into the king's room," said Boru. "We'll be letting in another servant in half an hour or so with breakfast."

They walked together to the king's bedchamber, where he hung the robe back in the closet and got back under the cover, resuming the invalid's role.

"Are you ready for a briefing now?" Golovin asked.

"Sounds good to me."

"Let me start with a brief description of your route to the throne," Golovin draped himself on a large chair. "It begins with Bhiksu Tanaka."

Uncle Bhiksu, Boru thought to himself, *I never realized you were such an enigma.*

"Bhiksu Tanaka was at one time a young idea man in the Foreign Ministry. He really didn't fit there; he was too intelligent. FM does in fact recruit some very intelligent young people, but typically they leave. It had not always been that way but it became so.

"Also he was too ethical. You raise your eyebrows, Your Majesty, but let me elaborate. This young idea man, Bhiksu Tanaka, suggested to his seniors that a proposal be made to Korbin, then King of Lokar. They would propose to Korbin that his second son, the infant Trogeir, be educated on Earth and returned to Lokar. He would then help the king move Lokar in the direction of the twenty-fourth century, planetary dominance, and associate membership in the Confederacy.

"Korbin was already very interested in modernization, and at that time very favorably inclined toward the Confederacy. But he was not a strong or particularly effective king, nor had he appointed forceful ministers. It was a case of progressive desires coupled with timidly conservative habits. So Bhiksu's suggestion was well received in the Ministry, the proposal was made, and Korbin agreed.

"Now, in the Foreign Ministry, certainly at the decision-making stratum, the levels of intelligence and particularly of ethics were not high, as I said before, and Department Eleven attitudes were very influential. Perhaps you are not aware of how elevation is achieved there. It is by politics—agency politics. And because it is politics hidden totally from public view, it means leverage, aggressiveness, ruthlessness. And of course, it is devious and covert.

"So naturally there is, or was, strong selection for those traits. But interestingly, selection was *against* high intelligence. High intelligence tends to be ethical, and tends to withdraw from such an environment or else deteriorate."

Boru's brows raised again and Golovin smiled. "The action of intelligence, Your Majesty, is computation and creation based on perception of the way things actually are. To the extent that one chooses unethical options in an area of operation, one subsequently withholds one's perceptiveness from it. One then dubs in, so to speak, imagined or altered data in order to rationalize what one has done and make it all right. And to the extent that one becomes psychotic in an area, even this gesture toward rationality tends to be dropped. Thus, in the in-house politics of FM, success is essentially a function of aggressiveness and ruthlessness.

"So Bhiksu Tanaka's simple, ethical, workable idea was

altered at the command stratum. They decided that the child would be brought to Earth, and at an appropriate time murdered, and replaced by a selected Terran child. This replacement child would be implanted to follow FM orders. I presume you're familiar in a general way with implanting? It constitutes a felony under Confederate law, but that was no problem for the command stratum of the Foreign Ministry.

"Interestingly, it wouldn't be particularly advantageous to them to install a false prince. The real prince could be implanted if implant they must. But that was the way their minds worked."

Boru frowned. "Maybe they felt the real prince wouldn't be bright enough for them."

Golovin nodded. "That may be how they rationalized it. But regardless of native intelligence, what they had planned for him—extensive implanting—would have reduced his intelligence significantly. Implanting interferes with reasoning and rational decision by introducing heavily enforced arbitrary data and responses into areas of computation, decision, and action.

"We all operate with arbitrary data—assumptions that we make when facts are inadequate. But to the extent that we are sane, we can evaluate such arbitraries, discard them, hedge on them. In implanting, those options are taken away by pain. The implanted person cannot resist or even recognize the implanted arbitrary.

"In addition, implanting fixes, sticks, a certain appreciable amount of the person's basic mental—let's call it his mental energy—to the area of the implant. Sticks it there in the form of *fear*. A normally low intensity, unrecognized fear that becomes galvanized into compulsive obedience when the implant command is activated.

"Meanwhile the mental energy that is stuck in the area of the implant is not available to thought and rational action in any area, so the person is hampered in every area. His reasoning and decision-making become at least a little slower.

"But FM plans went beyond an implanted false prince. They wanted an implanted king. So after they replaced the second son with an implanted puppet, they'd arrange for the death of the crown prince by seemingly natural causes, and finally do the same for the king. The implanted puppet would then become the ruler of Lokar."

Golovin held up his hand to forestall Boru's objections. "I know it makes little sense. They already had a king who was in agreement with their basic purposes, or at least with what those purposes seemed to be. They had the means, and the royal agreement, to install a prince of the realm, educated by themselves, as a minister plenipotentiary to forward those purposes.

As far as I can discern, their reasons for these atrocities were the compulsion to control. Clearly, those in charge were reasoning psychotics: they would make psychotic decisions and then apply reason to carry them out.

"Finally they added insult to injury, apparently without even realizing it. And this was where they undid their game. Had they been sane enough, they would not have done what they did next, for it both invited counteraction and made it possible. They assigned Bhiksu Tanaka to carry out key actions in the perverted program they had made of his original idea.

"Not only did they assign Tanaka to provide a child for the exchange; he was also to arrange a suitable, well-equipped and very private situation in which the child would be prepared. And Tanaka, not surprisingly, decided to foil their intentions.

"So he selected a child of the James Keenan clone, with a known resemblance to the royal family of Lokar, and for the child's training he employed a young student of N.A. Kubiak, providing him with a false history and a false security check. I, of course, was that student. Which meant, as he knew and fully intended, that there would be no implanting, while the child's education would include areas both extraneous and counter to FM intentions that he be a puppet. The boy would grow up broadly educated and deciding for himself."

Boru broke in. "Just a minute. If you trained Trogeir to think and decide so independently, how come you're still with him as an advisor?"

Golovin smiled with no trace of embarrassment or irritation. "Speaking of independent minds, Your Majesty makes me very optimistic regarding your reign. But if you'll allow me, I'd like to continue chronologically. I promise we'll come to your question shortly, and explain Albert Haas at the same time."

Boru nodded curtly.

Tanaka selected three twelve-month-old infants from the James Keenan clone, whether randomly or intuitively I'm not sure, and observed and tested them for eight months. Actually we both observed them. At twenty months he selected one to become Trogeir and found homes for the other two.

"From then on, I was responsible for the boy's care and training. The training included how to respond to the tests—the code words that were supposed to trigger certain implant responses. For he would, of course, be tested, and it was necessary that he respond in the tests as they intended. But he would do it from understanding, not compulsion.

"I'll tell you, the child had to know things that were hardly fair for children; he matured early. Yet it was not an unpleasant childhood; it was far more interesting and challenging than most, and happier. With Trogeir and me it was a game. And the advantages were with us, actually. We knew what was going on with them, while they did not realize what we were doing.

"Meanwhile the real Trogeir arrived on Earth when both were five Terran years old. The counterfeit Trogeir never met the real one, but as time went on, learned much about him and his associates.

"When he was six, I felt it necessary to lie to him for the first and only time. I told him that the real Trogeir did not want to be a prince, that he wanted to live on Al-Bakri's World as a hunter. And that we'd agreed to take him there, replacing him so his father wouldn't know and feel bad.

"I thought at the time how easy it was to fool a little child like that, even such a perceptive one, when his experience says he can trust you.

"The real prince, of course, was known by quite a few people, but no more than necessary, and was well-known by only a handful. At age thirteen—an age when many physical and psychological changes are occurring—he set off on a sixteen-month tour of the Confederacy. He actually made the trip, and I suppose he enjoyed it. I hope so.

"Up until then, everything had been done in such a way that, should Korbin call him home before FM was ready to replace him, he could go, eventually to function more or less as Bhiksu originally envisioned. But near the end of the trip, he was murdered and the body jettisoned, and the craft he'd been traveling on picked up *our* Trogeir in a ship-to-ship transfer, out-system.

"From that time, our surrogate Trogeir was the only Trogeir, until last night."

The black eyes had been on the thoughtful Boru almost continually. Now Golovin broke his attention for a drink. *The man is as calm as a neozen master*, Boru thought. *Kabashima himself wouldn't be any more at ease, any more matter-of-fact than this guy.*

"It is interesting," Golovin continued, "what Trogeir said to me after the transfer, in private. It quite surprised me, and not too much does. He said, 'Kyril, the prince wasn't left on Al-Bakri's World, was he?' And I said, 'What do you mean, Your Highness?' And this boy who wasn't quite fifteen said, 'The prince was murdered, wasn't he, Kryil.'

"He wasn't asking a question, you understand, he was making an oblique statement. And when I questioned him, he told he that when I told him the lie, he knew that I was lying. At age six. And more than that, he'd realized I was lying to spare his feelings.

"Some two years after the substitution, a Department Eleven agent arranged the death of the crown prince here on Thegwar. And immediately after that, of course, the distraught Korbin called for Trogeir's immediate return, for Trogeir had become heir to the throne.

"Department Eleven hadn't intended that his tutor accompany him to Thegwar. Tutoring was done with as far as they were concerned, and they had another man on site in Lokar to be the puppet master, so to speak. But Trogeir insisted that he wanted me there too, and FM saw no compelling reason to deny him.

"This was not a matter of dependence on Trogeir's part. It's true that he was confronting a new environment, and that I was his lifelong friend, in truth his only friend and confidant. But the major reason was the research we were engaged in."

"Research? What research?"

Golovin's eyes gleamed at Boru's response. "Ah, that's another subject. Let me continue with this one. When we talk about the research, we can easily spend a day on it. May I go on?"

"Okay."

"Haas was Trogeir's contact in the embassy here, which at that time was housed right here in Krogaskott. Haas was to be Trogeir's control, a stupid choice, for the man was too arrogant. As part of the assignment, he was to be Trogeir's close associate and confidant, but when we arrived, I continued to fill the role. Which Haas resented.

"So of course he tried to activate the control mechanisms that he assumed had been implanted, to have me dismissed. Trogeir responded in part, because he recognized what was going on, but didn't dismiss me. This gave the superficial appearance of agreement, but no action. I presume that Haas must have rationalized this in some way or other, perhaps on the grounds that implanting is not an exact technology."

"At any rate, Trogeir as crown prince established his own coterie of young or youngish Lokaru whom he'd shrewdly selected and cultivated. He rejected courteously but firmly the people Haas had preselected for him, at the same time privately voicing observations to Korbin which caused the old man to notice and reevaluate things for himself. Korbin had already cooled somewhat toward the embassy, and by association toward the Confederacy.

"Then Trogeir sent for the ambassador for a private audience at which, he told me, it became clear to him that the ambassador was quite ignorant of the Ministry's Trogeir Project. So Trogeir complained to the ambassador of Haas's arrogance, and said he would not tolerate the man's continued presence in Lokar—that if he wasn't removed at once, no later than the next day, he'd complain to his father. Not to appear hostile to the embassy or the Confederacy, he explained that Haas imposed himself in Trogeir's friendships, thereby offending his friends and weakening him in their eyes. Which in fact was true. And that these were the men he would rule with, for they were progressive, and eager to move toward association with the Confederacy.

"So Haas was reprimanded, and the embassy courier craft left with him for Earth the next day.

"Korbin's health had been poor since before we'd arrived, and we were never sure whether this was natural or the result of some Department Eleven action. We examined his food handlers ourselves, in a way I'll show you later, and none of them were other than they seemed. But at any rate, Korbin died of a heart attack less than four months after our arrival, and after the funeral, the seventeen-year-old Trogeir was crowned king.

"Only days later, he sent for the ambassador and informed him that he was removing the embassy from Krogaskott to a handsome villa on a bluff overlooking the river. That there was quiet resentment of them at court, and it would be better for the embassy and the king if they . . ."

Golovin was interrupted by the knocker on the door, and got up to answer while Selena picked up her flute and began to play. Boru closed his eyes and prepared to feign a coma. If there was to be no breakfast for him, at least he had a craw full of interesting information.

After Selena and Golovin had eaten—and Boru, who had a piece of dry fruit and a crust to give his belly something to work on—Golovin left. "For a few minutes," he said. "I'm going to find Larsa and have him brief you."

When he had gone, Selena sat on the bed and took Boru's hand. "I tried to read his thoughts last night," she said, "but I didn't have much luck."

"What do you mean?"

"He didn't think at all in words and pictures. He only verbalized to talk; there was no subvocalizing. People generally think in concepts but they tend more or less to verbalize them to themselves."

"Do you know if he was telling the truth just now?"

"I think he was. He might have been withholding some things, but I don't think he was lying. I don't really think he was withholding, either. But his concepts hardly surface. It's as if his thinking is entirely subliminal and only surfaces as action or speech."

She gestured at the two bell cords by the bed. "You know, he could have called someone else to bring the prime minister, but I got the impression that he left so you and I could be alone to talk."

She paused then, as if there was more. Boru waited.

"Darling," she said after a moment, "be sure to have him tell you about the research. It's important—that's one thing I'm sure of. I want to be sure we learn about the research."

TWENTY

There'd been no difficulty in preserving the bodies of the king's valet and "Barni of Jussvek." They'd simply been put in an unheated loft in the palace.

Meanwhile the king's recovery was faster than expected; he was, after all, a quick study. After only twelve days, looking weak and gaunt, he was carried in a chair out into the winter day to attend the funeral. Some ten thousand of his subjects thronged the square, but the king sat alone by the caskets on a low platform, isolated by protocol and respect. A light breeze played with his uncovered hair as he listened to the speakers, and all eyes went to him at least occasionally.

After the ceremony, other thousands, lining the avenue through the city, watched the funeral procession—the low open hearse, the party of chairborne king and walking dignitaries, the military band. And as the procession passed, a part of the onlookers closed in behind it, forming an ever lengthening train of followers.

It was not a military funeral, but both the public and the royal viewpoints were that the dead had died in defense of the crown. And that was sufficient warrant for the wild skirl of bagpipes, the deep resonant boom of kettle drums. Voroth would hear, and know that these had been worthy men, mourned by the realm.

Although Voroth clearly knew already, for not only had he given them a day that was sunny, but a temperature barely below freezing, with a breeze suggestive of a spring still months away.

The king's four porters walked in step as smoothly as they could, but still the royal chair bobbed and jounced. He rode it calmly, pale and unreadable, a symbol to a people used to symbols and to a royal symbol. Some held children overhead to see the passing monarch and open caskets. For some of those children this would be their earliest memory, some recalling only the white-faced corpses, some only the king with his bare blond hair and reddish beard. Others would remember it all, in detail that would gather meaning later— king and corpses, pipers and crowd.

The avenue became a country road, a highway by the standards of the land, flanked on each side by a rank of great-boled *byoltu*, with shreddy bark like eucalypts. Farther back some thirty paces, evergreen windbreaks, more black than green, had captured blowing snow in artistic ridges before it could drift the road full, helping to keep the way open for wagons. Or hearses. Or kings.

At last they took a side road, and the now-lengthy procession climbed a long and gentle slope to the burial field. There were no monuments, just low chiseled blocks of stone, now mostly winter-hidden except where wind had scoured away the snow. The ground, in summer soft and loamy, green and flower-flecked, lay stony hard beneath the white.

There was a building there, of timber, resembling the churches of Tonlik and like them the property of Voroth, blue trimmed with white, but in this instance lacking red. It received and protected the empty bodies of the winter dead, for until spring the soil could be dug only with sledge and long chisel, and rarely was. The hearse pulled up before it, and the crowd of several thousand closed up in a massed and quiet semicircle. The king stood, and walked slowly to the hearse, where he waited as patiently as the caparisoned peernu for the stragglers to join the crowd.

At length he looked up at the sky and spoke, and if his body seemed weak, his voice was not.

"Voroth," he called, "you have already received the spirits who gave nobility and life to these bodies. And considering the kind of men they were, I'm sure they have no grief and no regrets. If we feel loss whom they have left behind, we'll soon recover, for we have our lives to live, and duties of our own."

Then he turned his face to the crowd. "And now, my countrymen, I speak to you. Mark my words, and repeat them to others who are not here.

"This kingdom has its enemies, and one of them did this. We know now why; we know what they had in mind. For this was not the act of an isolated madman. The kings of Garvas and Prozhask, and the state directors of Bleesbrok, intend to attack our land and make it theirs. Not next spring when the roads and fields have dried, but this winter.

"They have long been jealous of what Lokar has made of itself, our commerce, our granaries, our success as a people. But instead of following the way of self-discipline, of orderly and productive activity, instead of building their own prosperity, they wish to steal ours.

"Yet even joined together, they are not our equal, and they know it. So how would they challenge us?"

He paused to let them consider the question.

"There are certain off-world criminals who have connived with them, people I expelled years ago. Criminals who dare not attack us with their off-world weapons because they would be punished by their own government. So instead they conspired with weak-minded rulers to the south, and sent an assassin to murder your king, thinking it would leave you leaderless and confused. But the assassin failed, and has been buried in a lime pit as befits his kind.

"And what if he had succeeded? What if I lay in a box like Barni there, and Valnor? What then? Even then Lokar would not stand confused. Our government would continue. Our people would not become a leaderless mob. Orderly production and commerce would have gone on, that our people still would eat, and laugh, and watch their children and grandchildren flourish and prosper.

"Perhaps my survival and return to health will confound the rulers to the south of us, make them doubt, and fear their own defeat. If they are intelligent enough, they will decide to stay home by their fires, rejecting war.

"But we will not assume their intelligence. We will prepare to defend our land. And should they attack—if they make that foolish and costly mistake—we will whip them soundly and drive them home. And the restitution and penalties we will impose will make those greedy rulers weep. We will hear the gnashing of their royal teeth across the miles and hills.

"But even so, we will treat them justly. We will take full restitution, make just examples of the guilty and ensure our continued national safety. We shall not, however, we shall *not* wreak angry vengeance or punish the innocent, for then we would be as evil as their rulers. That road leads away from Voroth, away from honor, to evil and eventual decay.

"But enough of that." The king turned and looked long at the bodies, then at the sky, feeling the eyes of the people on him. "Barni and Valnor, though you are missed here, we will not regret your present happiness. And I make you a pledge—one I believe that these our people share. Should you decide someday to wrap yourselves in the veil of forgetting and come again among us in new flesh, you will find that we've kept your homeland safe and well and happy. I have spoken!"

Then the king, still looking skyward, joined his palms before his face and raised them, hands separating in a graceful outward-sweeping gesture as they moved overhead in the salute to Voroth. In less than perfect physical unity but with a very large measure of agreement, the crowd followed suit.

And in a society where speeches did not see print, a society with a considerable oral tradition, Trogeir's speech would be widely repeated with considerable verity.

But just now the crowd waited, mostly avoiding the cheering that would be unseemly in this place. The king reseated himself in his chair; four fresh porters raised him, and the crowd parted to let them pass. The royal party left, followed by the now-silent pipers and drummers, and after them the crowd, whose increasingly busy tongues made a considerable if subdued hubbub back to town.

The king *was* tired; exhausted in fact. Over nearly two weeks he'd eaten two bread crusts each day, two pieces of dried fruit, and a morsel of cheese, washed down with water. And spent much of the time in bed. *I've had it with this invalid act,* he told himself. *It's time for a quick recovery.*

And striding nearby, Golovin actually verbalized to himself. *Our new Trogeir is a much different man than the old. But we are blessed with another genius.*

TWENTY-ONE

"Thank you, Farlin," said the prime minister when the minister for Quality Control had finished. He turned to Boru. "Your Majesty, that updates us on current activities. You indicated earlier that you wanted to discuss war preparations."

"That's right. I'd like to say first that having defense and the military in the Ministery of Foreign Affairs is taking some getting used to. I can see the rationale behind it, but I'm glad it's not that way in the Confederacy. I'd hate to see their Foreign Ministry controlling the fleet."

The foreign minister smiled wryly. "If I may, Your Majesty, that's because they have no effective quality control. I doubt that the possibility has even occurred to them. Also, their Justice Ministry lacks necessary authorizations in some areas and necessary constraints in others, and their Office of Support Services and Controls has no ethics branch.

"Basically," he concluded, "they have not enjoyed the organizational genius of a Kyril Golovin."

Boru glanced toward the tall advisor sitting out of the way by the door. The Russian smiled slightly.

"I'm afraid, Your Majesty," said Golovin, "that I have not been terribly original in this. It is an application of principles demonstrated by my old mentor, N.A. Kubiak. It is available to the Confederacy, but unfortunately the establishment there has been resistant to it. Nikolai Alexeevitch was a center of controversy of course. Here it has been relatively easy to establish it in government because there was no entrenched hostility and because the rationality of the system is quite attractive."

"Maybe I need a crash course to understand more fully how it works," said the king. "But right now we're going to

153

talk defense. Palek, you've planned to call up drafts of yeomen from the peasantry to form the usual archery support units. I disagree with that.''

Palek stood up to answer. "Your Majesty, it's a well-proven system and tradition. The bow is almost as much a part of the yeoman's life as his spade and hoe, his sickle and axe. Our military superiority derives in no small degree from the difference between the self-reliant Lokarn yeomanry and the serfs of Garvas and Prozhask. The yeoman is his own master in most of life, and fights stalwartly, with pride. The serf lives under arbitrary control by others, and fights with little heart.''

"I'm not questioning that. I gathered it from your briefings, and I understand it. But when is the last time Lokar defended its territory from invasion? Any serious invasion?''

"In 607, sire, seventy-five years ago. At that time it was against an alliance of . . .''

The king stopped him with a gesture. "In what season?''

"Late spring and early summer, Your Majesty.''

"Cavalry, right?''

"Primarily. But with yeomen archery in support.''

"Of course. When's the last time you fought off a serious invasion in winter?''

Palek frowned slightly, unsure where this was leading. "In antiquity, sire. In legend, or more correctly, myth, during the reign of Vastur the Mighty, when the Balnu hordes swept out of the deserts of . . .''

"Okay, okay, hold it. I'm not doing a very good job of asking leading questions, but bear with me. You've made it clear that, for various geographic reasons, we'd be inviting disaster to preempt the initiative by invading either Garvas or Prozhask. And to move adequate forces a couple thousand kilometers north to strike the barbarians in their own territory while hostile armies are being gathered to the south of us would almost guarantee defeat.

"So you've really convinced me that it's going to be a defensive war on three fronts, at a time of the enemy's choosing.

"I also appreciate the concern in this group that there may still be a hidden factor against us, beyond the alliance with the barbarians and the attempt to leave Lokar without her king. If there is another hidden factor, it will probably be military—some weapon or tactic not really out of place on Thegwar but simply not invented here. If the river wasn't frozen, I'd half expect some of Bleesbrok's fleet to sail up from the bay with primitive bronze black-powder cannon.

"Which brings up the question of why *we* haven't done something like that. We know about cannon and how to make them, and unlike the Confederate Foreign Ministry, we don't need to be concerned about the Cultural Ministry busting us.

"But it's too late to initiate something like that. And I'm not going to worry about unknown factors on the other side. We have one of our own I'm going to tell you about. Gentlemen, when the enemy moves in, we are going to stomp his ass, to use the time-honored Terran vernacular. Let him have any surprise factor he comes up with; we will outsurprise him."

The king of Lokar grinned around at the members of his cabinet. "And now that I have your thorough attention, if not your belief or confidence—for after all, the king has been both wounded and ill and is not the man he was—now that I have your attention, I'll tell you what we're going to do. If you have any disagreements or misgivings, sit on them till I'm done. Then we can debate if we have to.

"First, we can expect this to be an infantry war, for the most part. Against the barbarians it sure as hell will be. The snow was already hock-deep on a peeran last week, as far south as the Tilkenmor River, and we've all seen what the weather is like today. So here's what we're going to do, and we need to do it fast. Palek, you are going to organize the country north of the Tilkenmor into defense districts, to the edge of major settlement. Maybe you can base these on administrative districts. It is these defense districts, *not* army units, that will be the basis of military planning, organization, and action. And your military units will be made up largely of peasants—the yeomanry."

He held up a hand to forestall Palek's objections. "Hear me out," he said, and gave them a moment to settle down, to gather their attention back to his plan.

"You'll have military units made up of archers then. Their immediate officers will be noncoms and other experienced soldiers from the regular army, who will start working with them next week, or as close to next week as humanly possible. Their ranking officers will be commissioned officers or senior noncoms. Their function will be to shoot hell out of invading barbarians—use their bows en masse and avoid close combat. When in danger of being overrun, they move back under an umbrella of archery from behind them.''

He looked around as he continued. They were really listening now, not just waiting to argue. "The army will attach support units to the yeomanry units. And that's what they'll be, support units: kitchens, supply, things like that. The main strategy will be yeoman archers in large numbers, and tactics will be built around their archery. If you can think of some way to use mounted troops in deep snow, you might attach some army combat units to them. Otherwise we'll keep them for other fronts.

"So we're talking not about the offensive war of movement that's been the Lokarn tradition, but a district-by-district defense. In the north, surely. That will allow us to hold more of our army units to fight the Southern Coalition, where a cavalry war is more likely.

"Any comments?"

Palek looked thoughtful. "Your Majesty," he said, "I believe it can work, and it looks like the answer to the problem of too few regiments. It will take intensive preparation, but it can be done."

Boru grinned. "All you'll need to do is perform miracles of organization and training. And while you're doing that, look at how you might apply modifications of it in the south.

"And Palek?"

"Yes, Your Majesty?"

"I'll want to see a working draft of the plan by noon tomorrow. Something rough and ready."

"Yes, Your Majesty."

The king turned to the minister of National Services. "Mako, we can't have fighting men running out of arrows. We need the immediate emergency production of large quantities of arrows, even more than you might have anticipated. Find out everyone that makes arrows. Find out the sizes you need. Locate sources of shafts and heads and feathers and whatever. You may need to set people up in business, people who know how to make arrows. Go out into the countryside and find people who make arrows now and then for their neighbors as a winter sideline and get them making lots and lots of good arrows that'll go where they're aimed.

"And Mako, do this yesterday. They need to be made and in the farmer's quivers and the quartermaster's supply chests before any invaders arrive."

Boru looked around again and realized he was grinning, exhilarated. *Damn!* he thought, *I'm going to like this king business!*

"The rest of you expect to be called on for support. And Larsa," he added, turning to the prime minister, "if there are any serious slowdowns, I know you and your senior ministers will see them corrected quickly and smoothly.

"Now, is there any further business that needs to be taken care of at this time? No? Is it appropriate for the king to move that the meeting be adjourned?"

"No, sire. It is the cabinet's prerogative. Gentlemen?"

Edbar spoke. "I move that the meeting be adjourned."

"Seconded," said Mako.

"In favor? . . . The meeting of the third day of Winterhere, 683, is adjourned."

"Well, that was interesting," said the minister of Quality Control to the senior minister for Operations as they walked down the hall. "What did you think of him, Alf?"

Alf Mergalf smiled. "I'm very optimistic. He's not the Trogeir of old: he's no longer above his own left shoulder. But he will be, with good cousin Kyril's assistance. Meanwhile he's smart as a whip, with a lot of crude power and not too many rough edges. What a create he did on us!"

The smile widened to a grin. "And do you realize that his approach will strengthen the social dynamic of Lokar? His understanding is deeper than he realizes.

"And on top of that, he's enjoying it! I'd say he's the right man at the right time."

Kyril Golovin entered the king's office and stopped before the desk. "Yes, Your Majesty?"

Boru grinned at him. "Went pretty good, didn't it?"

"It did, Your Majesty. Your innovative defense proposal made a strong impression."

"I felt like I was in front of a personnel review board. A friendly one though. That's an interesting bunch of people Trogeir put together. There was no feeling at all of the little resentments, rivalries, hostilities you might expect between ministry heads. It felt—clean. Interesting as hell.''

He shifted to the matter at hand. ''I've got Army Personnel hunting up the three best skiers in the Tonlik Regiment for a project. I'm going to send them out one at a time, a day apart, to deliver copies of these letters. To make sure they get through.'' He picked up two large parchments and held them toward Golovin. ''I want you to know what I'm doing, in case there's another assassin hanging around.''

Golovin took them and read. The first was to the Lord of Jussvek.

> My dear Karn Kinjok,
>   May you, with Voroth's acquiescence, prosper, and may prime gontru grace your stretching frames.
>   I am aware that we at Krogaskott do not enjoy your undiluted approval. At so great a remove from us, you do not know us as well as might be. And likewise, in your remote location, self-sufficient as you perforce must be, you feel a certain independence of your king and of our laws.
>   Your good friend and ours, Lord Richard O'Bannion, has made clear to us a certain justice in your point of view. (He has known us since our childhood, and obtained your amnesty before he named you.) We will re-examine our tax laws with regard to those whose location separates them to some degree from the benefits of our expenditures.
>   But as remote as you are, I believe you appreciate how much more demanding are certain foreign monarchs and their lackeys, and how unjust. In that regard, the kingdoms of Garvas and Prozhask intend to invade Lokar this winter, with the help of Bleesbrok and certain other allies. It is our happy intention to provide them with certain surprises that will send them home like whipped curs.
>   We do not ask that you bring your people south to fight. That will not be necessary.
>   However, we do request that you pass the enclosed envelope to your good friend, the formidable trader and traveler, Wan Kubia-Dek Larmet.

Wan Larmet can be of inestimable assistance to our plans.

Please send your reply by the bearer of this letter, and treat him as my valued personal representative.

Cordially,
Trogeir, King

P.S. Lord O'Bannion would like to be assured that Vinta, Britto, and Narl returned safely to Jussvek. He says that any lord with a man like Vinta is fortunate indeed.

P.P.S. We hope that the person who followed Richard O'Bannion, whom we believe called himself Herman Heidemann, was not offensive while at Jussvek. We have had Mr. Heidemann properly corrected.

Kyril Golovin raised an eyebrow at the king, smiling, then read the second letter. Unlike the first, it was penned in Terran.

To: Wan Kubia-Dek Larmet of the Kansas Feedlot
From: Trogeir, King

Dear Wan Larmet,

As you know, men who sail your particular sea have been unwelcome on our shore for some years. However, a friend of yours, your co-traveler and fellow tavern brawler, Richard O'Bannion, has provided us with extraordinary services, and has risen to a very high position in our court and in our royal esteem.

We had known him in our childhood.

Mr. O'Bannion has convinced us that your services can be valuable to us and to our Kingdom. In turn, we would see you well rewarded and in a unique trading position. We can also offer you what we are sure you will find a most interesting and strangely honest game.

We trust that you will be interested enough to explore with us a possible co-action.

Please drop your anchor at the Royal Game Park, an extensive wooded area on the coast east of the city. The landing place will be marked by a large beacon fire nightly for several weeks. We will have a man there who will ride rapidly to us to notify us of your arrival. We will hurry there at once so that you can depart again by dawn.

Mr. O'Bannion wants you to know that Mr. Heidemann, until recently an employee of Department Eleven through a front firm, has met with a severe accident and will not need further transportation.

We appreciate the very major service you have already given us in bringing our friend to Lokar.

Cordially,
Trogeir, King

P.S. If at some time you need shelter, our harbor is open to friends.

Golovin handed them back. "Interesting and well done, Your Majesty, a fine blend of familiarity, mystery, and altitude. A high speed transportation service will be extremely useful."

"The trick is for Larmet to get his letter," said Boru. "I'm gambling that he's Department Eleven's liaison. And that at this stage of the game he's parked up there somewhere where he can receive orders and information from agents from barbarian territory to Garvas or Bleesbrok. But he could also be five hundred parsecs from here with some illicit cargo and no plans to return till spring.

"Or he could be parked overhead somewhere and not be in touch with Kinjok."

He looked at Golovin's calm eyes, shiny and black. The man had taken total charge when Trogeir was killed, but only long enough to get someone else in charge. And now that he'd gotten Boru on the job and functioning, it could be hard to get even an opinion out of him.

"What do you think, Kyril? Am I whistling in the wind?

Do you think he'll get it? D'you think he'll go for it if he does?''

"How did you feel about it when you wrote it?" Golovin countered.

"Huh! I didn't even wonder. I just assumed he would."

"Fine. Why don't we leave it that way."

The husky ex-barbarian wore his best clothes—those least workworn. His good wife had combed his hair and brushed both it and his sparse beard. His face and neck were already cleaner than most, for he had built a barbarian steam hut behind his house and made frequent use of it.

He'd been quite astonished, the evening before, when a kingsman had knocked on his door. The man had been most courteous, calling him "Master Sunto," and his wife "my good lady." Sunto was to be at the great gate of Krogaskott when it opened at seven in the morning, if he was interested in a rewarding contract with the government.

The man had not elaborated, but it seemed unquestionable that the contract involved hauling wood for Krogaskott, a matter of considerable prestige. So it had been a surprise and a mystery when the same man, after meeting him at the gate, had led him to the waiting room of the royal audience chamber. Sunto knew the place; he'd been there once before.

But he was naturally cool-headed, and he had been raised a northern barbarian. Among them, patience was a survival virtue well-drilled by hunting, fishing, and working with *Pseudobos subarcticus* D^H-211, known colloquially as tundra cattle, or riisuntaksi. He would wait calmly and see what this was all about.

A slender, sharp-eyed man came into the waiting room, and his attention went directly to Sunto, ignoring the other two who waited there. "Master Sunto," he said, "His Majesty will see you now."

Sunto followed him into the audience chamber. He hadn't been to the funeral; stoves and woodpiles knew no holidays in winter. But he'd been told that the king looked wasted and weak from his ordeal by poison. He didn't look weak now, just a bit thin. The eyes that watched Sunto approach were the same blue as seven years before, but they were somehow different.

Sunto remembered having heard the proper way to approach the king: he'd entered hat in hand. Now he swept it before him as he bowed. "Your Majesty!" he said.

The eyes and mouth smiled. "Sunto! My friend from the north! You told me once that you preferred to stay with us till spring. I'm glad you stayed longer."

Sunto's glance sharpened. *After so long, and so many visitors!*

"Most of the people I receive here," the king went on, "have petitioned to see me. They want me to do something for them. That is one of the duties of a king—to hear petitions. It is less usual for the king to ask to see one of his subjects.

"So let me thank you for coming, and tell you what I called you for." He turned to his aide. "Varix, bring a chair for my guest. I will not have him stand while I talk with him."

The slender man was stronger than Sunto would have thought. The chairs here were large and heavy, but he brought one from its place without apparent effort. The slim sword at his waist seemed suddenly more meaningful. When Sunto was seated, the king continued.

"My friend, you are not the only one of your people who dwell or have dwelt among us. One later returned to his homeland among the Siiksun, only to come back to us recently. He told us something most surprising.

"Would you care to guess what it might have been?"

"Your Majesty, I got no idea. What was it?"

The king's eyes twinkled at the straight, blunt reply, but his mouth did not smile. "He told us the tribes had united. That they plan to come down on us on skis, all their warriors, and attack us. When they attack, we will also be invaded from the south and the sea by Garvas, Prozhask, and Bleesbrok." He stopped then for Sunto's reply.

"King," said Sunto, "my people aren't usually liars, but I don't believe him. The tribes never got together yet, not even two of them. It's hard enough to get all the clans in one tribe to agree on something. A tribe isn't like a country, don't have a government, a king. A tribe is a bunch of clans, with a council that settles arguments between them. Sometimes—once in a long time—the council makes a law or changes one. And its clans have a big meeting each fall where people trade, and find a wife in some other clan. That's what a tribe is. That's *all* a tribe is.

"So the fellow that told you the tribes united to make war—I think he lied."

"I understand," the king said. His eyes were very direct. "But suppose a new medicine chief came along, a giant, whose medicine was much greater than any that the tribes had seen before? Suppose he made miracles? Could a man like that unite the tribes?"

This time the reply was not so quick. "I don't think so. Anyway, who got such big medicine?"

"It would be an off-worlder."

"My people know about off-worlders. A long time ago, off-worlders come down from the sky and two of them live with my people a year, watch and watch everything and ask lots of questions. Old people still remember them. And the off-worlders didn't have big medicine. They couldn't do medicine things. At first people thought they could, but they just had tools my people didn't have.

"And those off-worlders didn't even know our tongue when they come here, only Kuutonsisik and their own. They had to learn ours. And they be very old now, maybe forgot already. Probably dead. Also, my people watch them all the time, too, learn very much about them. If an off-worlder came to them again, the old people would know them right away. I would too; everybody would. Off-worlders don't even know how to ski! We had to teach them!"

The king nodded thoughtfully, never withdrawing his eyes. "My good friend, your people did not learn *all* about off-worlders. I lived on one of their worlds; I grew up among them, and know them well.

"There are many different tribes of off-worlders, and they are very different from tribe to tribe. Those who visited your people long ago belonged to a tribe called *anthropologists.* They are pretty honest; mostly they try to tell the truth. There is another tribe called *secret agents;* they are dishonest. They lie whenever they feel like it, which is very often."

Sunto watched the king's attention turn inward so that, for the moment, he hardly saw his visitor.

"And the secret agents have different clans. One clan is called *agents provocateurs.* They are the worst. They exist only to make trouble among other tribes. That is their only wish and purpose. A few of them will enter among some other tribe and with skill and great cunning will try to cause that tribe to do something that will destroy or degrade it.''

The king's eyes came back to Sunto, seeing him again. "The agents provocateurs could know much about your people. You know about writing; you may even have seen a book. Well, the anthropologists would write down in books all they learned about your people, for others to read and learn. And they also have little boxes that catch words and other sounds and keep them, and the anthropologists would have all the words your people said to them or near them, stored in little boxes for anyone to hear and learn.

"Anthropologists keep nothing secret. They let anyone learn what they learned. They're pretty good people, most of them, but they tell everything when they get home.''

Sunto gazed intently as the king continued.

"So secret agents could learn your language and your ways, and come among your people, bringing with them their evil intentions and their clever tricks.

"The report we had is that two strange medicine chiefs had come among your people—one among the barrenlands tribes and one among the river tribes. That their medicine was very great, and that they had united the tribes to make war on the Kuutonsisa. Do you still think that is impossible?''

"Maybe not,'' Sunto conceded, "for that tribe you talked about that lies.''

"Secret agents.'' The king pronounced the foreign syllables slowly and carefully, and explained it in Lokarit. "Now Sunto, if I could send you in an off-world sky ship and put you down somewhere near your people to ski to your village—if I could do that, would you go there for me? Because I want to know if the story is true or not. You would find out and then return to the sky ship and come home.

"Your wife and child would be well cared for while you were gone, and we would pay you well when you came back.''

Now it was Sunto's eyes that turned inward a moment, losing their focus on the king.

"What I will require of you,'' the king went on, "if you agree to do this, is that you learn all you can about any plans for invasion and about the strangers who claim to be medicine chiefs. Be interested; ask questions of your friends. Then, after a certain number of days—not more than four or five—

you would be back at the place where the sky ship let you out, and you would come back in it."

Their eyes met. "My friend," said Trogeir, king of Lokar, "I want to stop this war before it starts, if I can. Otherwise many men will die. And I have told you that the southern kingdoms plan to attack us when your people have come down and struck us. If Lokar is defeated, then the southerners will attack the northern warriors, who will have lost many dead, and drive them out. The southerners intend to share only the fighting, not the land.

"But if I can learn enough about the secret agents, I may be able to do something about them, so that the tribes will not attack us.

"You know me well enough, I believe. I hope you know that I am not cruel or vengeful. If the tribes attack, I will defeat them, but I will not hunt them down and root them out. Still, they and we will be much better off if they stay home.

"Will you do this for me? For me and for Lokar and the tribes? Will you go north and learn what I have asked?"

Sunto did not hesitate. "When you want me to go? If the story is true or not, I will find out for you. But I need a few days to arrange for others to take care of my customers."

"You have a week. I do not have a sky ship yet, so it could easily be longer. But if it is, I'll pay you beginning a week from now, five ornu a day, to keep you available for when the ship comes. I will then pay you a korbin a day, starting when the ship takes you away until it brings you back.

"When you return, I will also pay you the price of a large wood wagon and a further sum of twenty korbin. And while you're away from home, a man will deliver three ornu a day for your wife."

The broad tattooed face nodded calmly. "I'll be ready in a week."

"Good. A week from today, when the sun comes up, a kingsman will be at your house with a peeran for you, and I'll see you soon after."

The king looked to the slender, sharp-eyed man and gestured; the man opened the door for Sunto.

"Thank you for coming, my good friend. Your king is grateful. And there are much worse things in the world than the friendship of a grateful king."

* * *

As Sunto rode home on a king's peeran with a kingsman beside him, it occurred to him that there was something strange about this king. Sunto noticed things; his father was a medicine chief. This king did not seem like the same man he had met before, even if he looked like him.

But Sunto was not concerned. This man, this king, could be trusted; he was certain of that.

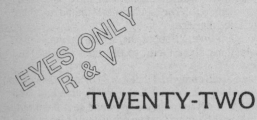

TWENTY-TWO

OFFICE MEMO

2392:09:16

To: Umbra

From: Corvus

I continue to have the feeling that there is something we should be doing about the situation on Siegel's World, with its bogus king whom we ourselves provided and nurtured to our long and continuing dismay. It is also unquestionably a hotbed of Kubiak-inspired activity and who knows what else.

Rumor even has it that we have sent two separate, highly touted assassins, one an old Lokar hand and agent of highest repute (you know who I mean), to reduce the situation. I've heard further that the head of one of them graced a pole in front of the royal citadel in Lokar for some weeks, while the other succumbed to unsophisticated interrogation techniques and was fed to the royal watchwolves or the royal swine, depending on who tells the story.

Now something *may* be in progess in some section or other to correct the situation. If so, my section does not know of it. And while security is ordinarily quite good in Department Eleven, I think if anything of consequence was in progress, I'd have heard or seen some indication of it.

So I worry. Admittedly our resources are not unlimited and tend to be considerably (I feel excessively!) committed to Cissy—especially CCCP—and to Sunrise. But we will never mature these ambitious, futuristic projects if we allow destruction present time situations to go seriously out of control.
If steps are being taken or planned, I do not insist on being apprised of them. But I *would* appreciate word to the effect that the situation is being acted on.

Corvus

The village looked cruder and more barbarous than it was. With one exception—the council house—its structures were entirely huts and outbuildings, the latter mostly food caches on legs, occasional common privies, and rude saunas.

There were no "dogs"—no domesticated "wolves"—trotting about in the bright cold morning sun. The natives had not tamed any animals except tundra cattle and the ubiquitous peernu.

The dwellings were hovels of small logs, hunkering snow-capped amid drifts and foot-packed paths. Thin smoke rose from chimneys only to settle to ground level, forming a thin haze that might or might not dissipate when the sun had been up awhile.

Snow not only capped the roofs; it had been banked around the walls as insulation. The large woodpile by each hut lay unprotected from the weather. It was only necessary to brush a piece of wood with a mitten or strike two pieces together to get the snow off them, for the snow was as dry as desert sand.

There was little activity outdoors. Hunters going out had mostly left before dawn, and those on herd duty lived apart in tents, following the cattle. An occasional habitant could be seen trotting through the ground haze to the nearest privy, or standing on a rude ladder taking provisions from a cache, or fetching firewood.

The temperature was minus forty-three Celsius, an ordinary morning; by early afternoon it might climb to minus thirty.

Inside each hut, the central feature was the brick stove, not unlike that in the king's bedroom except for size and a metal plate over the firebox for cooking. Most of the stove was the parental bed. Anyone else ordinarily slept on hides over a layer of dry grass on the packed dirt floor.

The introduction of the stove, some thirty years earlier, had caused changes that still had not stabilized. It had meant the end of moving the village every five or six years, and brought with it problems of fuel transportation and the over-browsing of nearby winter ranges.

But no serious thought—no thought at all—had been given to abandoning stoves for the crude and smoky firepits and drafty smoke-holes of before. The new comfort seemed abundantly worth the problems of a fixed winter location.

There were no windows, nor now any smoke-hole, to let in light. A small clay bowl or two of rendered tallow, with a wick of twisted bast fibers from the inner bark of trees, served as feeble lamps. The barbarians knew nothing of the gwalsu which provided excellent oil for the lamps of Lokar and other coastal lands.

The hut of Vasily Yakut was like the others, but sometimes, infrequently, it would be more brightly lit late at night by a cloudy white cube. Yakut kept this cube secret from the villagers, who might suspect his origins if they saw it.

His woman wouldn't tell; she was too afraid of him.

It was also secret that he was Vasily Yakut. He was known here as Kivi-Kotsu, "Sky Chief." And the hut had not always been his, nor the woman. Sky Chief had arrived that fall during the butcher's moon, announcing that he'd been sent by the Great Spirit, and proceeded to install himself as a new, supreme level of medicine chief. This had offended some tribesmen, but it was hard to argue against someone who gave strange and marvelous dreams and powerful visions, who commanded spirits and gathered to himself the unqualified support of tribal elders and medicine men.

Among those who disapproved was Tarksi, a prominent and respected man. Then his son, Piito, went mad and died after public dispute with Yakut. This hardened Tarksi's suspicion and disapproval into hatred, but Yakut would not allow open dispute, let alone hostility.

Yakut had then taken over the house and the woman of Piito. The Great Spirit had approved, and so had old Kivi-Tupos, the principal medicine chief of all the Siiksun. It was heavier reparation by far than had ever been awarded for an insult, but then, no one had ever before insulted the personal representative of the Great Spirit.

Aside from his great medicine, the words and voice and bearing—the very *size* of Sky Chief—carried power and authority. The Great Spirit had sent him to unite the barrenlands tribes and lead them out of the cold harsh north to a life of comfort, power, and ease in the south, where they would drive out the Kuutonsisa and take over their land.

At first the elders, though impressed with the man, had thought he was crazy. They remembered the army of the king. But Sky Chief had passed among them his skin of fermented mare's milk, blessing it, and cast powder into the council fire to call the Great Spirit, then chanted strangely, and afterward the Great Spirit himself had spoken to them.

And the word was passed that Sky Chief was indeed sent by the Great Spirit to command them and lead them to a new life.

Vasily Yakut had been busy ever since, expanding his authority over all three barrenlands tribes—thirty-seven clans in all. It was less difficult than might be thought, but it kept him constantly on the move.

At times he went out into the tundra hills alone to commune with the Great Spirit. At such times he also communicated with Marcel McKedrick, who was the Great Spirit's representative among the river tribes, the people who herded fish instead of cattle. Secretly, Yakut even returned to the sky on occasion, to visit the project leader in Garvas.

By and large there had been little active opposition, and Yakut had to abuse his woman to keep life interesting. He did not drug her much; that would make her too willingly acquiescent. He preferred to dominate her through force and fear.

TWENTY-THREE

The *Slengeth Büed* sat in knee-deep snow in a forest meadow near the coals of a dying beacon fire. Her pilot wore a clean jumpsuit and a cravat wrapped round his neck. For less noble guests the cravat would have been absent and the jumpsuit probably less clean.

He knew the king by the gold circlet exposed when he set back his hood, and by the cloak of gontar fur, a rich and lustrous near-black. They shook hands at the foot of the ramp, then the pilot and king and the king's two companions went into the ship. One of the companions was very tall, almost surely not a native; the other was as short as himself, dressed in back-country furs.

Wan Larmet was an unusually perceptive man—he had after all survived a dozen years in a hazardous profession. And at first he had the weird feeling that he'd known this king. During their first few exchanges, in his mind's eye he shaved him, but then he cancelled his suspicion: this man acted totally like a king, showed no trace of familiarity, and Larmet had certainly never met this king, or any king, before.

He gestured to the limited seating facilities—several strongly-built but comfortable swivel seats. "Have a chair, Your Majesty, gentlemen."

"Thank you, Captain Larmet," said the king. "These gentlemen are my advisor, Kyril Golovin, and Sunto of the Bear Clan of the Siiksun."

Larmet swiveled the command chair to face them, and sat down. "Your Majesty's letter was very interesting," he said, "but it left a lot of questions. What can I do for you?"

The king looked at him for a moment before answering. "I'm going to speak Terran. That surprises you? The vocabulary is better suited to some of what I have to say. Perhaps you didn't know I was educated on Earth. My father and the Confederate ambassador agreed it was desirable, and they were right, whatever the Foreign Ministry may think now.

"Mr. O'Bannion explained to me that besides being a trader, you are in the transportation business. Incidentally, feel entirely free to continue trading with Karn Kinjok.

"I believe you recently put two Department Eleven agents down among the northern barbarians." He paused for a second, noting the trader's slight reaction. "Do you know what they came for?"

Larmet shook his head. "They don't tell me and I don't ask."

The king nodded. "I thought they might have let something slip. Unlikely, to be sure.

"I was pleased, captain, but also surprised, at how quickly you came to us," the king continued. "Karn Kinjok must have been able to get in touch with you almost at once after receiving my letter."

Larmet said nothing, merely nodded slightly.

"In fact, I wasn't at all sure you'd get my message soon enough for my purpose. Perhaps you were parked in orbit where you could readily be reached by radio from the surface. It might even be that you're currently employed full-time as a courier and shuttle here on Thegwar, transporting people from place to place as needed.

"It also occurs to me just now that Karn Kinjok might have contacted you by radio, that you might have given him one so he could be warned if—if anything threatened him from the north."

Larmet shifted nervously in his seat.

"I'm not trying to make you uncomfortable, captain, believe me. I understand your situation. But I need to check my speculations when I can. I'm operating with a shortage of firm data and a lot of guesses.

"But to answer your question, what I want of you is to have Sunto delivered to a point near the same village where you put down one of the FM agents. It's a village of one of the barrenlands tribes, a tribe called the Siiksun."

Boru watched as Larmet examined and evaluated what he'd heard. After a few seconds the pilot met his eyes again. "I don't know the name of the village or the tribe, but I know the place. I let him off in the barrenlands, in the hills fifteen kilometers north of the nearest village. I can put your man down somewhere near the same village, but not at the same place."

So he meets him now and then, and wants no tracks to explain. "That's fine, captain. Sunto can take it from there. Just orient him before you set him down." Larmet was getting nervous again, so the king continued. "O'Bannion was right about you, you know: you're a man of considerable ethics. So I want to tell you two things right now, before I forget. Karn Kinjok is not your only friend on Thegwar. O'Bannion is another. And if you ever need a place to—get away from things, so to speak, the king of Lokar is also one. We're not like some of your clients, who might easily silence instead of reward those who work with them."

Then switching to Lokarit, he went over with Larmet and Sunto what would be done and when. Larmet would take Sunto tonight, now. Sunto would have three days to gather information. The moon was early in the first quarter, and when it went down on the third night, Sunto would be back where he'd landed. The computer aboard the *Slengeth Büed* could tell Larmet when the moon would set there. If for any reason either of them couldn't be there, Sunto would be back again when the moon set the next night. If they failed to get together both nights, Sunto would return on his own across country.

"I believe we've covered everything now except your fee," the king said finally.

"And one other thing," Larmet said in Terran. "You brought up O'Bannion, here and in your letter. Why didn't you bring him along?" The smuggler's attention was closely on the king now.

Boru stared at him. Larmet had put his ass on the line twice now when he hadn't needed to.

"You want proof that he's all right, Wan?" Boru said also in Terran. "You're looking at it."

Wan Larmet stared as things fell into place, then glanced at Golovin. The tall man's eyebrows had risen a trifle; otherwise he showed no response. The king's answer had not been explicit, but it seemed clear enough.

"Did—someone get hit?" Larmet asked.

"By Heidemann," Boru answered. "I'd have stopped it if I could have, but I blew it. But the party in power is still in power, and as long as Trogeir is on the throne, his basic philosophy and policies will continue."

Larmet gestured at Golovin. "Where does he fit in?"

"He was young Trogeir's tutor during a dozen years on Earth. Here he's the royal advisor. I brought him tonight because he's the best judge of character I've ever known. And then I didn't even use him; I size people up pretty damn well myself."

The king and the smuggler looked at one another for several seconds. "Okay," Larmet said at last, "I'm not so bad at that myself. If I was, I'd have been dead years ago.

"So I'm going to level with you. I've been scared lately; you put your finger on it. Because the things they've got me doing—the people I've hauled and where—I can't really see how they'd let me live when they don't need me anymore.

"The only reason I don't blow is that, knowing Department Eleven, every agent and informer they've got would have my specs and my picture, so it's safer to stay. So what you said earlier about friends—I may end up looking for a place to hide. That's my fee: a place to hide."

"Let's not talk about hiding. Let's talk about a place to live. There are worse than this one." The king got up and switched to Lokarit. "Sunto, go out and bring in your gear. Captain, we'll see you back here with Sunto three nights from now."

Five minutes later the *Slengeth Büed* was gone, and the two Earthmen began the ride back through the snowy woods to Tonlik and Krogaskott.

The royal apartment was empty except for the king and his nurse. He pulled off his fur-lined boots and set them aside.

"Honey," he said, "it's time for us to start the process of getting married again. Larsa says it's not okay for the king to have a mistress—kind of different from the days of kings on Earth. And giving you a room somewhere else in the palace won't cover it. Now that I'm healthy again, people are talking."

Selena looked at him thoughtfully. "That explains some of the disapproving looks I've gotten lately. Maybe I'd better move to the women's quarters temporarily, then, until we can get legal again. And just see you once a day to play for you. You could make me the Royal Musician. How long does it take for a king to get married?"

"Longer than you might think; there are prerequisites. That's what I meant by the marriage process."

She looked questioningly and he continued. "Remember when we were going to get married the first time and you asked if we had to post banns or anything like that? Well, for the king to marry, banns *do* have to be posted, in every town and village and church, which takes awhile, and they have to be there for three weeks. Anyone can deliver objections to the mayor or priest, who has them recorded and gives them to a royal messenger who gives them to the prime minister. The king then has to answer the objections to the Patriarch and then to the poeple in a well-announced public speech in the square.

"And that's if the girl is from a noble Lokarn family! If he wants to marry a foreigner or commoner"—he spread his hands—"it goes further than that. The banns have to be posted for *six* weeks. After the banns have been posted for six weeks, they hold an election. The king and the royal line being pretty damned important in Lokar, the people have to approve."

The king reached out and squeezed her hand. "They'll approve, all right, don't worry about that. When the time comes, I'm going out through the country and campaign—give speeches in every market town, with you beside me being beautiful." He grinned. "That'll clinch it, and it'll be good for the country to have their king get out and talk to them.

"I think they'd probably approve anyway; I'm their golden-haired boy in more ways than one. But I really like these people. They deserve a king that respects them enough to get out and talk to them now and then. With altitude, of course; they wouldn't want it any other way.''

The king fell silent then, and after a moment Selena spoke. "What is it?" she asked.

"What they really need is a king who can head off this war that's hanging over them. But it's not as easy as wishing it.''

She nodded. "Remember what I told you once? At our first breakfast I told you that the king and government here were as good or better than any I knew about. Well, they still are.'' She pulled the spread off his bed. "Meanwhile this had better be our last night together for a while. I'll arrange to move to women's quarters tomorrow.''

"Right. And tell you what: you might start considering what hats you might like to wear around here now that the king doesn't need a nurse. Maybe organize and direct a palace musical group: it's amazing there isn't one already.

"Meanwhile tomorrow I'll make arrangements to get those banns printed and posted.''

When he'd hung up his clothes, she went to him and kissed him. "Ah the weight of a crown," she said playfully, then her voice softened. "You're not only a good king, Your Majesty, you're also a very good person. In fact, you remind me very much of my late husband.''

She lay not troubled but not sleeping either. The king breathed in the easy even cadence of healthy sleep. *I wonder if I should have told him*, she thought to herself. *But my premonitions aren't infallible, and it might weaken his determination. He still might make it happen.*

And he really does want to prevent the war.

TWENTY-FOUR

Gneos—(*n. pl.* **Gnessr**)1. A citizen of the Khupraigneos.
2. The Cymlirian language of the Khupraigneos.
[Abbreviated from **Khupraigneos,** *supreme people*—
Khupra, *supreme,* from **khuf,** *superior;* **gneith,**
lineage—adj. **Gnesil.**]
—*Cassil's Compendium of the Languages of Siegel's World,* Cassil's Matrices AB, ¢12.30, Hel-
sinki, Terra, 2367.

The two slaves hopped from the gangplank down onto the
dock, holystones in hand, making way for the approaching
Gnessr.

Lean and sinewy, the slaves were adequately nourished but
rather lightly fed. They lowered their faces in respect, for two
of the three Gnessr wore the golden baldrics of nobles.

Despite the chill winter breeze—it was about eleven degrees Celsius—the slaves wore only breechclouts. Breechclouts were their entire wardrobe except for a long serape
they might don against storms.

The Gnessr likewise were somewhat exposed to the chill,
wearing only bleached and spotless kilts and soft mocassin-
like boots laced snugly over feet and ankles. Their baldrics
supported shortswords. These were not their war swords,
which were somewhat larger and worn on a harness.

They were notably large men for Thegwar, a result of
selective breeding and culling. They were also lean, muscular, and arrogant—more the results of training and indoctrina-
tion than eugenics.

The quartermaster, a man much like them but without a

baldric, his cutlass held at his waist by a sash as white as his kilt, saluted them at the head of the gang-plank. The visitors glanced at the kilt, approving its cleanliness. He barked a command; a midshipman not yet full grown saluted and disappeared into the poop to notify the commodore.

Commodore Koile vis Thelrai was almost a caricature—brown-faced, burly, and with one wooden leg. As he stumped out to meet the councilmen, he did not even think of looking about to check the condition and cleanliness of his flagship; it would, of course, be impeccable. He was a vis Thelrai, his officers and petty officers all family retainers, his midshipmen of good families.

He saluted the councilmen; they returned the salute, fists on breastbones.

"Commodore," said the elder, "we have come to inspect your progress on refitting the flotilla." He affected a bored tone, to communicate his opinion that inspection was undoubtedly a formality—that the commodore would certainly have everything well under control.

"Of course, your honors." He led them toward a companionway. "I have examined a Bleesbrokman in the harbor here to see the principles involved. It is primarily a matter of installing stoves in the troop quarters and of course in the slave ships. And providing the requisite blankets.

"The slaves will be quite accustomed to cold; they have lived their lives in northern climes. But as they will be freshly taken, it will be necessary to chain them. The lack of physical activity will make them chill more easily, and freshly captured slaves at best tend to die readily." He shrugged.

The companionway opened into a troop hold, its tiers of narrow sleeping racks in rows. At each end of the compartment were weapons lockers and a honeycomb of individual storage cubbies. Basically it was a typical Gnesil troop compartment, but in this instance each bunk had several blankets folded on it. And near each end squatted an iron-topped brick stove with a well-braced stovepipe leading through the overhead.

"Each top bunk," said Koile vis Thelrai, "will be used for the winter gear of the men who sleep below it. That reduces troop capacity by a fourth, but the two additional ships make up for it. And one regiment will easily show those northern bumpkins what real soldiers are like."

The councilmen inspected the flagship with knowing eyes,

visited another troopship and one of the five slave ships, and left content. The commodore was right, of course, and the council before him: one regiment would be quite enough.

Larmet had set him down in the barrens some ten kilometers east-northeast of the village. The sickle moon had set hours before, leaving the night to the distant stars, but the snowcover gave visibility more than adequate for travel. With pack and bow on his back and poles in his hands, Sunto strode off on the slender boards, their faint hiss the only sound.

He headed deliberately southward rather than toward the village, in order to approach it from the south, as if from the land of the Kuutonsisa. In a long Thegwar hour he was in the cover of scattered, stunted trees and turned westward. Finally he caught sight of a low but sheer rock ridge, a hogback that ran southwest-northeast for thirty kilometers. Not long after, he found the well-used trail worn by hunters who, homeward bound, funneled through a notch in the ridge, and he blended his tracks with theirs.

By the time he saw the village ahead, he was leg-weary; it had been years since he'd skied much. Pungent wood smoke piqued his nostrils as he approached, but no sound met his ears, even from a paddock of incurious thick-coated peernu that he passed. The village seemed unchanged. He went directly to his parents' hut, stood his skis and poles in the snow beside his father's, and after a moment's pause went in.

His mother saw him first. Seated repairing mukluks by a lamp, she looked up when he entered. For a moment her face seemed frozen in an expression of questioning, as if she didn't know him, but it was belief that was suspended, not recognition. The mukluk fell from her lap, and she wailed as she stood, a wail of joy driven by the charge of grief that lay beneath. They met halfway, mother and son embracing, she smiling through neglected tears, jabbering questions, he patting her shoulder, answering.

His father now was on his feet, his broad grin showing sound though well-worn teeth. He was sixty in Terran terms, seeming older than most tribesmen of sixty years because as the principal medicine chief he did not herd cattle through the summer or hunt the arctic peeran over winter's snow.

They all sat down then, close together, in low chairs of

cowhide laced into frames of stout saplings, the mother lean-
ing eagerly toward her son, still with questions. Sunto told
very briefly of his adventure southward with the hunting
party, his capture and release, of being a sailor, and certain
other things. He did not mention king or wife or child, or the
woodcutting business—any ties to the south. He was simply a
wanderer returned home.

Then he turned his eyes to his father and saw a man who
had markedly declined. Wisdom had become—something that
Sunto could not yet identify. Dignity was gone, replaced by a
sort of subsurface glee. The dark eyes, once so aware and
perceptive, missing little, still were bright but somehow out
of focus.

"It has been a long time, father."

"Yes, a dozen years."

Sunto nodded, although it had only been seven. Surely
senility should not have come so far ahead of time!

"The village, this house, seem unchanged," the son continued, "but there will have been marriages, births, comings
of age, deaths. . . . Tell me about the clan."

"Oh! Oh! You will not believe!" the old man said. "The
Great Spirit has greatly smiled on his people! He has sent a
grea-a-at medicine chief among us, who has given great
medicine dreams, great visions! Wonders are seen and done
far greater than ever before, greater than I ever imagined! He
is a *grea-a-at* chief with *grea-a-at* medicine, and he has gone
among *all* the clans of *all* the tribes who herd cattle."

The old man cackled then like a nokua cock in breeding
time. "And son, my son"—his voice lowered to an intense
hiss—"he is going to lead the tribes to a new world where
food grows *out of the ground* and summer lasts half the year!
The Great Spirit has decided that his chosen people will no
longer live in danger of starving, no longer in fear of a
wicked Kuutonsisa king. We will eat soft food and live in
great huts, and Kuutonsisa will fetch for us, and their women
will lie on their backs for us, and our old people will grow
young again and never die!" He laughed again, his bright
eyes vivid now.

"I hear you, father!" A glance showed Sunto his mother's
concern. "I hear you. Did the great medicine chief tell you
all this?"

"Not all! Not all! No. He told us some." Again the

lowered voice, the near-hiss. "Some I have seen myself in dreams and visions, and so have others! Since great Sky Chief has come among us, the chiefs and elders and many others have seen great visions. But I especially, for I am a medicine chief too, the greatest next to Sky Chief."

Then for a while he catalogued the wonders since the coming of Sky Chief, and described the man himself. Sky Chief was a giant, towering above others, and when he stripped in the ceremonial steam lodge, his muscles were like the skinned carcass of a bear, his soft penis as long as a wolf turd! Wah! What a chief! When the time came to conquer the Kuutonsisa, which would be very soon, Sky Chief with his own hand would strike them down by the tens and the tens of tens!

Before long, though, the old man ran down. It seemed he tired easily. Then both parents went to bed on the stove, and Sunto lay in his sleeping robe on a pallet of skins. Tired as he was, he lay awake with his thoughts and concern for a time, scarcely hearing the snoring of the older ones.

Sunto was relieved, the next day, to learn that Sky Chief was away from the village visiting other clans. Obviously the off-worlder was very dangerous, and might be suspicious of him. As Sunto talked with old friends, the picture began to take clearer form. A pattern of evil emerged: Kivi-Kotsu—Sky Chief—was no true medicine chief; he had them fooled. He was the great trickster, as the king had thought, using what the king had called "drugs" on the unsuspecting. And he was deadly to anyone who crossed his will.

The man was a corrupter. Since the Great Spirit had formed his chosen people out of steam from the smoking mountain and set them to inhabit the *riisu*, the prairie-tundra, warriors had fought only if their personal spirit advised it. When one clan prepared to attack a village of another tribe, each warrior consulted his spirit, and if it advised against it, the warrior stayed home. Sometimes fewer than one out of five went out to fight.

But Sky Chief had said that all the men, from age ten to thirty—seventeen to fifty-one in Terran terms—must go to fight the Kuutonsisa. Otherwise, the Great Spirit had said, he would abandon the tribes forever. They would be left to die, their cattle, their peernu, their women would become sterile, and their personal spirits would shrivel and live on as maggots in dung.

To prevent this, Sky Chief had ordered that any who refused should be roasted alive over slow fires until their spirit departed and they were no longer a danger to the people.

The time would soon come to leave. Sky Chief communed frequently with the Great Spirit, and he would tell them when.

Sunto's father, who still was called Kivi-Tupos—Great Medicine Chief—and the elders all affirmed that it was exactly as Sky Chief said. Many of the men were eager. Others were unenthused, but resigned to the situation and obedient. For who would wish destruction on the people?

Then Sunto heard about Piito, the son of Tarksi, who had opposed Sky Chief and afterward gone mad. He had run howling about the village, then fallen into convulsions so extreme that his bones had broken. Clearly the Great Spirit was adamant, and to offend Sky Chief was to offend God. The family of Tarksi were sullen about what had happened, and avoided councils with Sky Chief, but they were careful not to talk against him or against the war to come.

Of course, Sunto then visited the hut of Tarksi, but Tarksi was out hunting.

A single day told Sunto all he needed to know. Surely Sky Chief belonged to the Agents Provocateurs clan. He would be back in a day or two, or three or five, and then no doubt Sunto could meet with him and sample the blessed mare's milk and even speak with the Great Spirit, for Sunto was the son of Kivi-Tupos and had visited the land of the Kuutonsisa, and was therefore a man of importance.

Sunto earnestly hoped that Larmet would not be late, and that Sky Chief would be delayed for at least a few days.

Vasily Yakut skied with powerful strides up the long clearing. Overhead a layer of altostratos grayed the sky. He was tired of waiting, impatient. With his dominance established, with everyone accepting his orders, with the only opposition afraid and silent, there was still the chore of keeping things together until they moved south. He'd radioed the smuggler the night before and learned that it hadn't snowed in Lokar for a week; and project orders were explicit—he was not to move out until the snow was belly deep on a peeran as far south as the Tilkenmor. That might be next week or it might take a month—even two.

Meanwhile he had to keep these goddamn people in line and interested.

His flunky was having a hard time keeping up. Not only was Yakut a strong and skilled skier—the flunky was also—but he was thirty centimeters taller, much of it legs, and wore lightweight "medicine skis" whose magnetic plates bonded with others in the bottoms of his mukluks. This gave him better control and response than upturned mukluk toes hooked under ski straps in the manner of the barbarians and the Lokaru. As the two men skied past the first huts at the village edge, Yakut snapped an order and his flunky hurried to obey, glad to get away from Yakut's sour mood. The youth angled off to the hut of Vuuno-Nisso, the clan chief, with the command to come at once to Sky Chief's home.

Their approach had been seen, and word called into some of the huts. Some villagers came out to watch Sky Chief, mostly children. Sky Chief nodded to them as he passed, and went into his home.

Vuuno-Nisso, wiry, sharp-nosed, famous swordsman, did not keep Sky Chief, giver of dreams, great Kivi-Kotsu, waiting.

"Report!" said Yakut.

The shorter man's grin was like that of Sunto's father. "Great Kivi-Kotsu," he said, "the family of Tarksi persists in complaining. They have gone to the village elders and said it is not all right for you to live with the widow of Piito. By law, she should become the wife of Piito's unmarried brother. They have demanded a hearing, tonight, and because it is the law, the hearing has been granted."

Vuuno-Nisso tilted his tattoo-scarred face sideways, still smirking, waiting to see what Sky Chief would answer. Sky Chief simply nodded sourly.

"And Sunto," Vuuno-Nisso continued, "the living son of Kivi-Tupos, came back from the land of the Kuutonsisa three days ago." He paused, pleased by the flash of interest in Sky Chief's face. "He went on a long hunt southward in a winter of hunger, with other young men. Some did not return; they were thought dead. He was taken captive by the Kuutonsisa, then released, and has traveled about since then to many lands. Now he has returned to tell about it."

"Where is he now?" Yakut asked thoughtfully.

"I can have him found and sent to you, if you'd like," Vuuno-Nisso answered. Then slyly, "He was also asking many questions. He talked with me and later went to see Tarksi."

Yakut grunted. "He is nothing. Go and bring him to me. I will see if his years away from the Great Spirit have corrupted him. Speaking the language of the Kuutonsisa, he might be of some value to us."

Vuuno-Nisso was moving toward the door when Sky Chief stopped him. "But do not bring him here until time enough has passed to ski three kilometers. Find him and hold him until that time. Then bring him to me."

The chief of the Bear Clan nodded, still grinning, and sidled out the door. Yakut turned to his woman.

"Take off your clothes !" he ordered.

Sunto had heard that Tarksi was back from the hunt, so he went to Tarksi's hut again. The brawny Tarksi was twenty-nine years old—fifty in Terran terms—and still outstanding for his strength, endurance, and wrestling. In one more year he would be an elder, but for ten years already his voice had carried much weight in the clan at large, because he looked at things directly and his conclusions were usually firm and logical. His personal livestock, both cattle and peernu, were among the finest, by dint of wise trades and shrewd breeding, and he was famous as a hunter. He was less interested in clan feuds and raiding than many others, but in combat had made a reputation as a fighter and tactician.

He'd refused to drink mare's milk with Sky Chief and had forbidden it to his family; a few others in the village had followed his lead. Tarksi knew nothing of drugs; he had simply observed men become fools, seeing what wasn't there, and some had become slaves to a man who twisted religious lore to fit evil ways.

So when Sunto arrived in Tarksi's hut with questions about Kivi-Kotsu, Tarksi, after looking him over, nodded and took him outside. There they put on their skis and strode off toward the forest, passing a couple of inbound hunters on the trail. When they were among the trees and no one was around, Tarksi led him onto a side trail.

Sunto didn't get much information he hadn't gotten already, just a different viewpoint and an explanation. The tribes had no devil in their religious tradition, only minor evil spirits and the mischief maker. Sky Chief was too powerful to be acting for any of them. Tarksi had therefore decided that Sky Chief must be an off-worlder. If there was a world in the sky where the innocuous and friendly earlier visitors had come from, there might easily be still another where the people were evil.

Sunto didn't confirm or comment, he simply thanked Tarksi for his information and opinions. Then they skied back to the village beneath a thickening layer of clouds.

Vuuno-Nisso waited patiently outside the hut of Sky Chief. The time for returning was long past before he'd arrived, but listening outside the door, he'd heard weeping and whimpering and the harsh voice of Kivi-Kotsu, and decided it was best to wait outside. So he stood in the beginning of dusk and let interesting pictures come to his mind. He was fortunate, being the chief: Sky Chief had given him visions and dreams several times, and he could sometimes get some of them back.

After a time of uncertain duration, Sky Chief looked out, swore, and ordered him in. Vuuno-Nisso quickly removed his skis and did as he was told.

"Where is this Sunto I sent you to bring?" demanded Sky Chief.

"Gone."

"Gone? Explain!"

The woman huddled in a corner with a hide covering her head. Awareness of her and of her misery was a slight distraction. "I went to his father's house and he was not there. Then I asked around and someone said he'd gone into Tarksi's. But at Tarksi's, he had left, and Tarksi had too. Someone else had seen them ski toward the forest, so I took the main trail, thinking to find them, but I didn't. There are too many tracks leading out from it. I went all the way beyond the rock ridge." Vuuno-Nisso looked earnestly and worriedly at Sky Chief. "So I came back and found Tarksi in his house. Then I hurried to Kivi-Tupos, and he said his son had left again, taking his gear to go on a short hunt. By then it was so late, I thought I should come here."

Short hunt! thought Yakut. *The son of a bitch is running away—probably a spy!* He brushed past Vuuno-Nisso and out the door. He could send searchers to find the man, but it was almost time for the council, and there was no hurry. It was hundreds of kilometers south to the nearest Lokarn outpost.

Outside the first slow flakes of a new snowfall were wandering down. Perfect, thought Yakut. And any nearby hunters would come in for the council. So any fresh outbound tracks would be Sunto's. In another hour it would be dark. Two more and the council would begin, and he would settle the problem of Tarksi for good. In less than four hours from now—probably not more than three—it would be over and he would track the man himself.

He'd catch him easily: he could travel faster, and by not making camp he would catch him asleep. Inject him, question him, then either bring him back or leave him dead.

Kivi-Kotsu went back into his hut and sent the clan chief home. Vuuno-Nisso was glad to go, and relieved at the Sky Chief's unaccountable good mood.

Sunto waited in the night in the depression between two barren hills. Although it was cloudy, he knew he had a fair amount of time to wait before the moon would set.

They'd told him at Tarksi's that Vuuno-Nisso had been looking for him to take him to Kivi-Kotsu, and had left the village on the main south trail. So Sunto had hurried home, gotten his gear, and left without even waiting for a meal. That had worried his mother, but his father hadn't noticed. Sunto too had left the village on the main south trail, but detoured in the first fringe of forest, then paralleled the main trail through untracked snow. Thus he'd missed running into Vuuno-Nisso. After passing through the notch, he'd turned east on a convenient hunter trail for a way before curving northeastward into the barrens to the pickup place.

The new snowfall was still light, lying no more than the thickness of a finger on the mark that the skyship had pressed into the snow three nights earlier. It occurred to Sunto to wonder if perhaps he would be followed, tracked down. It wouldn't be difficult.

If he was followed, they'd either catch him or arrive too late. If they arrived too late, they'd still see the mark of the skyship, and when Kivi-Kotsu heard, he would know. But it was too late to do anything about that now unless he back-tracked and let them catch him nearer the village. That would protect the secret of the ship, but the king would not learn what he'd found out.

Of course, the king already knew, pretty much. All he would bring him was confirmation and details.

On the other hand they might well not trail him. And he had a wife and child.

So Sunto squatted stolidly on his skis, waiting. The flakes began to fall more thickly, but it was still not a heavy fall. Few were, this far north.

Vasily Yakut was grinning, his eyes gleaming, as he walked into the council house and scanned the interior. It was crowded; every man in the village who was the head of a household, who had a wife and child, was there, squatting in the firelight. There were well over a hundred.

There was no stove in the council house. The fire was open, large enough to bring sweat to those nearest, its smoke only reluctantly finding its way out the smokehole overhead.

Yakut was high on one of the drugs that were part of his tool-kit—an upper in this case. Looking around at the crowd of tribesmen, he saw them not as contemptible aborigines— his usual view of them—but as a flock of sheep waiting to be eaten by the wolf.

On his arrival, all eyes had moved to him. He saw the stool set for him on the far side of the fire, and strode toward it through the squatting throng, letting them avoid his feet and knees. When he was seated, he leaned forward, one big fist on his knee, leering. Already the heat of fire and crowded bodies had brought a sheen of perspiration to his flushed face to catch the ruddy firelight.

Without waiting for Vuuno-Nisso to open the proceedings, Yakut spoke loudly, and the bumble of other voices fell quickly to nothing.

"Men of the Bear Clan!" He looked around then, grin gone, head high. "We have come here to listen to the carping of rebels against the Great Spirit—men who would keep the People here in the cold and hungry north." Briefly his eyes found Tarksi sitting in the ring nearest the fire across from him, then passed on. "Let me tell you something, men of the Bear Clan, and this knowledge is powerful medicine. The one who complains loudest is the greatest offender. So let us hear complaints tonight. Tarksi! Have you anything to say to this council?''

Livid but controlling himself, Tarksi rose. ''I speak to the heads of households of the Bear Clan,'' he said slowly and deliberately. ''I do not speak to foreigners who come to corrupt the ways of the People.

''I do not speak to the foreigner nor ask his leave to talk to you. I follow the ways of the People as given to our ancestors by the Great Spirit, the ways and laws handed down to us in trust by our forefathers. By men who respected not only the Great Spirit and the law, but the People.''

He looked around the council house. Their eyes were intent on him.

''Now a foreigner has come among us who scorns both law and People, who disdains our ways. He claims to be sent by the Great Spirit, but he breaks and corrupts the laws of the Great Spirit! One of those laws says . . .''

As Tarksi had spoken, Yakut had swallowed a capsule taken from a pocket. From another pocket he took a capsule and flipped it unobtrusively into the fire. There was a tiny explosion, enough to throw sparks into the immediate row of listeners, and these jumped to their feet, slapping at their furs, a couple at their faces. Tarksi had stopped in mid-sentence, staring unbelievingly at Yakut.

The Sky Chief laughed long and loud. ''*The Great Spirit?*'' he roared. ''*The Great Spirit?* What do *you* know of the Great Spirit?'' He shifted from amusement to anger. ''Has the Great Spirit spoken with *you?* Has he chosen *you* to receive his power? You have refused even to drink the drink he has blessed! You are afraid to see and hear what the Great Spirit might tell or show you! And yet you *dare* speak about the Great Spirit to me!''

The agent swiveled his head about, confronting all, glowering. ''Who is this poor fool who speaks of what he knows not? Does he think I have my medicine from my own hands?'' He paused. ''*No!*'' he roared. ''I have it by the Great Spirit! The Great Spirit has given it into my hands. He has bequeathed his power on me to use for him, to unite his people and lead them out of the frozen lands to conquer and possess the land of the greedy Kuutonsisa!''

Abruptly then his voice fell to a hush that every man leaned to hear, even Tarksi.

"So the corrupter, the complainer Tarksi, says that I offend
the Great Spirit. He asks a *hearing* of this gathering that *it*
may judge."

He paused, letting their minds reach for what was to come.
It came in a deep, ominous rumble. "I say let the Great Spirit
himself judge."

With a sudden florid gesture he threw a powder into the
fire so that it flared lavender; then he began to chant. It was
not one of the traditional chants, but in the same form and
style. As he chanted, old Kivi-Tupos held a large drinking
bowl in one hand and poured fermented mare's milk into it
from a wine skin.

> "O Great Spirit
> who dwells in all things,
> clouds and plants and stones,
> who tells the buds to open
> and the cows to bear young
> and gives his People domain over them,
> who breathes life into the infant,
> hear my request!
>
> "Breathe justice into this milk!
> Let it select between the guilty and the just!
> Let those who speak the truth
> drink it and stand refreshed!
> Let those of evil heart
> drink it and know thy justice!"

Yakut stood tall and satanic, dark face shining with sweat
in the firelight, his arms spread overhead. Slowly he lowered
them, looking haughty and sure. Now old Kivi-Tupos looked
about him and spoke.

"Let Tarksi and his brothers and sons come to me."

Tarksi and four other scowling but nervous men stepped up
to the old medicine chief.

"And Sky Chief also."

Yakut stepped up on the old man's other side. Kivi Tupos
handed the drinking bowl first to him.

"Drink!" said Kivi-Tupos, and Sky Chief drank deeply,
then handed back the bowl, his mustache dripping white,
secure in the antidote he'd swallowed. The old medicine chief

looked into the bowl, grinned and shook his head in wonder
at the amount Yakut had drunk.

"Now you," he said, and handed it to Tarksi. Tarksi
raised it, then instead of giving it back, handed it on to a
brother. It made the round of them before the old man
received it again.

By that time the first brother was beginning to shudder.
Within seconds he screamed, wild-eyed, clawed hands striking about him, and threw himself on the ground in convulsions. Already the second was following suit. In less than half
a minute, of those who'd drunk or seemed to, only Tarksi and
Yakut were unaffected, and they were busy keeping the others out of the fire. A minute later the bodies had stilled, alive
but inert.

"You have poisoned them," Tarksi said at last, quietly but
easily heard in the stunned assembly. "As you poisoned
Piito." He took a skinning knife from his belt. "There is a
law among us for judging such things, which has nothing to
do with poisoned milk. It is combat by knife before the Great
Spirit."

There were scattered grunts of approval from the crowd,
and suddenly it occurred to Yakut that he was in danger of
losing them, that this could grow into sullen hatred. Tarksi
laid down his knife on the ground and began to strip. With no
gloating now, his face deliberately solemn, Yakut followed
suit. Shortly the brawny tribesman stood naked and shiny
with sweat. He was very large for a barbarian: a hundred
seventy-five centimeters tall and weighing eighty-eight kilos.
Yakut stood facing him, heavily muscled but sinewy, a highly-
trained martial artist who was also a gymnast and had trained
with weights. He stood one hundred ninety centimeters and
ninety-eight kilos.

"Take up your knives," said Kivi-Tupos, and his old voice
was eager. Tarksi picked his up; Yakut left his on the ground,
shaking his head.

"I will use no knife," he said simply. "I have no wish to
kill Tarksi. The Great Spirit will give me strength and quickness to win without steel." Tarksi paled at the utter certainty
in the words. He crouched, squeezing his hilt, staring at the
bigger man, and hardly saw the bare foot that slammed the
side of his head, sending him sprawling, stunned.

Still he kept the knife in his fist, and rolled clumsily,

groggily to his knees. After a few seconds he looked up to see his tormentor gazing somberly down at him, waiting for him to rise. Slowly Tarksi gathered himself, the raised tattoos squirming like worms on his face. Suddenly he sprang, blade sweeping. Yakut was ready. He spun, bending away from the stroke, driving a back kick into Tarksi's midsection, doubling him over, the wind driven out of him, the knife flying into the fire.

Calmly, powerfully, Sky Chief struck the bent-over warrior with his open hand, the sound of it like a gunshot, knocking Tarksi sideways to the floor again.

For a long minute the warrior lay there gasping, then scrabbled to his feet, screaming. For an instant he stared about him wild-eyed before running naked through the crowd out into the night and the snow.

There'd been no cheers, almost no sound from the crowd except for a few involuntary grunts. The beaten man had gone *ruotihaarsi*—he would run naked into the forest to die of humiliation and the cold.

Yakut didn't wait for their emotion to take its own form. He moved to direct and control it.

"My people," he said quietly, and their attention went to the gleaming giant by the fire. "I feel old and tired now, tired and sad. But I have grown in wisdom." He let the power of his voice grow a little. "I see clearly now what I did not see before. Tarksi was not evil himself. He and these his kinsmen simply withheld themselves from the Great Spirit, and thus were open to possession by devils. Devils possessed them, devils who wish to hold the People here to stay forever cold, forever far from the sun, forever at risk of hunger and starvation."

Yakut spread his arms low, beseechingly. "So pray, my brothers!" he said earnestly, "pray with me silently, each of us separately to the Great Spirit, to forgive these unhappy men and drive the devils out of them."

He fell quiet then, head not so bowed that he couldn't see part of the crowd through slitted eyes. They were not really with him, and would not be tonight, but the danger had deflated. Slowly he sank to his knees in an attitude of prayer. Around him, one by one, the others knelt to pray, led by the handful of elders who could not help obeying.

They stayed that way for several minutes, a barbaric tableau in the ruddy firelight, then slowly Sky Chief stood. When enough of the others had followed suit, he picked his way to the two large ceremonial skins of undrugged kumiss that hung long and full at the back of the council house, took one from the pole and carried it among the gathered warriors, giving each to drink, holding the skin for them. It took quite a while.

When all had drunk, he picked up his clothes and spoke again. "My brothers," he said, "there is the rest of this skin and another. Drink well, for tonight we have passed through the fire of danger and come through safely with the loss of only one warrior, for these four will probably live.

"We have all learned, I most of all. But now I must go and seek the further guidance of the Great Spirit, for I am deeply shaken by the hidden demons that had taken prisoner the spirits of our brothers."

With that, Vasily Yakut walked straight-backed and naked out into the dark and arctic cold. It was snowing harder now, and the wind was rising, sending clouds of flakes swirling in the night. He would hurry and get into his traveling furs, for he had Sunto, the old fool's son, to find and question and dispose of.

He trotted to his hut, dressed, packed his gear, selected the drug he would use in questioning, then went back out. The snow had thickened greatly, slanting steadily now on a south-west wind. At that rate, he realized, in two or three hours there'd be no tracks at all. Even the well-worn main trails would be drifted full, the country uniformly blanketed over.

Forget tracking tonight, he told himself. *When the storm is over, I'll take the best men, the best travelers I have, and sweep the country to the south until they pick up his fresh tracks. Then I'll send them back and follow him myself.*

He stood thoughtfully, then decided that storm or not, for appearance's sake he'd better ski into the forest and commune with the Great Spirit as he'd said he would. He was going to have to cultivate a new public image.

TWENTY-FIVE

It's interesting that an able person
can get into a frame of mind where he
thinks he has to do everything himself.
That makes sense if all you've got is
a bunch of turkeys around you, but in
that case you'd better straighten them
out as fast as you can or replace them
with able people.

If you think you have to do it all yourself regardless, then you're a little
bit nutty on the subject, and you've
put a close fence around what you can
accomplish. Kyril had the right approach: get able people and make them
more able. He and they performed wonders.

—*Reminiscences of a King* by Bjorn Boru

The weekly cabinet meetings had become twice weekly.
But this one was additional, unscheduled. Sunto had given
them his report, the secretary writing furiously, then been
taken to the official who would see to his pay and the
assignment of a wood contract between Sunto and the
government.

"Gentlemen," said the king, "the situation seems clear
enough and so does the solution. The agent named Sky Chief
is the key; eliminate him and the barbarians will not invade.

"And that makes me the key. I'm the one available person
who can be depended on to kill him.

"So what I'm going to do is intensify my workouts for a
week or two, borrow 'Hosar the Weaver's' nasty little dart
gun, and have Wan Larmet put me down near the village

where Sky Chief is. Then I'll temporarily resume my earlier profession as an assassin.

"Any questions?"

The calm faces around the table all were on him. He could not sense any barrier; the almost physical sense of resistance he had often been aware of when someone disagreed with him was absent. These men were different.

But he knew they disagreed, despite the absence of hostility, resentment, or censure. *Damn*, he thought, *I don't want to have to handle or convince these guys. I just want to get on with it.*

Larsa stood up. "Your Majesty," he said, "that's a most interesting scheme. But you're overlooking the other agent—the one with the river tribes. If you kill the one called Sky Chief, the other one might very well suffice to carry it off without him. In any event, it seems questionable that Department Eleven would engage in a program that could be wrecked by the loss of one agent."

Boru got up scowling. "I disagree. It is entirely possible that they would. This kingdom, this planet, is not urgently important to Department Eleven. It is merely an irritation that they've turned into a game. It isn't even important enough to use one of their own courier ships, which would entail a higher risk of being found out. Siegel's World is really only important to us. It is worth a major risk only to us."

He looked around the table. "I am not, gentlemen, a would-be martyr looking for a stake. I'm not even remotely inclined to risk my life wastefully. It's a matter of estimating odds. The odds are excellent that I can kill Sky Chief; he won't be expecting that kind of attack. And the odds are excellent that, having killed him, I won't be harmed by the tribesmen."

The prime minister had not sat down. His eyes met the king's calmly without flinching. "Your Majesty, I do not agree with your estimates. Department Eleven would not have sent someone for the job unless he was very alert, very quick, and very deadly. And some of the barbarians hate him, so he'll be on his guard.

"And as for the barbarians not harming you, I believe Sunto made it clear that most of them regard Sky Chief as the emissary of God. I'd say the odds were excellent of your being killed, whether or not you succeeded in killing Sky Chief.''

Alf Mergalf spoke without rising. "Your Majesty, we cannot risk you. If the odds were nine to one in your favor, I *might* say yes, but if we are invaded from both north and south, and Trogeir is missing or dead . . . My lord, you may not appreciate how important the monarch has traditionally been to Lokar, how central to its people. And in your, ah, years on the throne, in your wisdom and the strength of your being, you have brought this to a level not reached before. Regardless of invasions, with Trogeir on the throne, Lokar will win.''

Boru shook his head, unyielding. "You are overlooking two things. One is human lives. If I kill Sky Chief, there probably will be no war. Thousands of lives will be saved, many of them Lokaru.''

"Your Majesty," the prime minister put in, "those *ifs* are too large. If you go and do not succeed, well, Alf was right about the king and the people. If you fail and Lokar has to fight without you, it will be to the people as if Voroth had forsaken them. Lokar could very easily lose the war. Then people who would otherwise be free would be serfs for long generations.''

Free? thought Boru. *How free are they now, depending on a king and on Voroth?*

As if he'd heard the thought, Larsa went on. "And they would lose more then just the freedom they have now. They would lose the freedom we're working toward—they and the rest of Thegwar.'' He paused, then shifted gears smoothly. "Sire, you are all we could have hoped for, and more. There is not one of us, I think, who isn't deeply impressed by the quick and remarkable way you adjusted to the situation, at the intelligence and ethics you've brought with you to the throne, and the sense of responsibility you've shown to your new kingdom and your people.''

He paused again, sighed, then surprisingly grinned. "Your Majesty, you said we were overlooking two things. You told us one of them and then I interrupted. I believe we already know the second thing, but perhaps you still would like to tell us.''

The king looked inward, recollecting, then at Larsa and around at the others. Everyone at the table was looking steadily at him. "Maybe you do at that. The second thing I was going to say was that I am the king, and in the last analysis not subject to your veto. But even the king is subject to the laws of the universe, and hence to logic. I will not insist on going north to confront Sky Chief."

He sat down heavily, then spoke from his chair. "Gentlemen, this king business is hard work. I'd like you to leave now, with my appreciation for what you are and what you do. But Kyril, you stay here. I need to talk with you."

The others got up, some nodding to him, and left without saying more.

"Larsa was right, you know," Golovin said when they were alone. "About what you've brought to the throne. Each of them has gained certain abilities which you still don't have—these things aren't accomplished overnight. And Trogeir had gone further than any of them. But you have a certain genius—a genius for decision and action greater than any of them has displayed yet.

"Tonight though, something else intruded itself into your computations. I could see it there."

You could see it? thought the king. *It will be interesting to see what you see.*

"So why don't you get a nap after you hear petitions, and eat a lunch," Golovin suggested. "Then we can get together and sort it out."

The king of Lokar nodded. "You went through this sort of thing with Trogeir years ago, didn't you?"

Golovin smiled. "When he was still a boy we'd gone through a lot of it. He was bright to begin with. But as I continued my research, I learned a lot more. We did some new procedures, he and I, only the week before he was killed.

"I trained him to be an operator too. I would develop a procedure theoretically and *he* would test it on *me* first. Then I would test it on a couple of staff members. When it was debugged and I was satisfied with it, I'd use it on Trogeir and the cabinet. Development has been slower and more irregular than I'd hoped—there is something I've missed, haven't found yet—but we've made a lot of progress."

Boru nodded. "And what's the end of all this, Kyril? Where does it lead?"

"It leads to—greater rationality, increased competence,

even increased genius. And those, of course, lead to saner and less government, much less danger of war, greater security as man expands into new sections of the galaxy. What it eventually leads to, time will tell. Perhaps you'll have some thoughts on that yourself soon, Your Majesty.''

Boru looked thoughtfully at his advisor. "Why do you call me 'Your Majesty,' Kyril?"

"Why do you think, sire?"

"Hm-m. . . . Because—I'm the king and it goes with the job.''

Golovin grinned broadly. "Exactly, Your Majesty. You've hit the nail on the head!''

"Another question: they were reading my mind in there, weren't they?''

"If you mean telepathically, to the best of my knowledge, none of them were. Any one of them will occasionally know directly what someone else is thinking, in a sort of instantaneous knowing, but none of them does this routinely or controls it yet. Nor do I.

"But they are all bright. They began bright and they've become more so. So they could follow your reasoning and extrapolate—see where it was leading. Not very esoteric but quite effective.''

"What do you know about telepathy, Kyril? Selena says you've been exploring the phenomenon with her.''

Golovin smiled ruefully. "At this point I know quite a lot about it but not yet enough to do much with the knowledge. Telepathy is only one facet of ability, and I've never had anyone with Selena's talent to work with before, so I hadn't given it much attention.

"Apparently in the great majority of instances when someone is aware of a telepathic communication, it's from someone they have strong affinity with. And in most instances it's either an emotion that's received or a communication with a strong emotional content. It's as if emotion ordinarily provides the power behind the signal while a mutual affinity provides the channel.

"What makes Selena especially interesting is her ability to perceive thoughts that have little or no emotional force, and from total strangers. This is actually a different phenomenon.''

"I'd like to be a telepath," the king said. "Think you could deliver that somewhere up the line?''

"Possibly. I'd like to. But you have another talent that is more valuable; you ordinarily take the correct action at critical points, even without what would seem to be the requisite information. That's how you survived into your thirties in a very hazardous profession.

"So far as humankind is concerned, the ability to get intended results is the supreme ability, senior to every other. How it operates, the basic laws involved, were worked out by Nikolai Alexeevitch Kubiak. Here on Thegwar my self-appointed task has been to nurture and expand ability, starting with the ruling strata. It has involved some very interesting research.

"Ability, Your Majesty, is what has lifted humankind out of primitivism. Not idealism, not greed. Not opinion. Ability applied to intention. But our institutions—our cultures and governments and games—carry the seeds of their own destruction. We must also be able to understand what is happening and be able to correct as necessary."

Golovin got up. "This all sounds terribly serious, but it's nothing to feel concern about, sire. We're doing nicely. *You're* doing *very* well. However, it is possible to feel somewhat uncomfortable on occasion.

"If you will nap after hearing petitions, and then eat, we can look together at what was going on with you in the meeting."

Late that evening Boru stepped out onto the balcony into a light fall of new snow, carrying the pulse-beam radio Wan Larmet had left with him. It was already set with the parking coordinates of the *Slengeth Büed*; he simply dialed a beam width suitable for a hand-held instrument and turned it on.

"*Slengeth Büed*, this is Surface Five. Over."

"This is *Slengeth Büed*. Over."

"*Slengeth Büed*, the next time you're in contact with Surface Four—it's time to tell him about the impending barbarian invasion. Tell him to get ready to move his people south. As soon as the barbarians mobilize, let him know so he can get out of their way. And when he comes south, ask him to warn the other outposts along the river. Over."

"Understood, Surface Five. Will comply. And Surface Five, Surface Two is very anxious to start the invasion. Earlier today he had me check the snow depth along the

Tilkenmor River; it's snowing there now. Still short of the required depth by about thirty centimeters, but it's getting there. You don't have forever to get ready. Over."

"Thank you, *Slengeth Büed.* Understood. Surface Five over and out."

"You're welcome. *Slengeth Büed* out."

TWENTY-SIX

Looking down at the forest, a casual observer might not have noticed them at once. But at second glance he would have. Twelve thousand barbarian warriors moved through the trees in squad-size files, their traveling format varying somewhat with the terrain and the abundance of blown-down trees and other impediments. At any time they occupied from ten to twenty square kilometers of ground, sifting southward among the slim dense evergreens and occasional stands and groves of naked *osti* and *tuusari*, crossing creeks, bogs, burns, and occasional lakes—a long, irregular, dangerous horde like a migration of erect, frost-resistant army worms.

They'd been traveling for twenty-six days on a march anticipated to take twenty, and Vasily Yakut's usually poor disposition had grown vile. Not one of the warchiefs had ever directed or controlled more than two hundred warriors at a time—ten to maybe eighty was usual. And neither Yakut nor McKedrick had commanded or coordinated troops before. The clan chiefs wore no watches, the warriors had a markedly primitive sense of time, and it was a major project to break camp and get them underway as an army in the morning.

It was similarly difficult to keep the army from fragmenting. For one thing, the men were tired of eating jerky, jerky, jerky—had been tired of it for at least fifteen days. Lead units and flank units, when they came upon fresh tracks of big game, would not infrequently disperse and go hunting meat. Often they would stop to shoot at a partridge-like nokua in a tree. When they tracked down game and killed it, of course they stopped to dress it, and there had been fights, with men killed, over the carcass of a hreen or wild peeran.

Each Lokarn holding they'd come to along the river they had ransacked and fired. But the settlers, two weeks gone, had driven their livestock ahead of them, leaving nothing edible.

Finally even the jerky began to run low, which had three principal effects: the tribesmen started much more promptly in the morning, they traveled faster through the day, and they got in more fights. There was an increased sense of urgency to arrive among the Kuutonsisa and their livestock.

Initially the two agents found they could not rely on most of the existing clan warchiefs to coordinate anything with another clan. This was a contingency that had not occurred to the office-bound planners back on Earth; otherwise they might have included an ex-space marine officer among the Great Spirit's emissaries, to organize and direct the army. The assumption had been that barbarian warriors would naturally know how to mount an invasion.

Only belatedly, as the clans had gathered among the frozen groves of stick-like arctic trees to begin their trek south—only then in the quarreling and confusion had Yakut and McKedrick realized the horrid truth—they, unprepared, were the de facto field commanders as well as the instigators and overlords.

So they had coped, and made a maximum effort to identify chiefs and subchiefs who could function in larger unit commands. Gradually they had developed an organization and a set of recognized commanders. It had taken unyielding intention, a lot of roaring, and some clouts on the head.

Men of the Bear Clan would not, of course, take commands from a chief of the Wolf Clan or the Eagle Clan or . . . But within a tribe it began to be possible to get a *chief* of the Bear Clan and a *chief* of the Eagle Clan to accept orders from a chief of the Wolf Clan when the chain of command had been firmly established and insisted upon forcefully by Sky Chief or Sun Chief—Yakut or McKedrick.

To top it off, Yakut had broken one of his lightweight Terran skis partway through the trek. Snarling, he'd commandeered a ski from a barbarian, leaving him with a ski-maker to fashion a new one from the tough wood of a young tuusari tree. The magnetic binding on the broken ski was not removable, so he'd had to use the toe strap. Thus the new ski was not only twice the weight of the old, but exasperatingly awkward until he got used to it.

McKedrick had avoided talking to him as far as possible for two days afterward. Using the mismatched skis together was a nuisance, so after two days of muttered curses, Yakut took advantage of a meat fight among some warriors and scavenged the skis from a dead man.

He'd begun to suspect, when they found Jussvek abandoned, that the Lokaru had been warned. When a day later they found Jusstoniss also abandoned, he was sure of it. He'd radioed Larmet then and asked if there was any sign of military activity in the settled districts. Larmet had replied with malicious but concealed satisfaction that there was. He didn't say it was by farmers; Yakut hadn't asked, and Larmet was volunteering nothing to him.

Initially the situation had exasperated Yakut severely, but he'd adjusted. He had looked forward to descending unexpectedly on the settled districts, to overrun and waste a lot of territory and people. It would do warrior morale a lot of good. But the principal purpose of the invasion was to draw and tie up a major part of the Lokarn army, and that, he told himself, would be accomplished as well with the enemy forewarned.

Each night when the army made camp, he radioed Larmet. Finally in the pitch black of a winter morning, when the taciturn warriors were crawling stiff and surly from their robes, couriers spread the word through the encampment: they were almost there. They would descend on the land of the Kuutonsisa in just a few hours and indulge in their first fight.

Morale jumped: the monotony was about to end, and surely such a mighty force could not be withstood. They were the People, each man a skilled archer, a more or less practiced swordsman. And the Great Spirit was with them.

It was nearly full light, the sun about to rise, when the first squads, filing across a long strip of frozen bog, came under archery by a Lokarn patrol. Hissing arrows killed and wounded several tribesmen. Unordered, a number of warriors rushed toward the source among the trees ahead, several more falling before the shooting ceased and the Lokaru fled. The tribesmen pursued the patrol at first, but the warriors carried their full travel packs while the Lokaru were traveling light. So when the first fire of anger had cooled, the pursuers stopped and waited for the rest.

An hour later, with no further contact, lead elements came to the edge of the broad cleared district Sunto had seen seven years earlier. They stopped, impressed, and sent the shouted word back down the files to close up and halt, as Sky Chief had preordered. The dispersed horde began to condense, the warriors eager but unsure what would happen next.

Their lead officers looked out over a wall of loosely heaped stones that the farmers had, over some years, picked from the fields and dragged there on sledges to pile out of the way. The wall was high as a man, for the soil here was a stony till plain. Now wind-sculpted dunes of snow lay along it, and spread out from it like fingers, and in places the top of the wall had been scoured so the stones could be seen.

Another wall, older and higher, lay parallel some hundred meters farther, and a series more beyond it. Occasional tall trees stood along the walls, their feet deep in stones. Saplings had sprouted along the bases of the walls and been chopped back, but in places formed low screens. Here and there, nearby and in the distance, groups of log buildings huddled— barns and sheds and houses—the barns in particular impressing the barbarians by their height.

At intervals the stone walls had gaps wide enough for haywagons to pass through, and through one of these the Lokarn patrol had passed, far enough ahead that only their tracks could be seen.

Sky Chief and Sun Chief arrived not long after the first ranks, with their party of principal officers and couriers. The two holy men stood on their skis, scanning the clearing; the tracks of the patrol were the only sign of activity they could spy. Otherwise there was only the dry, windswept snowscape, perfect white in the morning sun.

"You wouldn't want to bet they're not out there behind that next wall, would you?" McKedrick asked.

Yakut glowered across the snow.

"Let's send a patrol through the gap where the tracks go," the Canadian suggested. "See what happens."

Yakut shook his head; he was the one in-charge. "They're

either there or they're not, and we came here to fight.'' He turned, looking into his memory for the tribe and clans leading the march that day. ''Paaro-Kaati,'' he said, ''have the Kolu Tantar, clans one through eight, spread out along the wall.'' He spoke over his shoulder to McKedrick. ''They're not out there. The patrol isn't that much ahead of us, and they haven't had time to man a line. They wouldn't crouch out there in the snow day after day on the chance we'd show up. Hell, they'd all freeze to death!''

When the designated clans had lined up, a shouted order was passed along the line, and the warriors clambered on their skis over the drifted wall or funneled through its gaps into the field behind. The lead rank had gone maybe twenty meters when the first flight of arrows arched toward them along the whole line. Men began to fall. Some of the warriors still behind the wall stopped to return the fire, but the distance was long for their short cavalry-style bows; their leaders shouted them angrily over the wall and into the field.

The arrows soon stopped as the defending yeomen took up their ski poles and retreated. When the barbarians surmounted the second wall, they could see the fleeing Kuutonsisa hurrying across the snow toward the gaps in the wall beyond. They weren't many; a few hundred. They could easily be defeated. Some of the warriors set aside their ski poles to send out arrows of their own, but most, under the shouts of their leaders, spurred on.

Only to discover that another line of Kuutonsisa waited behind the next wall, and their long bows easily reached the attackers. More and more dark bundles lay staining the snow.

A strange and stupid assault, it was no battle, and by midday the losers had conquered the district all the way across to the great forested swamp on the other side. If anyone had counted, he'd have found more than five hundred dead men out of the north, and as many others more or less disabled, with more than a few who had minor wounds.

The Lokaru had left forty-three dead behind them, most of them killed when they stayed to try to help some wounded comrade. A similar number left the field with wounds. Nowhere were they brought to bay to stand at close range on their skis atop a hundred and ten centimeters of snow exchanging point-blank archery—the ''infighting'' of ski troops in deep snow, a sword charge being impossible while both hands were occupied with ski poles.

When the tribesmen reached the forest on the south side, they stopped, as ordered by their leaders. The timber there had been heavily logged, was littered with treetops impractical to ski through, and in places was almost impenetrable with osti saplings that had sprouted in the openings. The Lokaru had left the field via a wagon road and major log-skidding trails, along which ambushes could be expected.

A few minutes later the emissaries of God arrived, dour and brusque. Their army had just won thirty-five square kilometers of snow and six hundred empty buildings exclusive of privies. Virtually no food was found. The warriors were glad to crowd into the buildings, make fires, and lick their wounds. Yakut and McKedrick prepared to question the two wounded prisoners they'd gotten.

And one question stuck in the back of Yakut's mind: how had the Lokaru known in time? How had they been able to have their people in position?

The Lokarn farmhouse was almost luxurious: it had three large rooms, each with its own stove, its own exit, and a floor of boards. Yakut decided it must have been the home of the district's headman, and declared it his command post. He and McKedrick shared the main room; their eight principal war chiefs occupied the others. The two had put their boots on boot pegs on the wall behind the stove; they'd hardly had them off for twenty-six days, and the place smelled of them.

The principal chiefs, called in for conference, stood with expressions ranging from surly through glum to apprehensive. They expected a chewing out from Sky Chief, who viewed them from a fur-lined chair. He surprised them: though he scowled, he was neither hostile nor antagonistic.

"Warriors, chiefs," he said, "it was not a good day for the People."

They murmured assent.

"The Kuutonsisa beat you up today. But not because they are better fighters; they are not as good."

There were grunts that could mean anything. The chiefs could not see where this was leading.

"They beat you up because your tactics were wrong." He

turned to his co-agent. "Sun Chief, tell the chiefs what we will do tomorrow."

McKedrick had been sitting; now he got up. He was a hand shorter than Yakut but almost as heavy and extremely strong. His hair was off-blond, not unlike many of the barbarians, but his eyes were blue against his tan. His hardness, ruthlessness, was less naked than Yakut's, his occasional brutality entirely tactical, not compulsive. When he spoke, his tone commonly was slightly bored, rarely truculent or overbearing.

Bastard, he thought toward Yakut, *you can't figure it out so you dump it on me.* But there was no heat in the thought, and he looked the assembly over casually. "Chiefs, here is what happened," he said. "There were not nearly as many of them as there were of you. If you had closed with them, you could have killed them all. But at a distance you were at a great disadvantage because their bows shoot farther. The Great Spirit has a law that longbows shoot farther than short bows, and they have bows much longer than yours. And they did not let you get close enough to shoot many of them.

"You captured this place, which grows much food in summer, because you are very brave. You refused to let them stop you. But you lost too many warriors because you attacked along a long front all at once.

"Now listen to me, and listen closely: you should have attacked at one point, so that only a small part of the enemy could have reached your warriors with their arrows. You should have kept pouring warriors at one gap in their wall until they were pouring through. Then *all* the Kuutonsisa would have had to hurry away to get behind the next wall, most of them without having shot an arrow. If they did not run away, the warriors would have caught them between the walls.

"Do you see that?"

Heads nodded. Agreements were grunted. All eyes were on McKedrick. Yakut was grinning now, somewhat bemused.

"All right. So when the first warriors went through the gap, the Kuutonsisa would either all run away, or they would come from farther along the wall to help fight the warriors who'd broken through. You would have kept a steady stream of men flowing through the gap. Then you would have attacked the next two gaps, one on either side. You see? The soldiers there would either have gone to help fight the warriors who had broken through, or they would have already run away, or they would have stayed to shoot at the two new attacks. If they stayed to shoot at the new attacks, they could not help their friends, and more and more warriors would pour through the first gap. Then the warriors would have many of them caught between the walls, and would have killed them.

"Do you see how that would have happened?"

There were more nods, more murmured agreements. Eyes and faces were lighting up. McKedrick continued.

"At the same time, back out of sight of the Kuutonsisa, you should have sent some clans around the end of the open land through the forest, to see if they could get behind them.

"But today is over, and that is not the way it happened. The Kuutonsisa bloodied your nose; too many warriors died."

He scanned them again, hard-eyed but not accusing. "That is all right. Tomorrow is coming and you have gained knowledge, the knowledge that you need. Now you know that you must close with the Kuutonsisa, because their bows are long. You learned that the Kuutonsisa like to shoot and run away before your arrows can reach them, and that where possible it is well to get behind them. You learned that the Kuutonsisa are clever; they take advantage of things like stone walls, and forest that is hard to ski through. And they like to use ambushes.

"So you must be clever too. Sky Chief and I are not your war chiefs; we were not sent here to do it for you. We made Paaro-Kaati the principal war chief who would command all the People. We made the rest of you the war chiefs of tribes, and certain other men the war chiefs of clans, so that Paaro-Kaati's commands are obeyed by *all* the warriors. We have made it so the warriors of *all* the clans obey the commands of Paaro-Kaati.

"Each warrior must fight to carry out the objectives Paaro-Kaati gives to you. Each leader of a group must give the orders and leadership necessary so that the commands of Paaro-Kaati are carried out. Because Paaro-Kaati cannot personally go throughout the army and throughout the battlefield, and be everywhere throughout the forest and order each warrior. He cannot be in this fight and that, with this group and that, all at once."

He looked around. "Do you see that?"

They nodded and he continued. "The Great Spirit has decided that the clans of the north are his chosen. But you must be worthy of him. Tonight the Kuutonsisa"—he paused, then went on more slowly for effect—"tonight the Kuutonsisa are *laughing* around their fires, saying how many of the People they killed while losing so few of their own. But tomorrow—tomorrow they will not laugh. Tonight before you sleep, you chiefs will decide what to do, and tomorrow the army will find the enemy again.

"Now go to your own place and do not disturb us. Sky Chief and I will make medicine and commune with the Great Spirit."

TWENTY-SEVEN

When the war chiefs had left, Yakut grinned at McKedrick. "You should have been a bureaucrat," he said in Terran. "You do a great job of passing the buck."

McKedrick didn't flash at him, just walked around as if restless. "Pass the buck? All we've got with these people is elevation; we've told them we're higher than they are. If we give the battle orders, we make a certain number of mistakes." He turned and eyed Yakut. "Like you did this morning."

"In case it didn't occur to you, we're goddamn lucky none of them understood Lokarit when we interrogated the prisoners this afternoon. What would they think if they knew they got beat up by a bunch of shit-kicking farmers and haven't hardly seen any king's soldiers yet? Beat up because of a stupid dumb-ass order from you-know-who. And they remember who.

"Dumb mistakes *are* going to get made, you can depend on that; that's a part of wars. So those mistakes had better be theirs. Because if *we* make mistakes, the next thing you know they'll start asking themselves questions, and there goes the elevation!''

He stopped, stuffed an old briar pipe with stale tobacco, and lit it. Remarkably, Yakut said nothing, just waited.

''We're in a war now, Yakut, not playing games with some ignorant chiefs and shamans. Giving some poor bozos a few dope trips and hypnotizing a few leaders isn't going to cut it anymore. Not here. And ninety-nine out of a hundred of these guys didn't even get any dreams. Even some of their war chiefs didn't—practically none of the subchiefs. And there's nothing like skiing fifteen hundred kilometers to burn the drugs out of the system and get back in the real world again.

''We're living on our goddamn reputation, brother. They're taking us on hearsay, on word of mouth from medicine chiefs and elders, most of them fifteen hundred kilometers from here. So if we start looking bad, we're not going to last long.

''And if they tell us to go fuck ourselves, or if we have to cut out to keep from getting lynched—if these guys decide to cut their losses and head north for home, and the Lokaru go back south and beat the snot out of the southerners, I for one don't like to think about the reception we'll get in the Department. Or what will happen if we try to drop out of sight.''

He fixed Yakut with a flinty eye. ''We can get away with not being winners here, but we sure as hell better carry out our assignment of tying up a sizeable piece of the Lokarn army. That means we don't give dumb-ass orders. It means that any orders we do give are broad, general orders like 'tomorrow we move out before dawn and hit the next district.' Then, if the battle gets screwed up, it's their fault, not ours. But we give them the best damn critique we can so they don't get discouraged and don't get butchered.''

His pipe had gone out, and he relit while Yakut brooded. ''You think I gave a stupid order today?'' Yakut asked.

''I don't think it, I know it.''

''It would have worked fine if they hadn't been waiting for us, all lined up and ready.''

''But they were. 'Would have' doesn't buy whiskey; it won't even get you a cheap beer. Maybe if you hadn't been high, you wouldn't have been so stupid. What were you using? Zippos?''

Yakut's face darkened but he did not retort; his eyes went

elsewhere. *How had the Lokaru been ready, waiting in the snow and morning cold behind their stone walls as if they knew we were about to hit them?* The prisoners hadn't had the answer to that one. They'd just followed orders.

He put his attention back on McKedrick, who was standing in a thin cloud of tobacco smoke. The Canadian was his junior on this job; but Department Eleven policy allowed a subordinate to take over, at his own risk, if he felt he could prove that gross errors had been made which endangered the mission.

At last Yakut spoke, ignoring McKedrick's rhetorical question about the drug. "The prisoners said the king is running the war. That means whoever was supposed to hit him missed. Killing the king was a key part of the overall plan; that's what they told us."

"Killing the king's got nothing to do with us," McKedrick answered. "Our job is to keep a big piece of the Lokarn army tied up in the north."

Yakut got slowly to his feet and without comment dressed for the outdoors. McKedrick watched without questioning. At the door, Yakut turned and spoke. "I'm going for a run on the skis. To blow that rotten pipe smoke out of my head."

McKedrick watched him leave, and snorted. *Pipe smoke's not what's wrong with your head, psych-bait.*

His pipe had gone out again. He laid it on the table, stripped, and began stretching exercises preparatory to his kung fu forms.

He was asleep when Yakut returned, but woke at his entrance. He expected to see the sweat start on Yakut's face, once in from the cold, had assumed he'd been out pushing his body, running hard over the snow.

Instead he carried a bundle of furs under one arm, a longbow and quiver over his shoulders, and a grin on his face.

"What's up?" McKedrick asked.

Yakut chuckled. "I hunted around for Lokaru bodies; had some of the gooks do it, actually. Until they found one big enough—husky and not too short." He held up a parka and pair of fur pants in one hand, a woolen shirt in the other. "Had a hell of a time getting them off him. He was frozen solid. Had to get help and break both shoulders."

Yakut's eyes were as strange as his mood. "My friend," he began confidentially . . . He paused, head bobbing slightly as if examining the phrase and approving it. "My friend," he repeated, "I'm going to the Lokaru and find the king. Then I'm going to kill him. Because this job here is the shits." He began to change into the new clothes. "I've got a few warriors to go with me as far as the riverbank so one of these gooks doesn't accidentally shoot me in my new clothes."

The mittens had gauntlets which made up for the shortness of the sleeves. The fur pants were also short, but tailoring was scarcely for style in the wardrobe of the typical Lokarn yeoman. The boots were too small, so he put the similar barbarian-style mukluks back on. When he was fully dressed, Yakut turned again to the Canadian, who was sitting up now with his feet on the floor.

"You got anything to say?" Yakut demanded. It was a challenge, the dark eyes bright in the lamplight.

This time it was McKedrick who grinned. "Be my guest. I wouldn't be surprised if you pulled it off."

Again Yakut chuckled, picked up the Lokarn longbow and quiver of nearly meter-long arrows, and went out.

Maybe he can, McKedrick said to himself. *I wouldn't be surprised a bit. It's the sort of thing he's best at. And I won't have to worry about him screwing things up here.*

He lay back down. He'd tell the chiefs in the morning that the Great Spirit had sent Sky Chief to kill the Kuutonsisa king.

The moon was more than half full, the snow on the river reflecting its light shadow-free, illuminating the night with marvelous clarity. But Yakut was only vaguely aware of it, imperceptive of any beauty. Somewhere to the east he heard but did not heed the shrill distant keening of a wolf pack, so different and yet so like the wolf songs of Siberia and Canada.

There was actually very little of Yakut himself that was aware at the moment. What was functioning was primarily a body and the man's psychosis, the psychosis driving the body to carry out its commands.

Approximately at midstream he stopped, and from an inner pocket took his pulse-beam radio.

"*Slengeth Büed*, this is Yakut. Over."

There was a lapse of fifteen or twenty seconds, and he'd

begun to fume before the answer came. "This is *Slengeth Büed*. You caught me on the pot. Over."

"Larmet, where is the Lokarn command post around here? Over."

"Hell, I don't have the faintest idea. I don't pay attention to things like that. Over."

Anger clanked in hard on Yakut; he suppressed it. "You know where we fought today. You know where I'm calling from. Where's the nearest Lokarn military concentration? Over!"

Yeah, thought Larmet, *I saw where you fought today. Your guys got chopped all to hell. It should have been you, not them.* "Okay, I can give you that," he said. "It's the next settled district south. About ten kilometers down the river on the same side. The west side. There's an area of farms that starts there, about two to three times as big as the one you hit today, but with scattered woods in it and a regular town. The town is on the high bank above the river; that's probably where the command post would be. Over."

Yakut lagged for a moment, looking for further questions he should ask. He didn't find any. "Okay," he said, "Yakut over and out."

"*Slengeth Büed* out."

I wonder what that was all about, Larmet said to himself. If they were thinking of trying a night raid, they'd get a surprise: the command post was at a tiny village about six kilometers west of the river.

He sent a tight beam pulse to the command post coordinate, but Kinjok didn't have his set on; he was sparing his power cell. The Lokaru would just have to take care of themselves; they were good at that. But they wouldn't have creamed the barbarians the way they had today without old Larmet looking out for them.

Fifteen kilometers of skiing the river's sweeping curves in the moonlight did a lot for Yakut. Fifteen kilometers without a bunch of damned barbarians to herd, he told himself, and keep out of trouble with each other. McKedrick could have the fuckers! Fifteen kilometers with no blowdown areas to pick his way through, just unobstructed river, no god-awful brushy swamps. No marshes to cross, where the reeds kept the snow from settling and you sank to your knees every step, then had to lift your ski clear for the next. Here was only firmly settled snow with a wind slab on top, and cold enough for best traction.

By the time Yakut could see the town hunched in the cold on the high bank a kilometer and a half away, he was feeling better than he had for a long time. He was even enjoying the moonlight, the snow sparkle, the silence only broken now by the hiss of his skis.

As he approached the town, its low buildings and stone fort began to individuate in the night. Closer up he saw shore pilings for an absent dock, apparently a floating dock removed in the fall so it wouldn't be crushed and torn away when the meter and a half of ice went out in the spring.

At the shore, Yakut knelt and tied skins on his skis to climb the high bank. By the time they were secured and his mittens back on, his fingers were numb and wooden. He couldn't imagine settling this country by choice, sweating in summer, freezing in winter, laboring long hours with ax and grub hoe and shovel, clearing the forest, grubbing out stumps and boulders, building houses and barns—and all so you could bust your ass farming.

They had to be tough and they had to be dumb, he told himself, without looking at how he'd lived the past few months, or the past dozen years.

Near the top of the bank, a strong voice halted and challenged him. "Who's there? What're you doing?"

He could see them, bows in hand, standing above him beside the cart road that angled across the steep slope. Yakut's Lokarit was rather good, but unpracticed and accented, so he feigned a stammer to cover it.

"My, my name is Ya-Ya-Yakut. I, I, I w-was cut cut cut off by by th-th-the barbarians. I skiiied . . . around . . . in in in the w-woods until they they they stopped following me."

They let him come the rest of the way. He didn't have a unit, he explained, and they began to get a picture of a big retarded farm hand who'd hung around the militia, no doubt willing and maybe even good with a bow, but who couldn't understand or follow any but the simplest orders. They told him where he could find a place to sleep, and hoped he'd find it, then returned their attention to the river ice.

*　　*　　*

In thc predawn morning, waiting in line with a bowl he'd been given, Yakut asked if the king was there. The man he was talking to raised his eyebrows at that.

"The king? The king ain't around here. He's way off down at his palace, probably, looking after things. They're expecting another war down there too, you know, even bigger than the one we've got up here."

"H-h-h-his p-palace? Wh-wh-where is . . . that?"

The wiry little farmer pursed his lips. *Strong as an ox*, he told himself, *and just about as dumb*. "Well," he said patiently, "if you was to follow the river south and went for about seven days hard, you'd come to a *big* town. *Way* bigger than Arnoless here. It's got lots and lots of buildings. One of them is like the fort here, but a lot bigger, and that's where the king lives, in that big fort. That's his castle."

He peered curiously up at Yakut. "How come you're interested in the king?"

"I waaant . . . to be his f-f-friend, and prote-te-tect him from the bar-bar-bar-barians."

"Well . . . That's good. I'll tell you though, the king's already got a lot of friends around him." The man looked around mentally for some place to send the big dummox, where someone would look after him. He was probably great for loading sleighs or wrestling boulders out of the ground. But the barbarians were expected today, and the lad would probably get confused and killed.

"But even a king can always use another friend," the farmer went on. "Yeah, that's a good idea, Yakut, it surely is. Why don't you go on south after breakfast, go on south and find the king. A big strong fella like you, you'd be a good protector."

When he'd done eating, Yakut got a large field ration of beef jerky and cheese and hard bread, put them in a pack he'd been issued, tied on the sleeping furs he'd used that night, and started south again on the river.

And now he had something to pass the time with. He held conversations with himself to practice speaking Lokarit with the northern accent he'd been hearing.

TWENTY-EIGHT

"Interesting how war plans usually don't work out," said the king. "Ours, theirs, anyone's."

He stood with Palek in front of a large window, in a villa overlooking the Great River. Five kilometers south, cut off from view by a hill, was Tonlik. The villa, Hyos, belonged to the family of senior minister Gundith Vattenkarm. As a location for the war office, it had two principal advantages over Krogaskott: there was a break in the west-shore bluffs directly across the river, and the highway from the southwest came down there. With headquarters at Hyos, couriers from the southern front, or to the southern front, didn't have to double back south or ride through the city. Also, general government operations at Krogaskott were not subject to the distractions of war traffic, war affairs, and to a degree, military rumors.

There was actually another important advantage neither Trogeir/Boru nor Palek had looked at yet: if the city should be threatened, their location here would facilitate a more objective, exterior, point of view.

The principal disadvantage so far had been that the king commuted. He rode out openly from Krogaskott each predawn morning and returned openly after dark; hence no rumor could be credited that the crown had fled or abandoned the city. But commuting, he was not constantly available to the war office, as he would have been had he simply moved into Hyos. And of course there was a certain risk of being attacked while traveling, even though he rode with a sizeable troop of guards.

They'd moved operations to Hyos three days earlier, after the armies of Garvas and Prozhask had attacked across the border. In the north, Larmet reported, the barbarians now were fifty kilometers into the settled districts, moving south in a broad spearhead movement west of the river. Yeomanry from the districts on both sides of the barbarian thrust had moved in behind to harry and distract them.

In the southern border region, a four-day thaw had shrunk the snow cover to about twenty centimeters, but the ground beneath was still frozen, giving a free fast field for cavalry. The invading southern armies were fighting notably better than expected—even those of Prozhask, whose soldiers were traditionally reluctant fighters and ready retreaters when outside their home districts. Apparently the war had been effectively promoted to them, no doubt thanks to Department Eleven. It also undoubtedly helped that their conscript infantry enjoyed the unusual, for them, protection of chain mail.

The Lokar cavalry, generally superior to the southerners, had been favored by the lack of deep snow. But that same lack did not permit the yeomen archers to be nearly as effective as hoped for because they were more susceptible to being charged and overrun by mounted southerners. Also, the unexpected willingness of southern pikemen to hold ranks and confront the cavalry had briefly proven costly to Lokarn mounted forces.

The tactic which had quickly evolved was to match Lokarn archery against southern infantry—both pikemen and swordsmen—with the yeomen falling back as necessary when hard-pressed by the southern foot troops. Lokarn cavalry then were used primarily to protect the bowmen from southern cavalry, which otherwise, under the conditions, might utterly destroy them.

Both in the north and the south, the Lokaru were giving up ground rather than committing the forces necessary to hold it, allowing the enemy to advance but charging him dearly in blood, holding back sizeable reserves to strike heavily the expected Bleesbrok seaborne assault on Tonlik.

But in the south there wasn't a lot of ground available for the trade; Tonlik wasn't that far from the border. Thus more of the army had been committed there than the Lokarn high command felt comfortable about.

Now Larmet had radioed that a fleet of about a hundred ships was approaching Tonlik Sound, a day or so away unless an offshore wind developed.

A rider had been crossing the ice from the west bank, but

as the two men watched, he turned south on the river road instead of riding up the slope to Hyos. "True, Your Majesty," Palek answered. "While certain elements of war plans often survive events—goals, purposes, even policies—the steps of carrying them out commonly get changed all over the place. Enemies of any consequence and ingenuity seldom cooperate, and of course you can't rely on the weather."

The king turned from the scene outside and looked at his minister. "Where did you learn about war, Palek? Until now, Lokar's only had two in your lifetime, and neither more than a few border skirmishes."

Palek smiled ruefully. "In my generation and that preceding, I am probably the least martial male of a military family. I served only briefly, in my teens, not long after the brief conflict with Prozhask. But I was exposed to the family tradition and the family library. Perhaps, sire, you do not appreciate the role books played in Lokar among the professional and merchant families, even before the recent advent of printing.

"Then also, of course, some of us in Lokar learned to read Standard Terran and were able to import books—something we look forward to renewing in the future. So I've studied much of war, from Alexander to Adolphus, even Marlborough and Charles XII. Of later periods I have read only casually."

He smiled. "So in the comfort of my study I've become quite a general for paper wars. Fortunately we have real generals for the real war."

"And what makes a 'real general'?"

"Um. Knowledge of course. Experience in moving and coordinating large numbers of men in military evolutions. Toughness. The ability to give commands that are followed without hesitation. . . . And not being stupid."

"Where does military genius fit?"

"Ah! Military genius goes beyond that, sire. A Hannibal, an Attila, a Genghis Khan operate *in* the general reality but *from* a different reality."

One of Kyril's people, thought Boru. "And where does that leave us? And Lokar?"

"With generals who are probably competent but who've never had a chance to demonstrate genius."

Boru nodded, eyes hard. "Let's check with Larmet," he

said, "and see if he's finished his examination of the fleet." He switched on the radio. "Wan, this is Trogeir. Over."

"Right, Your Majesty. I have a ship count and some other observations for you. The ships fall into two categories. The bulk of them—seventy-seven—are stubby, blunt-nosed, broad-beamed tubs that are almost all two-masted and square rigged. They carry a blue, yellow, and green flag—three vertical bars. They're full-decked, and I can't tell what's below but I don't see any sign of hay or anything else that suggests cavalry. They've got stacks of boats secured upside down on the deck, for landing I suppose, and they'd never accommodate peernu.

"Typical dimensions are thirty meters long and seven across the beam; I don't know how many troops that might come to. But they've got to have room for supplies and crew, and they've all got to sleep somewhere where they don't freeze, so I suppose it's less than one hundred soldiers per ship, even though they're probably crowded in pretty tight. Say seven thousand troops and equipment.

"Then there's another category of ships, fifteen of them. They're longer and slimmer, with three masts rigged fore and aft. They're keeping a little separate, and their flag is white with some sort of yellow emblem. No signs of peernu on them either.

"And that's all I've got. Any questions? Over."

The king looked questioningly at Palek, who looked as if he'd just been hit. Palek shook his head no.

"No questions now," the king replied, "but there may be when we've talked it over here. Thanks a lot, Wan. Trogeir over and out."

"Any time, Your Majesty. Larmet out."

The king deactivated the set, his eyes on Palek. "What is it?" he asked.

"The seventy-seven are the Bleesbrokmen we've been expecting. But the others . . . Have you ever heard of the Khupraigneos? . . . Usually shortened to Gneos. They're the only nation I've heard of whose flag is white—white with a gold escutcheon.

"They're reputedly the best soldiers on the planet—very skilled, very disciplined, very arrogant. Culturally they're rather reminiscent of the Spartans of Terran antiquity, but maritime instead of agricultural. They live on an island in the sea of Cymlos, elitist seafaring soldiers who raid and trade primarily on the southern continent.''

Boru pursed his lips in a silent whistle. ''There,'' he said in a subdued voice, ''is another hidden factor. A sort of twelfth or eighteenth century commando, depending on whether you look at the weapons or the ships. Are you familiar with the concept of commando?''

''Yes, Your Majesty: a small, highly trained military force used for special missions, or a mission by such a force.''

''You've got it. And you don't send a commando to assault a routine objective. So what are they for, Palek?''

''It could be to assault Krogaskott.''

The king frowned thoughtfully. ''Try this on for size. They're here to take care of any problem situations—strong defensive positions, serious counterattacks, anything that's threatening or stopping the invasion force.''

''It sounds eminently logical, Your Majesty, but I wonder if the enemy high command is that astute. They certainly haven't been very astute in the north.''

Boru shook it off. ''The north is a throwaway campaign. All it's for is to tie up some of our forces. This is different. They're going to land in our back yard. This is the strike at our jugular,''

Palek looked at it. ''You're probably right, sire. I suppose we'd better give the information to General Vorss and see what action he takes.''

TWENTY-NINE

The nearly full moon was low, lighting the west-facing roof slopes, limning chimneys and chimney pots against the black sky. The street itself was in shadow, its old snow grayed by soot, thaw, and traffic.

Yakut rode a rough-coated, stiff-gaited peeran whose previous owner would no doubt go undiscovered until the snow melted. The agent had ridden a hundred kilometers since he'd taken possession the day before. His gait too would be stiff when he got down, but he was a man relatively insensitive to pain.

There were a few people, mostly pedestrians, already on the street; in an hour, dawn would pale the eastern sky.

Yakut rode with his parka hood thrown back, for the night was warm and damp, at about the freezing point, with the feel of still-distant spring. Tonlik was southern, by Lokarn standards, and there were no coastal mountains this far south to cut off the occasional encroachment of warm marine air.

In addition to a few coins, Yakut had found cheese in a saddlebag, and a hard cake of what seemed to be cornbread. (Like the potato and certain Earth-exotic plants, maize threatened to become galactic.) So he was not immediately concerned about food. He wanted a place to sleep under a roof, and as he rode, he cast about, watching for anything that suggested cheap lodging for travelers.

From up the street he heard hooves, and saw a largish group of mounted men coming. For some reason that he did not examine, he reined off to the side, pulled up his hood, and watched them approach. A beam from the lowering moon slanted between two buildings, lighting the riders as they passed voiceless in the night. They were helmeted and well-armed, rode erect and alert; their eyes touched him and went on.

All were in uniform except one. That one rode with his hood back, as Yakut had, and for a moment the gold circlet on his head was illuminated by the shaft of moonlight. Then they were past, their horses jogging south toward the outskirts of town.

Yakut didn't reach for his bow. He had never been a practiced archer, and had he been, he would not have tried just then for the king. For at that moment it occurred to him that he wanted not simply to kill this king but to talk to him, find out about him before he dealt the blow. Then he would strike him dead in some manner more suitable, more personal, than an arrow from ambush.

When their hoof falls had faded, he turned his own weary mount, kicked it into an unwilling trot, and followed them.

*   *   *

The sun had just set when the fleet anchored. They had not gone as far as they might have; they could have sailed several kilometers farther west before harbor ice would have stopped them. But here there was little risk of an arctic air mass freezing the ships into the ice pack.

And they had reason to assume that the time of their arrival had not been foreseen—that they could land and begin their march uncontested.

The Lokaru of course would surely know that a seaborne invasion was intended; they had their spies. And no doubt some lookout was galloping westward now, to alert the defense and bring them hurrying to battle.

Actually, of course, the Lokarn First Regiment—the Tonlik Regiment—which was regular army, and four reserve regiments had been sent out on foot before dawn from the military reservation east of the city. Like the rest of the Royal Army, all five were cavalry units trained to fight on foot when necessary. They'd hiked to the Royal Game Park that covered a large area of hills along the coast, bivouacked in the forest, and waited, a few men watching from the naked treetops.

They were impressed by the invasion fleet when it hove into view up the Sound. When it was seen definitely to have stopped, the army was quick-timed along the hill crest to a stretch opposite the fleet. From there they moved down the slope to take positions among the trees just above the beach. There they waited in the gathering dusk, not noticeable from the ships, which were anchored well off shore.

By that time boats of soldiers were rowing toward the beach, and the yeoman archery detachments took the foremost positions. When the first irregular rows of crowded boats were within effective bowshot, the archers stepped into the open—some twelve hundred of them—and sent flights of arrows that sleeted down deadly and unexpected, devastating those within reach. But warned now, the passengers in the boats that followed made a virtual roof of shields.

The archers held their fire then for a bit. The surf was not heavy, but the boats were small and the shallows rocky. Some boats, carried by the breakers into rocks, capsized or foundered. Once the invaders were out of the boats, whether they were dumped or disembarked more conventionally over the sides, the archers resumed their murderous point-blank fire.

Then the Lokarn soldiery charged through the line of archers and fell upon the landing Bleesbroku. The true battle began, the yeomen moving back up the hill away from the fray.

The Bleesbroku fought desperately, knowing they had to secure a sufficient beachhead to land reinforcements or be wiped out on the slippery shingle. By full dark they had two thousand men on land, fighting their way up the hillside from the beach, but progress was slow and terribly costly, and their success was not assured.

That was when the Gnessr hit. They'd landed unnoticed and uncontested eight kilometers northeast, the separation simply a precaution. From there they had quick-marched along the crest and now rolled up the Lokarn flank with savage surprise. Half an hour later the invaders owned a two-kilometer length of hillside and a sizeable zone along the top, pressing outward against a regrouped but shaky defense. By then the final invading troops had landed, and pulled their boats through and over the bodies on the beach up out of reach of any possible storms. The third front was a reality.

After Yakut had watched the king's party ride up to Hyos, he'd turned his worn peeran back into town and put it up at the livery stable on the square. Then he'd taken a room in the Three Bulls and slept.

But not all day. Later he robbed an affluent-looking house in the city's perimeter, clubbing to death the two domestics, wife, and older child, then ransacked the place for money. There wasn't as much as he'd have liked, but enough, he thought, to refit and last him while he made his way to Rosten, the lovely vacation palace of the king of Garvas.

He'd been to Rosten three times, flown there by Larmet—it had been his arrival point on Siegel's World, and he'd been taken there twice from the barrenlands. It was the command location for the project—convenient for the Garven king whose greedy cooperation was a key ingredient, and private and remote enough that the smuggler could land there secretly by night.

After the robbery, Yakut gorged himself at Tonlik's most prestigious eating place, which hadn't yet found a suitable replacement for its departed dancer. After that he bought a new wardrobe—sturdy and warm, but civilized, and in a dandified style that in Lokar would be considered a trifle florid.

To top it off, he'd bought a matched sword and dagger. He was not truly a master of the sword; it had no special attraction for him. But he had been trained in it during his years of martial arts instruction and was a superb natural athlete. He could have beaten ninety-nine percent of Thegwar's swordsmen, whose techniques were less sophisticated and whose standards of excellence not comparable to the oriental school in which he'd learned.

Next he'd tried to buy a better peeran but hadn't enough money left. Good saddle animals were always expensive and the war had inflated their value. He shrugged it off; when he was done with the king, a better mount would present itself one way or another.

During his meal and his bargaining, he heard people talking about the war and especially the enemy army that had landed on the Sound the night before. But he gave it little attention; he was interested simply in his own purpose, which he regarded with a sort of detached amusement. He had no doubt at all of his success.

Finally he went looking for his evening's entertainment. He had no intention of hiring it; he would find more pleasure in coercing it and strangling the evidence. By Tonlik standards, Yakut was a crime wave all by himself.

It was morning, the sun well up and slanting through the south windows. They'd just heard from a second courier, the second bearer of bad news from the new front since daybreak.

"So it's that bad," said the king to his principal general.

"I'm sending a courier to Klinta," Vorss replied, "ordering him to pull the Second Regiment at once and send it here on a forced march."

"The Second Regiment?" said the king. "Wait a minute. Let's look at that."

Vorss did not suppress his frown as the king went on. "The game park is forested hills, some of them rugged. Not cavalry country. Do you think it's a good idea to bring in twelve hundred of the best mounted troopers on the planet to use as infantry? Why not bring in another of the reserve regiments?''

''Your Majesty, the reservists simply aren't good enough. On foot or on horseback, we need the best in there. At the rate the enemy is advancing, they'll be at the city in three or four days.'' The general's wide square face was grim. ''If it was only the Bleesbroku, that would be another matter. But the Gnessr are too good.''

''You've already got the First Regiment there. They're regular army; they're as good as the Second. And there must be about as many of them as there are of the Gnessr.''

It pained Vorss to answer. ''They're not as good as the Gnessr either,'' he said, ''but they're considerably closer to it. They've been much more effective than the reserve regiments.''

The king walked to the window and looked southward toward the unseen threatened city. ''If you bring the Second Regiment here, that leaves only one regular army regiment on the southern front. And you've already said it's the regular cavalry that's made the difference there—that the reserve regiments aren't much better than the Garvnu. And the Garvnu and Prozhku outnumber us seriously there.''

''Your Majesty, we have no real choice! In three or four days the Bleesbroku and Gnessr will be ready to attack the city unless we can hold them, and with the Second Regiment we have a chance.''

''How good a chance?''

''Good. Fair at least. Just their arrival will make a big difference. The troops there now are desperate, and desperate men may fight hard, but usually not intelligently. And if we let things get worse . . .'' Vorss spread his hands to complete his statement.

''How long will it take them to get here?''

''A courier can reach them soon after nightfall, sire. They can be here by dawn, sleep in the barracks a few hours, and be in action late in the day.''

Jesus but I hate this, thought Boru. *We're spread so damn thin!* He looked around mentally for an alternative. There were only three regular army regiments; full time soldiers were an innovation on this part of the planet.

''Bring in one of the reserve regiments from the south,'' he said at last. ''They may not be as good as the regulars, but they're twelve hundred more good men, trained and willing. I will not risk our yeoman defense forces getting slaughtered by Garven cavalry."

Vorss matched eye contact with his king, groping through his exasperation for words. Then Palek spoke, and both the others turned to him.

"Your Majesty, if you please. Do you recall that the Gnessr did not unload troops from five of their ships?"

The king's reply was wary. "Yes. Larmet mentioned it."

"Does it make sense that they'd have uncommitted reserves on board? When and where could they use them more profitably than in battle last night and today?"

"What are you getting at, Palek?"

"Your Majesty, I believe those five ships hold only crew. They weren't sent to bring troops, they were sent to carry away cargo."

"So?"

"The Gnessr are notorious slave traders, Your Majesty, though in the past they have raided mostly in the tropics. They can probably jam two hundred or more captives in each ship. The capture of Tonlik could be a very profitable venture for them."

Boru stared at him, mouth slightly open, thunderstruck for a moment. Then he turned to Vorss. "My apologies, general. You've got your permission. Send for the Second Regiment."

Vorss's discipline was not enough to hide his relief. "Thank you, Your Majesty!" He saluted and strode from the room. They both watched him leave, and continued to look toward the closed door briefly after he'd gone.

"Palek," said the king, thoughtful again, "how are the Gnessr about champions? Do they put a lot of emphasis on certain special men? Would they take a severe morale loss if a Lokarn killed their greatest fighter?"

"I'm not sure, sire. I do know that in reading about them, I read nothing about any champion. Apparently they don't eulogize them."

"Um. Tell me, what would you have told Vorss if you were king and the danger of slaving hadn't come up?"

"I'd have let him bring up the Second Regiment. If we defeat the seaborne invasion, it won't be difficult to drive the Garvnu and Prozhku out of the country. But if we defeat Garvas and Prozhask while losing the city—well first, if we lose the city, we might well not defeat them. It would lift their morale and damage ours severely. But if we did lose the city and win on the southern front, it would be very difficult and costly of lives to take it back again, other than in ashes. Leaving forty-five thousand citizens homeless in mid-winter. Negotiation would be possible of course, but if anything is worse than the pride and arrogance of the Gnessr, it is the stubbornness of Bleesbrok in matters of conflict. Either of them is a much more difficult opponent than our southern neighbors.''

Boru stared at his minister of foreign affairs. ''You're right,'' he said. ''And I just realized a problem I've had. If I saw something I thought of as really undesirable, like risking the yeoman defense units, my attention was likely to stick there. It would trap my attention, and I couldn't look past it to evaluate the overall scene.''

Palek smiled. ''Maybe now that you're aware of it, it won't be a problem. At any rate, I notice you talked about it in the past tense.'' He stepped to a west window and looked out.

''Speaking of changes, Your Majesty, perhaps you'd care to look at the sky.'' He pointed northward.

The king looked. A band of high thin clouds had appeared over the northern horizon.

''Perhaps the weather that Wan Larmet mentioned in the north is going to visit us,'' Palek added. ''That's the first break in the perfect blue in a week.''

THIRTY

Brother Kyril was not a trained, interned, licensed physician. He wasn't even a registered nurse or paramedic. But he practiced medicine and even surgery without a qualm because he was the most qualified person on the planet.

He'd prepared for it on and off for several years back on Earth. It had occurred to him that the homegrown medical/surgical services on Siegel's World would be pretty horrific. And he could already see that FM would have to be kicked out, and the palace would then lose the ambassadorial clinic. So of course, being Kyril, he'd put together a small selection of medical books, and read his way through them with the help of a medical dictionary for laymen. Then he outfitted himself with a chest of equipment, including an antique pressure cooker to use as an autoclave.

A lot of his medical reading was from the late nineteenth and early twentieth centuries. Medicine and surgery during that period were already pretty rational, and you could do a lot with them, but they didn't depend on sophisticated facilities and equipment that wouldn't be available. He also read up on modern military field medicine and had an interesting paramedical handbook for the colonist on a pioneer planet.

He knew better than to try to provide a medical service for the entire palace; there was a limit to what even Kyril could get done in a day or week or year. But he quietly treated his key people.

Of course his non-medical skills helped a lot, and so did a strong constitution on the part of the patient. And the little packages that came to him occasionally from Earth made a lot of difference—especially certain dried, vacuum-packed antibiotics. Larmet didn't know where they'd come from or who wanted them, and neither he nor Kinjok knew where they ended up. But after a while they'd arrive at Krogaskott and find a home in Kyril's medical chest.

Without antibiotics, semi-professional internal surgery would have been a high risk activity, and a sword thrust through the guts would almost amount to execution.
—*Reminiscences of a King* by Bjorn Boru

After the decision to bring in the Second Regiment, the king and Palek played the game of "draft the peace treaty." It was based on the assumption that Lokar won on all fronts, and definitely better than looking over Vorss's shoulder, even if the assumption was questionable.

But under the circumstances it was hard to really get into

it. So when the sun began to dip behind the hill across the river, Palek wasn't surprised that the king decided to leave early for Krogaskott.

Yakut had concluded that the only way he was going to get close to the king was by going to the villa. The gimmick would be his radio: he'd show it to the entry guards, tell them what it was, and offer to explain it to the king. It was a thin and incomplete ploy, but he'd come up with nothing better and was bored and restless. So he'd decided it would work.

He'd taken his next to last zippo.

No way was the king going to stop on the road to shoot the breeze with some stranger. And there were all those guards, on peernu a lot better than the agent's; Yakut figured they'd kill his ass for sure if he tried. The dangers at the villa were not as obvious, although unquestionably serious, and there were always one or more courier peernu saddled and ready at the front entrance. He could jump one and ride zig-zag down the road, he thought semi-facetiously—see how good they were with those bows.

So he was on the road to Hyos when he spotted the king and his party riding toward him. For a moment he determined to accost the king then and there, regardless of the danger, but sanity intervened and he rode past them, not turning until they were out of sight behind a hedgerow on a curve.

Glowering, he jogged his mount back into Tonlik, keeping sufficiently behind the royal party that mostly they were out of sight. He wasn't actually following them in the sense of intending to go where they went. Mostly his mind was cycling repetitively through an old anger not related to the king or Lokar. Almost he failed to notice that king and guards had jogged past Krogaskott. They were riding out of the square on the far end as he entered it and saw them.

It snapped his attention at once to present time. Instead of going to the livery stable as he'd intended, he rode across the square, now their deliberate follower. He had no idea where they were going—did not even know where the street went in that direction beyond the next few blocks—but he was intensely interested.

*   *   *

"Where is the battle, captain?"

The soldier, weary, grimy, turned to him, then almost jumped backward into the fire. "Your Majesty!"

The king smiled. With the blurted words, every pair of eyes in the vicinity, even around other nearby fires, had turned to look, for it was a quiet company. Men hunched over their supper bowls got quickly up, some spilling hot thick pottage on their hands. And the whisper spread outward: "The king is here!"

"That's right, captain. Where is the battle?"

"Sire, half an hour ago it was right over there." The husky reservist pointed at the woods on the east side of the long narrow meadow. "In a line right along there in the trees."

The king looked where the man pointed, at woods that in the night might have passed for a forest in Vermont or Schwaben or Michigan back on Earth. A forest dark and no doubt bloody now. Light from the soldiers' warming fires lit the edge; moonlight paled the naked upper branches.

"But right now they've broke off attacking for a while, Your Majesty. Even the enemy needs to rest and eat."

Even the enemy. Boru considered the man's words. *That's a virtual admission that he's come to look on the enemy here as superior.* "I understand, captain." The king glanced over the troops. *They're willing to fight, but they no longer expect to win. They're not taking things into their own hands, not making things happen. If the enemy stops, they're willing to stay and wait.* "How far away are they?" Boru asked.

"Oh, ah, I don't rightly know, sire. Maybe thirty or forty meters from the edge. If one of 'em was to laugh loud, we might hear him. But we gave 'em nothing to laugh about," he added grimly.

"I'm sure of it. Thank you, captain. Carry on."

He'd assigned four reluctant guards and the peernu to help evacuate wounded. With the other two guards he moved now among the men who filled the meadow in fire-centered groups. Almost all eyes were on him, as he intended. He said little— "good evening, sergeant," or "at ease, men"—as he passed. He asked no questions, mainly wanting them to see him calm and confident here, to put himself in their thoughts, preparing them.

And he observed. He'd slipped into the neozen aware state as they'd ridden here; it came more and more easily as

Golovin worked with him, and he no longer thought of it as unique to neozen.

A soldier wearing a wooden yoke came up to him. On each end of the yoke a large bucket hung, and a man with a ladle walked beside. The yoked man grinned broadly and bobbed his head.

"Would you like supper, Your Majesty? Mighty good, sire. Lots of good meat and grain and taters in it."

His sober-faced ladleman nodded emphatically and offered a bowl from a bag at his shoulder. Several hundred eyes watched the tableau in the firelight as the king accepted the bowl and the ladleman filled it.

It wasn't bad, the king decided, actually pretty good. He thanked them and waited while they served the two guards with him, then continued his stroll, drinking off the broth and plucking morsels from the bowl, inserting them into the royal mouth. As he walked, light from the fires gleamed on the ornate gold headband, for unlike soldiers and guards, he wore neither helmet nor mail.

Then his soup was gone; it was time for the next act. The ladlemen—there were several dispensing teams in the meadow— had begun collecting bowls, and he gave his up to one of them. He had picked up a small following—a colonel, with aids and couriers and a bugler. The colonel, not knowing what to say or whether his words would be welcomed, had said nothing. The king turned to him now.

"Colonel, what nationality are the enemy in there?" He gestured toward the woods.

The colonel's eyes were wide and dark, sober in the firelight. "They are Bleesbroku, Your Majesty."

"Ah." The king allowed his face to show disappointment. "When do you expect them to attack next?"

"It's hard to say, Your Majesty. They attack for a while, then disengage for a somewhat longer time. We know when they're preparing to attack; we hear orders being shouted. The attack itself is signaled by bugles."

"Um. Do you have sentries out in case they try to sneak up on you?"

"Yes, Your Majesty, all along the line. They're a short distance back in the woods—ten paces."

"And does the enemy have sentries out?"

"I'm sure they must, Your Majesty."

"Um." His eyes absorbed the officer before him who had not tested the enemy sentries. "Thank you, colonel. We have to beat those people, you know." He turned, and with his two guards wound his way toward the woods in the direction of the enemy. At the edge he turned and looked back at the soldiers, felt their eyes. Then he drew his sword and disappeared among the trees.

They stared after him into the shadowed woods. What was he doing in there? For four or five minutes he could have been an illusion, a dream.

Suddenly from back in the forest came an incredible shriek that stopped every heart for a moment, followed by shouts and commotion from the enemy line. Quietly the Lokarn officers began to form up their men into defensive ranks. After half a minute the enemy was quiet again.

They waited. In three or four minutes more the shriek repeated, a stunning sound, more shouts, more commotion, then silence again. Two minutes later they could hear enemy voices calling orders, and at that moment the king emerged from the trees with his guards, their swords in their hands, and passed through the first line of soldiers. Only the king's sword was bloody.

Moments later the enemy charged. The king was like a demon, moving up and down the line, entering the fight wherever his men were giving ground, wherever the front line broke. And wherever he entered, his shriek struck the Bleesbroku like a blow to the heart, his sword slashing and striking like something from an enchanted age, so that the enemy gave way, and shortly the Lokaru found themselves driving their attackers back into the woods, the hardheaded Bleesbroku backing away, leaving their dead in the wet and dark-stained snow.

The Lokaru might have let them disengage, but their king would not. He pressed into the woods, helmetless and without mail, cleaving and hewing. So willy-nilly the troops pressed forward until exhaustion set in and the bugles called a halt.

Most of the men slumped to the ground then to rest, sitting or kneeling or even lying in the snow, but one approached the standing king. Like the king he wore no uniform, no helmet and no mail. His sword and clothing were splashed with blood not his own; his grin was without fear, his eyes strange.

"A good fight, Your Majesty," he said.

The king looked at him in the dimness and shadow, frowning slightly.

"Where did you learn to fight like that?" the man went on.

There was a moment's lag; then the king spoke in Terran. "The same place you did—from Li Kit Yun in Peking. What are you doing here, Yakut? I haven't seen you since the fiasco on Belknap's World."

Yakut's grin dissolved in confusion, to be replaced after a moment by wonder. "Boru?"

"Trogeir, King of Lokar. Let's see now . . . Bhiksu fired your ass and the guild kicked you out. You had talent up the yingyang, but you'd get crazy. Who are you working for now? Let me guess: Department Eleven."

Yakut laughed, a sound dark but amused. "You got it, Boru. You always were a smart bastard."

"Trogeir," the king corrected. "Let me see if I can guess what you're here for."

"Don't push it, Barney."

"It's okay, Yakut, you wouldn't kill me. You owe me. Remember?"

"I'd have escaped."

"Nobody got away from one of Dag Chek's prison camps without help. The best and luckiest help. Except by dying. And if somehow you'd gotten through the fence alive, there'd still have been the problem of getting off the planet."

They murmured together for ten minutes, reminiscing, always with the flavor of old rivals. And then the sentries yelled, galvanizing the soldiers out of weariness, and the Gnessr hit in savage silence.

The reservists were forced backward at first, fighting desperately, but again the king was there with his blood-chilling shriek. He'd lost both of his guards in the earlier fight, but now a tall powerful man fought near him, and wherever they appeared, the Gnessr, even the Gnessr, fell or fell back.

Finally the tall man went down, and the king fought like some berserk propellor. In twenty minutes the Gnessr assault was broken, and the Lokaru stood panting, wet with sweat in the winter night.

The king went to where Yakut had fallen, and knelt by him. The man was conscious, clutching his belly with bloody hands, and he stank.

"Vasily," said Boru in mock exasperation, "you damn near got yourself killed."

"Yeah. I've been working on it. I get crazy, remember?"

"Oh yeah. I forgot. Look, don't die on me now, okay? I've got a job for you, something important. So hold on; I'm going to get you out of here."

After that the king talked no more to Yakut, who slipped into unconsciousness. Borrowing some soldiers, he took the agent out on a makeshift litter made of poles and the cloak of a fallen Gneos. In the meadow they ran into a file of litter bearers moving up, and he commandeered two of them, who stared for a moment at their sweat-greased, blood-splashed king before transferring Yakut to their own litter.

The troopers he sent back, and because Yakut was large, he spelled the bearers off and on until they came to a road where ambulance sleighs waited for wounded. They loaded Yakut, and as the king got up beside the driver, he saw snowflakes drifting down. For the first time it registered on him that the temperature was falling and that the aware state had slipped away after the fighting had ended.

The ambulance passed by the barracks that was serving now as a hospital and entered the city, and the king had Yakut taken into Krogaskott through the postern gate. By that time the temperature had dropped notably, and already twenty centimeters of new snow had fallen, riding down thickly on a wind.

Yakut was quite unconscious, but he would live; the king had decided.

And on the long ride through the storm, the king had also decided in considerable detail what he was going to do. Not about the war: his attention was off the war. The army and the weather would take care of the war now. The war was a nuisance, brutal and costly, and it would do little good to win it if he did not handle what lay beneath.

THIRTY-ONE

Over the years there'd been some heavy
sessions in the little room where Kyril
did his most important work. But those
two weeks in the month of Winterheart
683 must have been among the most interesting. I'll bet my crown they were
the loudest—especially the first one.

I went into his study one morning quite
innocently—I had a key—to borrow one
of his research notebooks. Good thing
it was winter, with the windows closed
and the drapes drawn: it sounded like
someone was being tortured, or maybe
like a religious service on New Para-
dise, or at least like the bandages
were getting ripped off Yakut's hairy
hide. I guess different people's cases
discharge differently to some extent;
I'm pretty sure I never hollered like
that.

When I took the notebook back half an
hour later, I didn't hear a thing. So I
put my ear to the door, and there were
their voices murmuring back and forth
as cool as you please. I even thought I
heard Yakut chuckle.

Being shamelessly curious, I dropped
back now and then over the next few

days. Weeping? I half expected to see
the tears running out under the door!
Laughter? Gales of it! Yakut was never
very inhibited.

Of course, after the first week he ran
a lot less loudly. And by the end of
the second week, he'd followed Kyril
on that road I'd dreamed about one
northern night beneath the aurora, but
without all the symbology.

—*Reminiscences of a King* by Bjorn Boru

After he picked them up at the Oaxaca spaceport, Bhiksu
Tanaka took Boru and Golovin to an exclusive restaurant
where, using an assumed name, he'd reserved a private room.
There they briefed each other and finalized their plans. Bhiksu
reviewed and signed certain documents and then they ate,
taking their time. He didn't want to arrive at the Justice
Ministry with them until late in the day.

Boru had some pointed questions for him, questions he
hadn't asked in his messages via Larmet after hostilities had
ended. He'd looked at some possible answers before he asked,
so he wasn't surprised at what Tanaka told him.

When Department Eleven had finally made up their mind
to kill Trogeir, they decided to do it through a justice contract
to be requested through Systems Mining and Manufacturing.
And it seemed poetic justice to them to tap Tanaka for the
job: they'd long since concluded that he'd chosen Golovin
deliberately to sabotage their intentions.

They'd threatened muscle, and Tanaka knew he couldn't
win a war, not that kind of war, with them. So he'd agreed
without argument.

If he could have, he'd have told Boru to install himself as
Trogeir's bodyguard. But Department Eleven was merely crazy,
not across-the-board stupid, and they knew Tanaka. So they'd
had everything ready—bill of particulars, briefing cubes, orders. . . . All Tanaka had had to do was fill in an agent's
name, and sign. Then they'd had him call Boru, put disguised
video cameras among Bhiksu's ethnic office bric-a-brac, and

stepped into the adjacent study to monitor the meeting. Boru had picked up his package and left.

Meanwhile they'd also arranged an unexpected vacation for Bhiksu Tanaka. To James Island in the Galapagos group. The only humans on James Island were at a meditation center run by the Roman Catholic Brothers of Bhaktananda, who didn't even have a radio there. Communication was via an ancient skyhopper operated out of the order's central office in Delhi.

Department Eleven had made reservations for the "ailing but very spiritual Mr. Soktai," and provided a male nurse to accompany him. He'd spent six interesting and very restful weeks there, meditating and studying: he could now discuss with considerable insight the value of raising spiritual consciousness through understanding the message of the Holy Redeemer. The Brothers' understanding of Bhiksu Tanaka and his nurse, however, seemed to remain somewhat incomplete, though Bhiksu thought they'd gained an inkling of it.

Tanaka had selected Boru not because Boru and Trogeir were of the same clone, but because he was confident that Boru would walk away from the hit. That wouldn't be the end of it, of course, but it would be a major setback for the department.

Department Eleven couldn't understand something like the walkaway clause. They genuinely didn't understand justice or ethics, only expedience. Therefore, to them the clause could only be a gimmick to get out of a contract without losing the fee. And of course the agent would be ordered in advance to take the walk. Department Eleven had made sure that the slippery Tanaka could give no such order.

When Boru's questions all had been answered, and Tanaka's as well, the three of them left the restaurant. At the great horseshoe drive outside the Hall of Justice, Bhiksu told his chauffeur (chauffeur-plus, actually) to park and wait for a call. Then the three walked up the broad landscaped walkway. The Confederated Sovereign Worlds could hardly have selected a lovelier place for its capital than Oaxaca, Mexico—always summer, always green and fragrant, and at sixteen hundred meters above sea level, almost always comfortable. And of course only minutes away from anywhere on the planet, if you had clearance and the price.

Inside they had to wait for someone to receive their complaint, but even in a confederacy of eighty-five planets that had legal commerce with more than two hundred others, kings aren't required to wait long, and Bhiksu had connections. They filed criminal charges against Department Eleven of the Foreign Ministry and numerous individuals, among the lesser names being Abdul Mahmoud, Siegel's World Project In-Charge; Kendall Reynard, Project Deputy; Albert Haas, agent (all deceased); Vasily Yakut, agent; and Marcel McKedrick, agent. The charges included perversion of office, illegal interference with a class D planet, conspiracy to commit regicide, regicide, murder, conspiracy to commit war, illegal war, and assorted lesser crimes. Extensive depositions in evidence were deposited on audio-visual matrices and in writing to support the charges, including detailed material by agents Yakut and McKedrick.

Tanaka had warned Boru and Golovin that technical identification would be required: both finger and retinal prints. In Golovin's case it meant little. In Boru's case, when the prints were run through the computer, he'd immediately be identified as Barney Boru of Earth.

Of course, he was identified in the full statement of charges, but they wouldn't know that until some senior official had seen and digested the full statement, which could easily be the day after next. But with charges that serious, involving current and retired Foreign Ministry officials, Boru's prints would undoubtedly be run by a junior executive right after the abstract was viewed.

Which would certainly enable FM and its allies to confuse, obscure, and delay the issue and harass the plaintiffs. Boru might well be jailed, and in jail might conceivably be murdered or implanted, though that was doubtful considering the public attention Bhiksu had arranged for the case and for Boru.

Certainly it was highly desirable that Boru not be charged, or at least not found and arrested, before ten o'clock the next morning, at which time he'd be out of reach at the hearing Tanaka had arranged with the Assembly's Committee on Cultural Protection.

And next to busting Department Eleven, the hearing was the most important business they had here. In the long run it was more important.

Thus the tactic of making the charges late in the working day. The charges were recorded now, but hopefully the abstract wouldn't be played until the next morning, and Boru not identified until too late to keep him from the hearing.

As a safeguard, Bhiksu had arranged to remove Boru, along with Golovin and himself, from the capital for the night. When they left the Hall of Justice, they went to a private landing park and spent the evening and night in Tahiti, dining and being interviewed by a well-known and widely listened-to investigative reporter.

THIRTY-TWO

Boru looked around the table. Six members of the Committee sat along one side. The seventh, the chairman, sat alone at one end. Boru and Kyril sat on the other side with a dapper Bhiksu Tanaka.

The Committee consisted of six hominids and one felid; only a relative handful of known planets had sapient felids. The Committee was reading the brief position statement Boru had prepared enroute to Earth. Boru, Golovin, and Tanaka were reading the Committee's concise rules of procedure.

The brief reviewed Department Eleven's activities first to subvert and then to destroy Lokar. It then went on:

```
The above has been presented in de-
tailed depositions to the Justice Min-
istry. Further testimony will be given
them as requested.

Our purpose in sketching Department
Eleven activities for you in this brief
is to point out what can occur despite
cultural protection law. Furthermore,
had Department Eleven succeeded in de-
```

stroying the nation and culture of Lokar, as it nearly did, it is doubtful that the Assembly or the Justice Ministry would ever have known of it.

However, our primary purpose in requesting this hearing is not to urge an improved system for detecting criminal off-world impacts on primitive cultures. Rather, we wish to propose a modified viewpoint of cultural protection which will result in improved *law*. Specifically we would like to see the law changed to speed and enhance the development of class D and E worlds, and hopefully F worlds, into technological cultures that are politically rational and ready for membership in the Confederacy.

A body of theory and historical data has been compiled, along with the limited experiential results obtained on Lokar. These clearly suggest that it is practical to influence and guide cultures without overwhelming them or enforcing a preconceived cultural template.

The government of Lokar is ready to cooperate with this Committee in the preparation of enabling legislation and support material if the Committee wishes.

One by one the readers finished and looked up. Chairman Chu glanced around the table. "I believe we are all done reading," he said, and looked at Bhiksu. "Knowing your philosophical affinities, counselor, I suspect that underlying the ideas and procedures referred to here is the work of Dr. N.A. Kubiak."

Tanaka's slight smile was bland and inscrutable; *he's being oriental for Chu,* Boru decided. "The chairman is very perceptive," Tanaka said. "However, the ideas and data can speak for themselves, independent of their origin."

Chu acknowledged with a single bob of his head, then looked at Boru. Boru could perceive the chairman's response to them in the man's tenuous electronic field. Its frequency and amplitude, which came across as a thin grayness to Boru, marked a slight distrust, a skeptical reserve which could grow or dissipate. Of the other six members, the attitude of four was similar to the chairman's. A fifth, a tall, very slender, forty-ish woman, had a very "clean" field, marking open interest. The name plate in front of her had only one name, *Spodigru.* The sixth, a large ruddy man, had a field and face that marked hostility. His name was Kurt de Vries.

"I am sure," Chu said, "that His Majesty's proposal will be examined with an open mind." He looked at the other Committee members. "Has any of this Committee a question or comment before His Majesty makes his oral presentation?"

The smallest of them, the reddish-tan felid, signaled with a rather human-looking hand. Her name plate was the longest—it read *Citizen 12 752 032 593.* "Citizen Twelve?" said the chairman.

"Thank you, Ming." Her words were a melodious victory of practice in articulating what, to her, were utterly foreign and unnatural sounds. She turned to the king.

"Your Majesty, are you the legitimate ruler of Lokar? It seems to me that the manner of your assumption renders you in fact an improperly constituted monarch. Your brief indicates that you were installed by Department Eleven as an impostor in place of the actual prince, became crown prince through the Department Eleven assassination of your older brother, and king after the suspect death of Korbin II."

Her steady yellow eyes awaited Boru's answer.

"Thank you for your question, Citizen Twelve. The manner of my becoming king is actually somewhat more complicated than described in the brief. I *did* become king illegally however. Although I am in fact a member of the royal family on my father's side, I was not in the direct line of descent and in no way eligible to inherit the throne. As Korbin died leaving no heirs, the throne should properly have been filled by public election.

"However, my legitimacy was recently resolved. After the

war ended, I had the full situation published broadly, posted in every town, village, and church, and read to large public gatherings throughout the kingdom. Then, after the called-for six weeks of public discussion, an election was held and I was properly elected. I am now the legal and proper king of Lokar.

"And while my legitimacy is not directly relevant to our proposal, it is interesting that in a free and open election, a very large majority of the adult population voted for me. It indicates broad popular approval of the policies and actions of my government, a government operating on the principles and policies which our proposal here would extend to other primitive worlds on a test basis. They have given us a mandate to continue."

"Thank you, Your Majesty," said Citizen Twelve, and turned to Chu. "Thank you, Mr. Chairman."

De Vries quickly raised a large and immaculate pink hand. "Mr. de Vries," said the chairman, "your question."

The assemblyman stared hard at Boru. "Mr. whatever your real name is, why do you imagine we'd accept your story of free elections? You, a tool of Department Eleven, who could not even retain your loyalty to them!"

The king turned from de Vries and spoke calmly to Chu. "Mr. Chairman, the court protocol of Lokar may not be appropriate here, nor is it necessary that this Committee agree with me, but as the legal sovereign of Lokar, I am not interested in replying to hostile and insulting language."

"Thank you, Your Majesty." Chu Ming Hwa turned blandly to de Vries. "Assemblyman de Vries, please restate your question with regard for the standards of courteous address expected by this Committee, the Assembly, and I am sure the electorate of Nei Frieslân."

De Vries's pinkness darkened. "Your Majesty," he said. The words were slow, distinct, heavy. "Why should we believe your story of a free election and a popular mandate? Particularly in the light of your confessed history."

The king's eyes met but did not challenge the man's, and when he spoke, it was mildly. "Thank you for your question, Assemblyman de Vries. I am not able to answer it as satisfactorily as you might like. However, while the committee is deliberating on my proposal—assuming it doesn't summarily reject it—during your deliberations, the Committee or its representatives are welcome to visit Lokar and travel around the kingdom freely with your own interpreter to judge its people and its government for yourselves.''

He smiled slightly, briefly. ''Considering the history of monarchs, whether kings or dictators, I understand your skepticism. I would like to stress, however, that my legitimacy is not a measure of my proposal.

''I trust that satisfies your question.''

De Vries nodded curtly, then turned to the chairman. ''My question is answered.''

Golovin had jotted on a small note pad; now he unobtrusively detached a page and put it on the table by his right forearm. Boru glanced down. In small block Lokarn letters he read: *Police waiting in corridor.*

''Thank you, Mr. de Vries,'' the chairman was saying. ''Thank you, Your Majesty. Assemblywoman Spodigru, I believe you indicated a question.''

''I did, Mr. Chairman. A connection has been implied between the philosophy of Dr. Kubiak and His Majesty's proposal. I'd like to know more about this.''

''Thank you, Assemblywoman Spodigru,'' Chu said. He scanned down the table. ''Are there any objections to having our guest present his proposal now? Perhaps while he is doing that, he can cover Ms. Spodigru's question. . . . Very well. Your Majesty, if you please.''

Boru picked up Golovin's note and passed it to Tanaka, then stood up, glanced around at the others, and began. ''Cultures change,'' he said. ''Rapidly or slowly, they change. Terrans three centuries ago were surprised to find how static certain cultures were, but even the Etas of Labatt's World had recorded significant cultural changes through the millennia. And historically, the end result of cultural change has been eventual collapse or dwindling away. One might say the existing cultures are those which haven't disappeared *yet.*

''The life cycle of a culture is in some respects analogous to that of an organism. It has an origin, perhaps in the ashes of a past culture. It develops, growing and changing. Then it begins to decay, as some trees do, while still growing. Later, unless it's been cut down, it declines and finally dies.

''Again like a tree, given time it dies little by little from its decays and diseases. Or it may be overturned by the winds of revolution. And at any time from infancy to senility, it may die in the flames of war.''

The king smiled then. "If my language is dramatic, it reflects the drama in the histories of nations.

"On many planets the dominant cultures seem stuck at D or E. Limited by wars, plagues, and other catastrophes, individual cultures rise and fall within those levels. But once one of them reaches C, it or some other which has caught and passed it is likely to move up to B within a few centuries.

"Usually though, without Confederacy membership, before one of them reaches A—before everyday operational space flight is developed—crash! They usually collapse through nuclear or biological warfare or resource depletion. Then they generally crash all the way back to E—subsistence agriculture or herding. Sometimes they fall all the way to F!''

The king looked around now, his eyes and voice abruptly and deliberately hard and sharp. "I'd like to suggest that this is not a set of phenomena to preserve, let alone encourage. But that is exactly what present cultural protection law does for worlds like mine which are not advanced enough to be allowed off-world trade or to receive technical missions."

The king removed the momentary hardness from his voice, speaking drily now. "I am not suggesting *laissez faire;* that would be a catastrophe to worlds like mine. I simply urge a more rational body of law on the subject.

"There is a tendency among human beings"—he turned to Citizen Twelve—"and I presume among sapient felids as well, to apply 'nonsolutions' to many problems. Existing cultural law is an example. As it stands now, and as it stood prior to existing amendments, it is not actually a solution at all. It serves to cope with, to hold off, the pressures that would otherwise swamp and destroy primitive cultures and turn their people into self-destructive caricatures. It does do that, but at the expense of the commerce which the Confederacy was intended to encourage. And in no way does it address the basic problems of culture; it simply provides time for a solution to be developed.

"But so far the government has taken no visible steps toward a solution.

"A *solution* would be to work out and work with the dynamics of human and group behavior, which are the dynamics of cultures. These have been worked out and described by N.A. Kubiak and his students, but their findings have been rejected by the establishment. His doctorate was in the wrong major and his results too unfamiliar. He refused sociology's version of the phlogiston theory. He has been unwilling to continue with psychology's equivalent of the medieval four humors: blood, phlegm, choler, and bile.''

Boru paused for the space of a breath, smiling ruefully as he looked around. "Ah well. On Terra, fortunately, change not only happens *to* the culture, it's a basic element *of* the culture. So for forty years, Kubiak's ideas have been seeping into the culture at large and out to other planets. Counselor Tanaka mentioned at breakfast that now certain universities offer courses in Kubiak, and hire his students as professors to teach them. Especially on Moraz, where I understand Kubiak's findings are widely applied in government, business, and personal life.''

Spodigru grinned at him, and he realized where she must be from. *A friend on the committee*, he thought. "Presumably then, the Assembly can be persuaded to consider its use on a small scale in this specialized area." *And that will get the ball rolling.*

"So far I've stressed the need for this from the viewpoint of someone from a class D planet. Appropriately enough. But it has a material importance to the Confederacy also, quite apart from and well beyond the expansion of trade.

"The Confederacy might be regarded as a superculture comprised of many constituent cultures, most of those with a set of subcultures. A superculture built around the FTL drive, a central if considerably limited government, vigorous commerce, a unified science, and a standard central language to communicate with.

"There is no reason to think that this superculture does not operate on the same dynamics as other cultures.

"Culturally, the Confederacy has major strengths. It is expanding into new space and has abundant resources. It is extroverted. It enjoys a government which is somewhat more rational than most governments historically have been, although Department Eleven demonstrates that pockets of insanity and stupidity exist in it. And the considerable sovereignty retained by its constituent worlds protect it from having to try to handle local problems everywhere with the ignorance and clumsiness of distance.

"But the fact remains, as certainly every member of the Assembly knows, that destructive attitudes and vectors have existed and operated in the Confederacy from the beginning. Still with minor effects, but looked at with the perspective of well over three centuries, those attitudes and vectors are growing, and so is concern about them.

"So the Confederacy *needs* a technology that can keep cultures healthy and vigorous, able to avoid or handle serious problems of those sorts without continuous repression that only gives rise to new serious problems."

The king stopped again to look his audience over. "And that is my case, my diagnosis. Here is my immediate or opening prescription. The Confederacy is well advised to authorize several studies on as many planets—call them research or pilots or demonstrations—of what can be accomplished in the rationalization and improvement of cultures, which is to say of worlds. I will continue the study on Siegel's World, of course, but more are needed under other conditions.

"Dr. Golovin"—he gestured to Kyril—"is very knowledgeable in this area. I recommend you make him your consultant. We in Lokar can proceed now without his further personal attention, although we'll miss having him to take our problems to.

"And that, ladies and gentlemen, is all I have to say. I'd like you to save your questions for Dr. Golovin. Counselor Tanaka and I have business with the Justice Ministry."

The Committee and three guests stood and moved about briefly, shaking hands and talking. Tanaka was different than Boru had ever seen him, grave-faced. Boru wondered if Kyril had passed him another, more sobering note after they'd gotten up.

It was time to confront arrest, he decided. He excused himself and Bhiksu, and leaving Golovin with the committee, they went into the small reception room adjacent. Only the receptionist was there. Tanaka put his hand on the knob of the outer door, stopped and looked back. "What is it?" Boru asked quietly.

Tanaka shook his head and motioned Boru away, then

opened the door and stepped through. There was a sudden, jolting flurry of shooting, Tanaka's shots loud and blasting, the others burner pulses that made popping sounds when they hit. The receptionist screamed once. Boru didn't move. All he could see was Tanaka sprawled on the floor, gun by his hand. For the moment there was no sound of movement from the corridor, but the door behind him opened as Citizen Twelve slipped in.

Then feet thudded, approaching up the hall, and stopped. Someone outside said, "Get the medics," feet hurried away, and Boru stepped out. A kneeling guard glanced up, then back down at the uniformed man he knelt beside. Two more men in uniform lay on the carpet, but it was obvious that nothing could be done for them.

The last mad hit by Department Eleven, Boru thought as he knelt by Tanaka. Perhaps the final violence by a clique uncovered.

He'd never imagined that Uncle Bhiksu would be so fast.

"So you returned after all." From a lotus position, Artemus Kabashima smiled up at his foster son.

The nonagenarian master had added a low firm cushion/stool to the sparse furnishings of the room, and Boru sat down on it before answering. "Yes," he said. "I've been back for a week now, and very busy."

"How long will you stay?"

"Here? An hour." It was all they'd need; it was all they'd ever needed since he'd grown up. "I'll be on the planet for a few more days."

"Ah."

"I suppose you still don't read the papers?" Boru asked.

"As before. On occasion I sense there is something I should read about. Then I order a newsfac and find out what it is."

"You read about Uncle Bhiksu?"

"Yes." He cocked a black and beady eye at the blond-headed son of his home. "And about you. A king!" The old man chortled. "I am the father of a king!" He appraised Boru. "Behind that beard you are greatly changed. I do not think you will be joining an order as you planned.

You must have found a great master to have come so far so soon.''

"True." Boru grinned. "A good thing, too. With thighs like mine, it's tough getting into the lotus position; I might not have survived a monastery."

He sat quietly then while Kabashima struck the gong, and did not speak again until Maralies had poured tea and left. "Do you know where Uncle Bhiksu is, now that he's been killed?"

"Very far away. That's all I know. *Very* far."

"Ah." The younger man looked thoughtfully past his cup. "I'm married, you know. My wife is going to have a baby in a few months."

"Is that so!" The old face grinned. "Tell the child hello for its grandfather." The expression changed, became sly. "I'm very old now. Perhaps you'll have another before long?"

"I'm sure we can arrange that."

They continued talking together, Kabashima asking questions, Boru telling him about Golovin, his methods, and the phenomena that resulted. The hour passed, and another. They ate, and at last Boru got up to leave.

"And son?"

"Yes, father?"

"Tell Bhiksu Tanaka hello for me." The soft parchment face grinned again, broadly, showing old teeth widely spaced.

Boru grinned back. "I will, father, I will."

EPILOGUE

It's assumed that readers will be interested in some of the outcomes and costs of the Lokarn War incidental to our story. Here is a summary.

	KILLED
Barbarians	3,407[a]
Gnessr	472
Bleesbroku	2,888
Garvnu	2,189[a]
Prozhku	1,823[a]
Lokaru	6,500[b]
Total (approximate)	17,300

[a] Body count. Actual number probably higher.
[b] Persons unaccounted for or known dead. Includes about 350 noncombatants.

CLOSURE OF HOSTILITIES

Northern Front

When Marcel McKedrick was informed by Wan Larmet that the southern armies were beaten and negotiating, he ordered the tribes to stop fighting, and asked for negotiations.

When a meeting time had been agreed on and the warchiefs prepared, McKedrick left, surrendering himself to Lokarn forces. Sunto Woodhauler was landed as a negotiator.[1]

After terms were agreed upon, the barbarians, in severe distress from hunger, gathered with Sunto on the river ice. There they piled their swords. (No one below the rank of group leader was allowed to keep his sword.) One hundred fifty beeves were driven up the ice to them and butchered for travel rations.

The barbarians then trekked north up the river homeward. As they had previously killed or driven out much of the game in the river valley, they arrived at their villages hungry and weak.

Game Park Front

Fifty centimeters of snow, and temperatures estimated as low as –30C (–22F) totally and at once reversed the military situation. The Bleesbroku and Gnessr were beaten back in an immediate post-storm battle, then turned their efforts to survival, making rude shelters and cutting firewood. The Lokarn Second Regiment, arriving at Tonlik from the southern front, was issued skis and bows and sent to harry the immobilized enemy.

Civilian volunteers set up a large tent camp in the forest, kept warming fires fueled, and provided hot food. Skis were brought to the regiments already in the area, and all units began rotating: two days in the field and two in the barracks east of Tonlik.

The invasion forces took heavy losses during eight days of hit and run attacks, with five days of temperatures that, for the area, were unusually severe. Many of the surviving invad-

---

[1]In negotiating, Sunto explained to the chiefs about *agents provocateurs*, and a new word entered the barbarian vocubalary—*ISS-sahn RO-vu-KAH-tu*, their pronunciation of the French, twice removed—which was assigned the meaning "false medicine chief." Their rules of speech do not allow a *pr* sound, and *r* seemed especially appropriate to replace it because it is used as an initial sound only in words having a connotation of danger or evil.

ers suffered severe frostbite and were rendered ineffective. Their morale utterly collapsed.

On the morning of the ninth day post-storm, the Gnesil force surrendered and gave up their weapons. Inexperienced at coping with severe cold, many had suffered crippling frostbite that required amputations to avoid gangrene.

The Bleesbroku surrendered later the same day.

Southern Front

Here the actual snowfall was probably less than at the Game Park, but much of the country was open, and drifting was severe. And temperatures that far from the sea were undoubtedly colder.

The combination of drifts and severe cold halted cavalry activity almost entirely for five days. Most of the hostilities then were hit and run attacks by Lokaru on skis, mainly burning barns where enemy peernu were sheltered. Hundreds of enemy cavalry were converted to infantry because their peernu were lost. Except when built of stone, farm houses sheltering enemy soldiers also were subject to firing, and their fleeing occupants to archery attack.

The Coalition forces began a limited offensive on the seventh day, but on the twelfth, three regiments of Lokaru arrived, having been two days on the drifted road from Tonlik. The Lokarn general, Klinta Hessler, met with the commander of the southern forces, displayed for him the captured regimental banners of the seaborne invaders, and showed him the surrender terms drafted for him by King Trogeir. After a short staff conference, the Coalition commander agreed to the terms except that commissioned officers should be allowed to keep their swords and horses. Klinta acquiesced and they piled their weapons in great heaps, then began their dismal march home on foot through the snow, bellies growling.

Within three days of that surrender, the only enemy troops still in Lokar were the Bleesbrok and Gnesil prisoners in a hastily set up internment camp near Tonlik, where they spent a bitter winter in tents in the snow.

The Rosten Commando

The final act of war was carried out by Lokar on the same day that the Garven and Prozhkan armies accepted surrender terms. Wan Larmet, following the time-honored policy "cover your ass," had maintained his working relationship with the Department Eleven project while covertly giving information and support to the Lokarn high command.

But on that day he played a combat role: he transported a ten-man commando, led by Trogeir himself, to Rosten. The commando, dressed in captured Bleesbrok officers' uniforms complete with plumed hats, were allowed to enter the palace, where they were taken to King Heigelt as a Bleesbrok delegation. At that particular moment it happened that the Department Eleven Project In-Charge and Deputy were with Heigelt. Trogeir shot both agents to death with a spring-operated dart gun. Then Heigelt, a knife at his throat, was taken to the *Slengeth Buëd* and transported to prison in Tonlik.

PEACE TERMS

Garvas and Prozhask

Garvas and Prozhask jointly paid reparations adequate to compensate Lokarn property holders, the injured, and survivors of the dead, for damages. The Lokarn government was compensated for wages paid to reservists called to duty, and all other expenses of war on the southern front. Compensation was from a fund provided by Garvas and Prozhask in a ratio of two to one because of Garvas's leadership in the Coalition.

In addition, each nation paid a penalty of eighty kilos of gold.

Because their principal military forces had been disarmed, the threat of a punitive invasion by a Lokarn army was sufficient incentive for acceptance and payment.

The Lokaru did not expropriate or even temporarily occupy any enemy territory.

Bleesbrok

The Bleesbrok prisoners were held until the Directors General paid a ransom equal to the damages—mainly survivor and disability benefits, the wages of reservists engaged against them, and costs of sheltering and feeding prisoners—a penalty of forty kilos of gold, and an agreement to purchase all their timber imports for the next three years from Lokar. Previously, Bleesbrok had bought most of their timber imports from Prozhask and Garvas.

Khupraigneos

The Gnessr refused even to discuss ransoming their captured prisoners, who by surrendering had become unworthy. They did agree to buy them back as they would slaves, paying twenty kilos of gold.

It had been Heigelt of Garvas who thought of involving the Gnessr by offering them Lokaru as slaves. Therefore the Gnessr were also required to ransom Heigelt for a payment of one copper coin, and to sell him to a mine in Dżuk Bom Ka, where imported slaves were used with notorious severity. The Gnessr were happy to do this. They felt humiliated by their defeat, and considered that Heigelt had greatly misrepresented the military situation to them.

The Gnessr also agreed to buy furs from Lokar, and ten shiploads of sawn lumber annually for five years.

The Barbarians

The barbarians were considered to have been the gullible though willing and avaricious victims of Department Eleven. Relative to their populations, the tribes had suffered far more from the war than any other people involved.

No reparations were demanded of them. Their penalty was to give back all the gifts the king had given them, including the surviving white peernu and all white colts.

A trade agreement was made with each tribe whereby they

would sell certain quantities of furs to a consortium of fur traders at agreed-upon prices. Agreed-upon trade goods would be available at trading posts at accessible river locations.

The Confederated Sovereign Worlds

The government of Lokar developed a list of civilian and military damages and other costs. Trogeir took these to Earth with him. Civil action was filed by the law firm of Ramirez, Tanaka, and Hertz against the government of the Confederated Sovereign Worlds as the responsible entity.

The Confederate Justice Ministry ruled that the charges were justified, and all costs and penalties were paid.

VASILY YAKUT

One result of the mental and ethical salvage of Vasily Yakut was his realization of responsibility for his crimes. The Lokarn Ministry of Justice in private hearing agreed to accept his proposed reparations.

The prostitute he'd strangled had no known family. By Lokarn mores, as a prostitute she had been disowned by her family. Therefore, as reparation, he was required within five years to endow a home for orphans.

The rider he'd killed for his peeran was a widower, with three grown children who then inherited the family bakery. The merchant family he'd savaged had left a widower, and their murdered household servants had left two grown children. Yakut authorized Trogeir to sell his personal goods on Earth, cash in his pension, draw his backlogged Foreign Ministry salary, and convert it all into gold.

Trogeir brought this back with him to Lokar, and it was delivered anonymously to the survivors involved, as ''from one who appreciates your loss.''

Meanwhile, under an assumed identity, Yakut went to the library of the University of Cornfields and studied pertinent texts and references on fur farms, on the primitive manufacture of bog iron, and on the refining and alloying of low-grade iron. He then planned and set up a technical development program, including research, to establish these as practical tribal industries. The program was funded from Confederate reparations, and required a degree of unification and cooperation of clans.

Marcel McKedrick agreed to do the on-site training and supervision. It was believed that Vasily Yakut would not be accepted by the tribes and might well be murdered if he went among them. Certainly he would restimulate old angers, griefs, and losses much more than McKedrick did.

KEITH LAUMER

GORDON R. DICKSON